MYSTERIES *of* MARTHA'S VINEYARD

MYSTERIES *of* MARTHA'S VINEYARD

A Port

in the

Storm

ELIZABETH PENNEY

Guideposts

New York

A Port

in the

Storm

CHAPTER ONE

Martha's Vineyard in the winter. Piles of warm covers on the bed, curtains pulled tightly shut against the cold, and a dog with cabin fever.

At barely seven o'clock Jake jumped on the bed and stuck his chilly wet nose right in his owner's ear. Priscilla Latham Grant pushed him away with a groan. "Give me a few more minutes, okay, Jakey? It's too early for you to go out."

In answer, he plopped down on her legs and curled up with a sigh. She reached out to stroke his silky ears, thinking once again what a blessing her adopted dog had been. Especially during this first winter on an island in the Atlantic, far from the Kansas farm that had been her home. For more than three decades, she and her husband Gary had worked together raising wheat, corn, and soybeans, an endeavor that ended with his untimely death a little over a year ago.

The inheritance of a lighthouse and cottage from her aunt Marjorie Latham had given Priscilla an opportunity for a new life, one she embraced heartily. Her daughter Rachel, thirty-two and living in Kansas City, hadn't been so sure about her mother's decision, but Priscilla had found peace in it. Until these short, dark days had set in, filled with relentless storms battering the island, one after another. Friends and neighbors hunkered down, reluctant to go out in the inclement weather, and Priscilla found herself alone—and lonely.

"Enough of that," she muttered to herself. Indulging in self-pity wasn't healthy, and in a faith-filled life, certainly not a godly pursuit. Restless and annoyed at herself, she gently nudged the dog aside and slid from under the covers. After a cup of hot coffee and a hearty breakfast, she'd work on her plans for the small museum she was going to open next summer. She wanted to create an exhibit of family history for visitors to enjoy. The local tour company had added the lighthouse to their itinerary, and the museum would offer an additional piece of Latham history.

Priscilla slid her feet into fleece-lined slippers—a necessity with the icy wooden floors—and pulled on her fluffy robe. Next she shuffled to the window and opened the curtains. Monitoring the weather was a time-honored tradition for island residents, as it had been on the farm. Whether derived from land or sea, family livelihoods depended upon reading the signs correctly.

Instead of the expected overcast skies, blinding sunlight streamed through the window, making Priscilla blink. Joy and gratitude flooded her heart, sending her spirit soaring. *A sunny day at last.* Once her vision cleared, she drank in the view. Sparkling blue water frosted with tiny whitecaps lay beyond the rocky shore, which was blanketed with a pristine layer of snow. Nestled next to the cottage, the lighthouse stood proud and stalwart, a beacon of safety for the past one hundred years.

What a beautiful place to live, even in the dead of winter.

Jake had jumped off the bed and was waiting at her heels. She bent and ruffled his furry head. "Come on, boy, I'm taking you for a walk." In response, he leaped about the room. She laughed. "You know that word, don't you?"

First she washed up and put on long johns and a turtleneck under wool pants and a sweater. Warm layering was a must during a bitter New England winter. Then she and Jake went to the kitchen, where she fed him and made a pot of coffee. While it brewed, she threw on her outdoor gear: a down parka, boots, and hat. After filling a travel mug with steaming java, she pulled on mittens and grabbed Jake's leash. "Come on, boy. Let's go." He didn't need to be told twice.

The phone was ringing when Priscilla stepped back inside the cottage a short while later, her cheeks scoured by fresh air and Jake panting with happy exhaustion. She unclipped Jake and shrugged off her coat, then hurried to answer.

Her cousin Joan was on the line. "Good morning, Priscilla. Did you notice that strange yellow orb in the sky?"

Priscilla laughed. "I sure did. I needed to wear sunglasses against the glare." Getting to know Joan, Gail, and Trudy, her Latham cousins, had been one of the best parts of moving to the island. All three were different in personality and temperament, and while she loved each equally, Priscilla was closest to quiet, practical Joan.

"Want to meet me at the bakery for breakfast? I haven't been able to get there for days." Joan's droll tone expressed what she thought of that state of affairs. Candy Lane Confectionery was one of the women's favorite haunts.

"Sounds like a plan," Priscilla said. "Great timing, by the way. I was just about to make something to eat."

After making sure Jake had food and water, Priscilla put on her coat again and set off for the village in her SUV, which had lovely heated seats. The ice on the roads was melting, puddles forming on the pavement, but tall snowbanks still loomed on each side of the winding lane, a reminder of the storms they'd endured.

Slowing for a corner, Priscilla caught a glimpse of her neighbor's historic Cape Cod house through the leafless trees. She admired the way the cozy home nestled between ancient maples, smoke drifting from the chimney in a lazy stream. It was a picture-postcard example of a classic New England structure, like many beautiful homes on the island.

She really ought to go see Rebekah Alden, the older woman who lived there. They'd met briefly last summer when Rebekah was puttering around in her flower garden. Priscilla had the impression the woman was isolated, almost a shut-in. That situation must be so much worse in the winter.

Resolving to go over soon, perhaps with some homemade baked goods, Priscilla turned her attention to the next tricky corner. Snowbanks not only impeded visibility, they reduced the width of the road to a narrow track.

Down in the village, she easily found a parking space on Beach Street near the bakery, one of the advantages of the off-season. In the summer, it was almost impossible at times to drive through town, let alone park.

Several of the gift stores and emporiums flanking the bakery were closed until spring, but a few had brave Open flags hanging outside their doors. Thankfully the bakery was open year-round. What would she and her cousins do without their frequent fix of Candy's treats?

Priscilla pushed the door open with a jingle of bells, entering a steamy warmth scented with vanilla, coffee, and cinnamon. Pulling off her hat and mittens, she glanced around and spotted petite, dark-haired Joan at one of the dozen small tables in the space. Every other table was filled with patrons chatting, reading the newspaper, or tapping away on laptops.

"It's been crazy in here," Joan said when Priscilla reached the table. "I was lucky to get a table. Everyone seems to have had the same idea."

"We all have cabin fever, I guess." Priscilla stuffed her hat and mittens in her coat sleeves and hung the garment on the back of her chair. She peered at Joan's plate. "What did you get?"

Joan displayed the pastry with a flourish. "A cream puff. They're not just for dessert anymore. Seriously, I thought I deserved it after being snowed in for a week."

Priscilla laughed. "On that note, I think I'll go for some of Candy's hummingbird cake, if she has any. Be right back."

A young woman with cropped brunette locks and elf-like features was loading the cases with fresh cookies. She gave Priscilla a brilliant smile that wrinkled a pert, freckled nose. "Good morning. Can I help you?"

"You must be new," Priscilla said. "I haven't seen you here before."

"I just started this week, as a baker and general gal Friday." The young woman set down the tray and smoothed her apron. "I'm Harper Jenson."

"And I'm Priscilla Grant, a devoted customer of this bakery. You'll be seeing a lot of me and my cousins." She nodded at Joan. "Joan is one of them."

"Good to know. What can I get you?" Harper stood poised to take her order.

Priscilla scanned the case. Good, they had hummingbird cake today, made Candy's way with cranberries and cream cheese. "A slice of the Tisbury Tizzy and a coffee."

"Great choice." The cheerful Harper beamed with satisfaction as she slid the case open. "That cake is fabulous."

"It sure is. I love everything here." Priscilla's gaze roamed over the muffins, crème horns, cookies, and other treats made on the premises.

She was getting ready to carry her breakfast to the table when Candy Lane, owner of the bakery, emerged from the kitchen, walking with her head down. In her mid-thirties, Candy was usually an irrepressible bundle of energy. Today it was as if her internal light had dimmed. Even her hair appeared lank and tired. She glanced up and noticed Priscilla. "How are you, Priscilla? Nice day, isn't it?" Her tone belied the cheerful words.

"It certainly is, for a change." Priscilla hesitated, then inquired, "Is everything all right, Candy? You don't seem like your usual self."

Candy ran a hand through her hair, disarranging it. "Is it that obvious?" She glanced around. Harper had darted back into the kitchen, and no other customers were standing nearby. "It's been a tough winter," she said in a low voice. "With the bad weather, we're way down in sales. And I've had one unexpected expense after another."

Priscilla's heart squeezed in sympathy. She remembered the anxious times when the weather hadn't cooperated on the farm and they'd lost crops. Or when equipment broke down—always at the worst possible time, it seemed. But God had always provided, sometimes in a miraculous way, if not the way she expected. "I'll say a prayer for you," she said.

"I appreciate that." Candy gave her a wan smile. "Enjoy your breakfast."

"I will." As Priscilla turned, she spotted a flyer taped to the counter. *Share a Little Love*, it read, with a picture of two intertwined hearts. The flyer gave details of a dinner and dance at the high school on Valentine's Day.

Candy noticed her reading the flyer. "You should come to this. It's a great event that benefits both the homeless shelter and the animal shelter. Everyone in town goes." She gave Priscilla a sly smile. "You can bring a date or not, up to you."

Priscilla felt heat flood her cheeks. Since moving to the island, she'd met a certain Coast Guard captain, Gerald O'Bannon, and they'd become friends. Others around her kept hinting that they should take the next step and officially start dating, but she wasn't ready. How could she be?

But what if he did want to go on an official date, a little voice whispered, *what then*? Priscilla shrugged off those unsettling thoughts. "I'll think about it. Going, that is." Her cheeks flamed even hotter.

"Go eat." Candy made a shooing motion. "I'll send Harper over with coffee refills in a while."

"Thanks, Candy." Priscilla carried her plate and mug to the table where Joan waited. She settled herself, then asked, "Do you attend the Share a Little Love event?"

Joan, cradling her mug in two hands, nodded. "Wouldn't miss it. Every year the event benefits a different organization. This year it's going to help your church." Faith Fellowship ran a homeless shelter from January to May each year.

"And an animal shelter, which helps dogs like Jake." Priscilla shared Jake's comical reaction to the snow with her cousin, how he'd dug his nose in and then flung the fluffy flakes off in surprise.

Joan listened, a wistful expression on her face. "You're making me want another pet." She'd lost her dog, Champ, the previous year.

"I heartily recommend it." Priscilla drained her coffee, and with impeccable timing, Harper came around the counter holding a pot. Priscilla waved her mug with a smile.

Harper bustled over. "How is everything?"

"Scrumptious as always," Joan said. "You're new, aren't you?"

"This is Harper Jenson," Priscilla said. "This is my cousin, Joan Abernathy."

The two exchanged greetings. "What brings you to Martha's Vineyard?" Joan asked the young woman.

Still holding the coffeepot, Harper cocked one hip to stand more comfortably. "I'm searching for my family."

CHAPTER TWO

Priscilla felt an immediate thrill of connection with the young baker. She'd been seeking the same thing when she'd moved to the island—family and a sense of roots and history. Her mother's ancestors had been the lighthouse keepers for more than one hundred years.

"Who are your people?" Joan asked. "I've lived here all my life, so I probably know them. Or of them, at least."

Harper bit her lip. "That's just it, I don't know. All I have is my mother's diary." She blinked away tears. "She never told me anything about her family before she died. Not even their names."

Priscilla was touched. *She's young to have lost her mother. And it sounds like she's alone in the world.* Impulsively she reached out and grabbed Harper's free hand. "I'm so sorry for your loss."

"I am too," Joan echoed. "But maybe we can help you locate your relatives. Right, Priscilla?"

"That's right, we sure will try." Priscilla felt bound and determined to help the young woman. "Mildred Pearson at the East Shore Historical Museum is a good source of information. She has lots of genealogy records there."

The young woman's brow creased in confusion. "Research? At a museum? I wouldn't even know where to begin."

"I'll teach you," Priscilla found herself saying. Joan gave her a look of approval. "I'm in the middle of working on my own family history, so I'd be glad to show you around the historical society's archives."

Harper's face brightened with excitement. "Really? You'd do that for me? I was just praying I'd find answers somehow, and here you are."

Warmth glowed in Priscilla's heart at the idea of being someone's answer to prayer, mingled with trepidation about being able to find the answers Harper sought. "I'll do my best. And Mildred will help too, I'm sure."

"I hope you find what you're seeking, Harper," Joan said. She hugged herself with both arms. "Are either of you cold? All of a sudden I'm freezing."

Priscilla realized that the room was chilly, even though no one had opened the door for at least fifteen minutes. "I'm cold too. And usually it's really toasty in here."

At the tables around them, other patrons had started to comment, glancing around as if that would help them figure out what was wrong.

Harper groaned. "The furnace must be on the fritz again. Excuse me, I'd better go tell Candy so she can get someone over here to fix it." She dashed away.

"I think I'll drink up and get to the museum," Priscilla said. "I have some ancestors to look up."

"For the lighthouse?" Joan asked. "How's that going?"

Priscilla pulled out the notebook where she jotted ideas and information and turned to the page showing the layout. She went over it with Joan. "I want to display a mix of nautical and light-house items along with family photos and artifacts. I'm calling the exhibit 'Life in a Lighthouse.'"

Joan beamed. "It's going to be wonderful. We've always been proud of our family history, but no one's pulled it together like this. I can't wait to see it."

"I plan to create a framed display with biographies of all the keepers, including pictures of them and their families," Priscilla said. "If I can find photographs for all of them."

The front door opened with a jingle of bells. Local contractor Beau Ortmann and a young man strode inside, each carrying a toolbox. Beau and Candy were engaged to be married, a story of lost love found again.

"Looks like the cavalry is here," Joan said. "That was fast."

"Who's the other guy?" Priscilla asked, watching as the duo passed the tables and entered the kitchen. The man in question appeared to be in his early twenties. Slight and wiry of frame, he had a pointed nose, watery blue eyes, and a patchy blond beard that didn't quite hide his acne scars.

"That's Jason. He does dishes and handyman work here and at the Marshland Diner." Joan pulled her coat off the back of her chair and slid her arms into the sleeves. "It's getting really frigid in here. Want to head out?"

Priscilla tucked her notebook into her bag. "Sure do. I'd like to get the rest of my errands done before lunch."

"And before the next storm comes in." Joan stopped winding her scarf around her neck and pointed. "Look at that sky."

The plate glass windows revealed a creeping line of clouds overtaking the blue. Priscilla sighed. "Is it really going to snow again?"

"It certainly is," a man reading his phone at a nearby table said. "They're calling for another six inches tonight." He tucked the phone away. "I'd better go gas up the snowblower."

"And I'd better stop by the store for milk and a loaf of bread," Priscilla said. "At first, when I heard that New Englanders did that before a storm, I thought you all were crazy. Now I'm doing it too."

Joan smiled. "You're catching on fast. When you live on an island, you have to hope and pray that the boat managed to arrive with the delivery." She ate the last bite of cream puff. "That's why I've started baking my own bread."

"Great idea. Maybe I'll buy some yeast and flour and try it too." Priscilla pictured herself in her cottage, baking beautiful loaves of bread. Life didn't get much cozier than that.

The cousins parted with promises to talk later, and Priscilla headed over to the East Shore Historical Museum. The small parking lot adjacent to the yellow Queen Anne was empty except for curator Mildred Pearson's automobile. Good, Priscilla would have her undivided attention. Priscilla pulled in beside Mildred's car and grabbed the tote she used for her research projects.

Mildred was dusting a china display in the 1850s dining room. She leaned over and peered through the doorway. "Good morning, Priscilla. Taking advantage of the calm before the storm?" Tall and thin, with her gray hair in a bun, Mildred was dressed like a character in *Little Women*. She always wore period clothing while at work—and sometimes during leisure time.

"You could put it that way." Priscilla made a face as she shed her outdoor garb. "It's going to snow. Again." She hung up her coat on a peg in the hallway. "I thought I'd get a little research done while I can."

Mildred sauntered out into the hallway, still holding the feather duster. "Anything in particular you're looking for?" She was a fount of knowledge about all things Martha's Vineyard and could put her hand on just about any piece of information upon request.

"You know I've been working on the lighthouse museum," Priscilla said. "I've got quite a good collection of family information, although I can always use more. I want to add something exciting to the display."

Mildred considered this, arms folded, foot tapping. "Like what? You've found treasure and solved a murder involving one of your relatives. Those are pretty exciting."

"I agree," Priscilla said. "But I was hoping for something related to the lighthouse itself."

The front doorknob rattled, and the figure of a man could be seen through the frosted glass.

"How about a shipwreck? A passenger steamer went down in 1884 right off your shoreline." The door began to open. Mildred pointed a finger at Priscilla. "Hold that thought. We've got lots of artifacts and stories about it. Even a painting."

Mildred turned her attention to the handsome man of about forty-five who stepped into the museum, and Priscilla wandered into the dining room to wait.

While she studied the lovely dishes a sea captain had brought home from the Orient, she kept an eye on Mildred and the new arrival. Dressed in an expensive wool overcoat, leather gloves, and a jaunty plaid cap, he had chiseled features and a short dark beard.

"How can I help you, Bradley?" Mildred asked.

Bradley stood just inside the door, not moving to take his coat or gloves off. "I'm not staying long. I wanted to tell you that my aunt isn't going to be making her annual gift this year."

Mildred's brow furrowed. "I'm sorry to hear that. She's been a wonderful supporter. Let's go into my office and talk about it."

He put up a hand. "There's nothing to discuss. The gravy train is over, I'm afraid." He touched the brim of his cap and pivoted on his heel. "Good day."

As Bradley exited, slamming the door behind him, Mildred stared after him, hands on hips, a confused expression on her face.

Priscilla approached. "I'm sorry, I couldn't help overhearing. Was her gift significant?"

Mildred's lips quirked in an ironic smile. "Only ten thousand a year. Rebekah Alden is one of my most generous donors. And a wonderful lady."

"Rebekah Alden? She's my neighbor." Priscilla moved toward the stairs. The archives were on the second floor, created out of three former bedrooms. "Maybe she'll change her mind."

"I doubt it, with Bradley at the helm." Mildred's tone was dark. "Let's go up. I'll show you the information on the *Edwin Fitzpatrick,* that steamship."

Upstairs, Mildred led the way to the file cabinet that held information on historic town events. She extracted a file, then pointed to a print on the wall. It depicted a foundering steamship in heavy seas and a variety of boats heading from shore to rescue people in the water. "Not a person was lost, which was a miracle. It went down so fast. Your ancestor Homer Latham spotted the wreck and summoned the rescue boats."

The painting was powerful and dramatic, perfectly capturing the moment of crisis. Priscilla bent closer to study it. "Do you think I can find a print for the museum?" The large work would make a perfect focal point for her information on Homer.

"Probably. I've seen copies for sale in the antique print shop and online." Mildred set the file on a long table. "You'll find clippings that go into detail."

"Thanks so much." Priscilla set her tote on the floor and prepared to sit down. "I'll get to work so I can make it home before the snow starts."

Mildred lingered. "Speaking of wrecks off your lighthouse, Bradley Alden was involved in one himself."

Priscilla turned in her seat to face the curator. "Really? What happened?"

A twinkle returned to Mildred's eyes. "Bradley might appear to be an upright, uptight businessman now, but when he was young, he was in all manner of scrapes."

"Go on," Priscilla said, more to humor her friend than from an interest in ancient gossip.

Mildred leaned against the filing cabinet, arms folded, and settled in to tell her story. "He was one spoiled young man, I remember. New cars, flashy motorboat, sleek wooden sloop. The sailboat belonged to Rebekah's late husband, Henry Alden. Henry adored that boat. Used to take his wife and daughter out all the time."

"And Bradley sank it," Priscilla said, chagrined at the young man's carelessness with a precious possession.

"That's right. Took it out when the forecast called for squalls. He had to be picked up out of the water. The boat was a total loss. Henry had a conniption, not just over the boat, but at Bradley putting himself in danger like that."

"I'm glad Bradley didn't drown. That would have been tragic."

Mildred straightened. "True. And since Rebekah is alone in the world now except for live-in attendants who are paid to care, he's all she's got." She frowned. "I wish I could be convinced that he has her best interests at heart."

Priscilla considered Mildred's words with growing alarm. Not that she knew her neighbor or that it was any of her business, but the idea of an elderly woman being taken advantage of didn't sit right. "I hope he does. I've been meaning to visit her. Maybe I'll move that up on my list of things to do."

The curator moved toward the door. "It probably wouldn't go amiss." She paused in the doorway. "I'll leave you be. If you need anything else, just give me a shout."

"I will." Priscilla opened the folder and was soon lost in the account of the sinking of the *Edwin Fitzpatrick*.

It's like driving in a snow globe. Priscilla squinted through the snow pelting her windshield, which either came straight on or swirled in a dizzying pattern. Despite the hour—about noon—the lowering clouds and dense snowfall made the day dark, reducing visibility to a few feet.

There was very little other traffic on the road. Occasional yellow headlights or red taillights appeared in the murk, drivers mutually slowing down to edge past each other. The pavement was white and slippery—greasy, as the natives called it—and it would take only an ill-timed tap of the brakes to send a vehicle into a skid or a snowbank.

Priscilla watched for familiar landmarks, breathing a sigh of relief when spotting each one. *Only a little farther....* She reached her driveway at last and turned in with a profound sense of gratitude. She parked the car, grabbed her tote, and slid out, then hurried to the house with head bent against the wind and icy flakes.

Inside, Jake greeted her with leaps and excited barking. "Hold on," she said with a laugh. "Let me get my coat and boots off." Once those were shed, she crouched down and gave him a thorough petting. "Were you afraid I was lost in the storm?" His answer was a lap of his tongue on her cheek. "Come on, let's get you a treat."

Before heading into the kitchen, Priscilla paused to look out at the shore. The curtain of snow obscured her usual view of water and Cape Cod's landmass. But the beam from the lighthouse cut through, a welcome sight to any sailors unfortunate enough to be caught in the storm. "Visibility less than one mile," Priscilla muttered to herself, thinking of the marine forecasts islanders lived by.

She gave Jake a treat, which he took under the table to enjoy. After tuning the radio on the windowsill to classical music, she opened the refrigerator to decide what to cook for dinner. Bad weather always inspired Priscilla to whip up nourishing, hearty meals, even now while living alone.

She had ground turkey, kale, carrots, onions, and a jar of homemade chicken stock on hand. Next she checked the freezer and found a loaf of artisan Italian bread. She would make one of her favorites, kale and turkey meatball soup, and have it with the toasted bread.

Priscilla foraged through the cupboard and selected a cast-iron dutch oven. Then she pulled out a blue pottery bowl and prepared the turkey meatballs, adding bread crumbs, grated Parmesan cheese, basil, and parsley to the meat. She shaped these into small spheres while olive oil heated in the dutch oven.

The meatballs sizzled when she slid them into the hot oil, releasing savory aromas that made her mouth water. Once the soup was set to simmer, she'd grab lunch. Keeping an eye on the browning meat, she sliced carrots and onions, then washed the kale and ripped it into small pieces. After removing the meatballs, she browned the onions with a little diced garlic, then added the carrots and kale to the pan. Once those were softened, the chicken broth went in, and the meatballs were returned to the pot.

Turning the burner to low, Priscilla checked the bubbling soup with satisfaction. Simple, but made with quality ingredients, the way food should be. "Now what, Jake?" she asked. "Leftover haddock sandwich? How does that sound?" The thumping of his tail on the floor was her answer.

Seated at the kitchen table, Priscilla was enjoying the sandwich, made with thick toasted bread and tartar sauce, when her phone rang. Rachel was calling.

"Mom. How are you?" In the background, Priscilla could hear the murmur of voices and the clatter of computer keys. "Martha's Vineyard was featured on the weather news. And not in a good way."

Glancing out the window at the storm, Priscilla laughed. "It's snowing, all right. But Jake and I are warm and snug inside. We're fine."

"You have enough food? What if the power goes out? What will you do then?" Her daughter's questions poured out in an anxious, fretful stream.

Priscilla took a deep breath, knowing that Rachel meant well. Concern was her way of showing love, even if it sometimes made Priscilla feel like a scolded child. "I'll light a fire in the fireplace. Besides, having the lighthouse here means we're high on the priority list for power. It's not islanders who are in danger, it's the ships passing by in bad weather. I was just reading today about a horrible shipwreck in the 1800s—"

"Mom." Rachel cut her off. "I know I'm a pain sometimes. But...but...I miss you. I guess worrying is my way of telling you that."

Priscilla pulled the phone away from her ear and stared at it for a second, not quite believing what she had just heard. She hadn't realized her daughter was so insightful about that particular trait. "I know that, darling. I miss you too." And just like that, she did. A wave of homesickness washed over her like a flood. So many precious times with Rachel and Gary were all in the past now, relived only in memory. A choking sound came out of her mouth, and she quickly covered it with a cough.

Rachel heard, of course. "What was that? Are you all right?"

"I'm fine." Priscilla took a drink of water. "A crumb went down wrong."

"Be careful eating alone." Then Rachel laughed. "Sorry, Mom. Look, I've got to go. I'll check in on you later, okay? Love you. Bye."

As quickly as she'd swooped in, Rachel was gone, leaving Priscilla holding a dead phone. The wind howled around the cottage and down the chimney, making an eerie whining note. Snowfall pressed close to the cottage, blocking Priscilla from the outdoors as effectively as an opaque blanket.

Loneliness draped over her, a dark, suffocating cloud. Why was she here again, thousands of miles from the only family, well, *immediate* family, she had left—

Something moved outside the window. A rush of surprised horror flashed over Priscilla, washing away her maudlin thoughts.

An elderly woman was staggering through the snow, wearing only a long red flannel nightgown.

CHAPTER THREE

Priscilla ran for her boots and coat. Thinking of the woman's inadequate attire, she snatched a second jacket off the pegs. Then she bolted for the door, hoping the poor thing hadn't wandered off a cliff or tumbled into the water. The tide was high, and waves were crashing on the beach and rocks, ready to soak the unwary.

Priscilla stepped outside, accompanied by an inquisitive Jake, who had insisted on coming with her. She was met by snow-laden gusts of wind that slapped her in the face, causing her to gasp in shock. Bracing herself, she took tentative steps, scanning the shoreline for a glimpse of the red nightdress. If the woman had fallen, she might already be covered with snow, it was coming down so heavily.

Jake whined, seeming to sense Priscilla's mission. "Where is she, Jake?" Maybe he could find her. As if answering her, he leaped into the snow like a swimmer diving into deep water. He began to plow through the drifts, leaving a wake of snowflakes behind him.

There she is. Priscilla looked in the direction Jake was "swimming" through the snow and spotted a flash of red on the other side of a group of boulders. In a wide-legged gait for balance, she followed Jake along the shore, moving as fast as she could in snow that reached her knees. The drifts also hid hazards: holes and rocks that could send her flying or twist an ankle if she wasn't careful.

Even in her heavy garb, the cold was numbing, the wind teasing at her collar and sleeve hems. Her feet already felt like blocks of ice. The woman had to be frozen, perhaps even hypothermic. Priscilla forced her legs to move faster despite the deep snow pushing against her.

She remembered a freak late spring snowstorm when she and Gary had to rescue young calves stranded in the fields. She felt the same urgency of racing against the falling temperatures and inclement conditions imperiling a vulnerable creature.

Priscilla reached the boulders at last. The woman huddled among them, her gown spilling across the white snow like blood. Jake had circled around and was pressing close to the wanderer, instinctively trying to warm her.

The woman gazed up at Priscilla with wide, pale-blue eyes. "Who are you?" Thankfully her voice was still strong, and she appeared alert, if confused.

Priscilla recognized the worn and weary but still lovely features. "I'm your neighbor, Priscilla Latham Grant." She included her island family's name in hopes it would place her in Rebekah Alden's mind. "What are you doing out here, Rebekah? Come on, let's go inside and get warm."

To her relief, Rebekah took the hand Priscilla extended, rising slowly from her crouched position with mutters and groans. "I could use a cup of tea, if you have it."

"I certainly do." Priscilla put a gentle arm around the woman's shoulders, noticing how fragile and frail she was. *Like Mom.* Priscilla's heart twisted in compassion and tenderness. Her mother had died a decade ago, and at the end she'd been tiny like this, all skin and bones, a formidable spirit lighting her sunken eyes.

Rebekah pulled her foot out of the snow, a sodden fleece slipper still somehow attached. "It's hard walking in the snow. I'd forgotten. But I wanted to..." Her voice faded.

Wanted to what? Priscilla attempted a hearty laugh. "I'll say it's challenging, hiking through snow. I'm using muscles I forgot I had."

"Me too." Rebekah leaned heavily on Priscilla's shoulder as they trudged back to the cottage using the tracks Priscilla and Jake had made, which was slightly easier than breaking the trail had been.

Priscilla was still exhausted by the time they reached the side entrance of the cottage, and it took all her strength to get Rebekah up the steps and into the house. Mind whirring furiously, Priscilla unzipped her jacket and kicked off her boots. Fresh clothing, blankets, and a seat by the fire—that was the protocol she remembered for treating possible hypothermia.

Rebekah's eyes darted around the cottage, taking in every detail. "I haven't been here in decades. But it hasn't changed much." She began to shiver, her teeth chattering. On the way inside, she'd lost a slipper in the deep snow.

"Come with me into the bathroom." Priscilla guided her into the room, then flew to her bureau to pull out underwear, thick wool socks, a thermal top, and a soft fleece lounging set Rachel had bought her for Christmas. All of it was too big but would work in a pinch. Wincing at the forced intimacy, she helped Rebekah out of her gown, rubbed her down with a towel, and assisted her in putting on the dry clothing. Again, she was reminded of her mother during her final illness, of her helplessness and dependence. She found herself blinking back tears. Didn't anyone care about this precious woman?

Where are her caretakers or her nephew? Hasn't anyone missed her?

"Let's go sit in front of the fire," Priscilla said once Rebekah was dressed. She seated her neighbor beside the fireplace and wrapped an afghan around her shoulders. "I'll make a fire and then go put the kettle on." Kindling was already laid, so Priscilla added balls of paper and lit a match. Once the kindling caught, she added a few small logs.

Rebekah leaned back in the chair, staring into the flickering flames. "I do love a nice fire on a cold day." She turned her head to look at her rescuer. "You're a good woman, Priscilla Latham Grant." The use of Priscilla's full name seemed deliberate, almost teasing.

Priscilla's eyes met Rebekah's, and she saw keen intelligence in their depths. A tingling ran up her spine, a warning that something was out of place. *She's no more senile than I am. What is going on?*

Out in the kitchen, Priscilla put the kettle on. Then she dug the local phone book out of a drawer. Rebekah was listed, as Priscilla had suspected she might be. Many older folks had kept their landlines. She picked up her own house phone and dialed the number.

The other end rang eight, nine, ten times. Priscilla was about to hang up when someone answered. "Hello?" a woman said in a raspy voice. "Alden residence."

"Hi, this is Priscilla Grant, your neighbor. I own the lighthouse." She paused briefly to allow the woman to absorb that. "I've got Rebekah in my living room." She paused again. "She was wandering around in the storm, wearing only a nightgown."

The woman gasped. "What? That can't be. Hold on." Priscilla heard a clunk as the woman set the receiver down. Then she heard people talking in the background, the raspy female voice plus a deeper male rumble. Within a minute or two, the woman was back. "You're right, she's gone. You say she's at your house?"

Priscilla bit back her impatience. "That's right. Sitting by the fire and warming up." With effort she kept reproach out of her voice. The kettle shrieked, and she pulled it off the heat. "I saw her walking along the shore in her nightgown, so I went out and brought her inside." Holding the phone with her shoulder, she opened a canister of teabags and plopped one into each mug, then poured steaming water over the bags.

The woman snorted. "She must have snuck out. I told Ed he oughta lock the doors and windows. She's been getting away from us lately."

Does Bradley know that? Priscilla cleared her throat, forbearing to comment. "Well, can you please come get her? I think she'll be happier in her own home." She set the mugs on a tray and added a sugar bowl and pitcher of milk. "And bring boots and a coat for her."

"Hmm. It's snowing real hard out right now...."

Priscilla remained silent. While she liked and respected Rebekah, her caretakers needed to fulfill their responsibilities.

The woman blew out an exasperated sigh. "All right. We'll be there as soon as we can."

Please, God, Priscilla prayed as she carried the tray into the living room, *don't let me ever be at the mercy of such people.*

After doctoring a mug with sugar and milk, Priscilla handed it to Rebekah, who nodded in thanks. Then she added another log to the fire, which was already radiating welcome heat. The cold material clinging to her legs reminded her that she should also change. The snow had reached well above her boots. "Please excuse me while I change out of my wet pants."

Rebekah saluted her with the mug. "I'll be right here by this cozy fire with your wonderful dog." Jake had plopped down right on top of her feet. She reached down to scratch his ears. "You're a love, aren't you?" He gave a grunting sigh of pleasure.

In her bedroom, Priscilla peeled off the pants and the damp long johns, hung them to dry in the bathroom, and then slid into a pair of cozy sweats and fresh socks. Not wanting to leave her guest alone long, she hurried back to the living room.

"How are you feeling, Rebekah?" she asked, sitting in the wing chair opposite. She reached for her mug of tea. Taking a welcome sip, the mug warm in her hands, she studied the other woman. Color had returned to her face, and a slight smile creased her lips as she gazed into the fire. Anyone looking at her wouldn't guess that only minutes ago she'd been drifting along the shore like a wraith.

"I'm fine." Rebekah extended one hand then the other, flexing her fingers, shifting the mug as she did so. "My hands and feet were frozen, but they're all warmed up now." Confusion creased her brow. "I don't know what...why..." She shook her head as though to dislodge her thoughts.

Priscilla didn't press, but she resolved to have a private word with Bradley Alden. Something was going on with his aunt, and it needed to be addressed. She changed the subject. "Would you like something to eat?" She thought of the dish simmering on the range top. "I have homemade soup."

Rebekah brightened. "Is that what I smell? I'd love some."

Priscilla was hungry herself after the ordeal of rescuing Rebekah, so she ladled out two bowls, added sliced bread and butter, and brought the whole thing in so they could dine by the fire. Standing trays made nice tables for that purpose.

They both dug in, accompanied by the crackling fire, snoring dog, and the hiss of snow against the windows. Once in a while the snug cottage creaked and groaned when a strong gust of wind hit.

"I've been meaning to come visit you," Priscilla said. "But time always gets away from me."

"You're welcome any time." Rebekah's smile was warm. "I heard you're creating a museum in the lighthouse. I might have some photographs you can use." She ate another spoonful of soup.

"My husband and I were good friends with your grandfather, Warren Latham. He and Henry, my husband, used to go sailing together. Warren also played the fiddle, and he'd sit on the boat when it was becalmed and play sea chanteys until the wind came up."

Priscilla was thrilled at this glimpse into her grandfather's life. Her mother had left the island as a young woman, and Priscilla had not known her grandparents well.

The rumble of a truck was heard outside, and a moment later there was a knock on the front door. Priscilla levered herself out of the comfortable chair, reluctant to move. "I'll be right back," she assured her guest.

A thin woman with long, straggly hair stood at the door, holding a pair of boots in one hand and a parka in the other. "Hi, I'm here to pick up Rebekah." Behind her in the driveway, a large pickup truck waited, headlights aimed at the house. Their glare illuminated the snowflakes cascading down.

Priscilla held out a hand and introduced herself. She wanted to find out who these people were, not just hand over Rebekah like so much stray baggage. "And you are?" she added when the woman didn't reply.

"Oh. I'm Maureen Moody." She jerked her chin toward the waiting vehicle. "Ed's my husband. We look after Rebekah."

Not very well. "Why don't you come in? She's just finishing up her meal."

Maureen glanced back over her shoulder, as if seeking Ed's approval. "Okay. For a minute. But we got to get going." She kicked her boots against the threshold and followed Priscilla inside to the living room.

"There you are, you naughty girl." Maureen dropped the boots and coat on the floor, then shook an admonishing finger at her charge. "Why'd you go off and do something like that? Had us worried sick."

Rebekah seemed to shrink under the onslaught of her caretaker's scolding. She waved her hands, her face a mask of guilty confusion. "I don't know...I'm sorry..."

Anger boiled up in Priscilla's chest as she hurried to move Rebekah's tray so she could get up from the armchair. Every drop of soup was gone, she noticed. Were they feeding the poor woman? She'd definitely speak to Bradley about this situation, sooner rather than later. While Maureen didn't appear mean, treating Rebekah like an errant two-year-old was condescending. Plus, the caretakers hadn't noticed her absence, so they certainly weren't worried, judging from the phone call.

Priscilla helped Rebekah to her feet. "You can keep those clothes for the ride home."

"We'll get 'em back to you," Maureen said. "Nice of you to help."

"No problem. It was a pleasure having you visit, Rebekah." Priscilla patted her neighbor's shoulder, wanting more than anything to give her a hug. "I'll be over soon to see you."

Maureen frowned. "She don't have too many visitors."

Priscilla regarded the caretaker levelly. "Well, that's about to change. Rebekah and I have things to discuss."

Rebekah shuffled across the rug toward her caretaker, who helped her put on the coat and boots. "Thanks for dinner, Priscilla Latham Grant. It was a pleasure dining with you."

"Same here, Rebekah Alden. Let me bag up your nightgown." Priscilla darted to the bathroom, where she'd hung the garment to dry.

From there, she clearly heard Rebekah's quavering voice say, "Don't tell Bradley, okay? I don't want him to put me in a home, like he's been saying."

CHAPTER FOUR

Priscilla's hand froze in the act of pulling the nightgown from the rail. *Bradley wants to put Rebekah in a home?* Perhaps appealing to him wasn't the wisest idea, since what she regarded as the caretakers' failure was likely to be used against their charge, as proof she needed more supervision.

She grabbed the nightie and folded it, then tucked it into a plastic bag. She also tossed in the lone slipper. Perhaps they'd find the other one when the snow melted.

Her desire to keep an eye on Rebekah hardened into determination. Perhaps if Ed and Maureen realized she was watching them, they'd do a better job and Rebekah would be able to live out her days in her own house.

After saying goodbye to Rebekah, with another promise to see her soon, Priscilla returned to her early dinner by the fireside. Her soup was cold, so she added more from the pot, poked the fire into life, and sat down to enjoy the peace and quiet. Jake stretched out on the hearthrug for a nap, and after eating, Priscilla picked up her latest novel from the library and opened it to where she'd left off.

Glancing outside once in a while to check the progress of the snowstorm, Priscilla realized she was content. Yes, she was a little lonely, but on a night like this, what more could she ask for? She had a sturdy roof, a warm fire, and a happy dog.

The sound of scraping and a rumbling engine awoke Priscilla early the next morning. She peeked out the window and saw a pickup truck plowing her driveway. She'd had to hire someone since there was no way she could shovel the long driveway herself, and she wasn't quite ready to operate a snow blower.

Next she checked the ocean view. The snow had stopped for the moment, and a line of pink and yellow etched the eastern horizon. Pewter-gray waves rippled under an overcast sky.

Instead of going back to bed, Priscilla made coffee and took a mug into the bathroom to drink while she ran a hot bath. Her cousin Trudy had given her two bottles of organic bubble bath for Christmas, and she hadn't opened them yet. Deciding today was as good a time as any, she cracked the lids and sniffed. *Yum.* Eucalyptus with citrus, and lavender with calendula. The second one might be too relaxing, so she chose the first, a livelier blend. While relaxing in the steamy water and bubbles, continuing to sip her coffee, Priscilla thought about the day ahead.

Without much on the agenda, she might as well spend the day making headway on the museum project. Her goal was to open up next summer, when the island tours began again. She was at the point where she could design the layout, she decided, and then fill in any blanks she discovered. That would focus her research going forward.

She'd heard the plow truck drive off a while ago, so when she heard scraping sounds again, she was puzzled. The water was getting cold anyway—and her fingers were wrinkled—so she stepped out of the tub, dried off, and slipped on a robe. The noise was coming from the side door, so she tiptoed across the floor and peeked out a window.

Eek. Gerald O'Bannon was shoveling her steps. Priscilla flushed, instinctively grabbing the neck of her robe even though he couldn't see her. She flew to the bedroom to get dressed, opening and shutting drawers before settling on a flattering turtleneck and sweater combination and her best pair of jeans. Striped hand-made socks completed the outfit.

Priscilla opened the door and peeked out, feeling slightly breathless. "Good morning, Gerald. How nice of you to shovel my steps."

He stopped with shovel lifted and smiled, his hazel eyes twinkling. "Thought you might need a hand. This snow just keeps on coming. We'll all be buried before long." He deftly tossed the snow onto the heap he'd made next to the porch and scooped up another shovelful.

"Please come in for a cup of coffee when you're finished." She hesitated. "If you have time, that is." Boy, was she out of practice! She was afraid of sounding too bold or, conversely, pushing him away by being too aloof.

"I'll do that." He tossed aside another load of snow. "I brought treats from the bakery. Guess I hoped you'd invite me in for that coffee." His grin was wide, with a hint of hopeful bashfulness.

Priscilla found herself returning his infectious smile, her heart lifting in pure joy. "Anytime. See you in a few." Inside, she hustled to the kitchen, where she made a fresh pot of coffee. She got out her best pottery mugs and plates, cheerful orange cloth napkins, and her good spoons.

By the time the hot brew finished dripping, Gerald was at the door, bakery bag in hand. Kicking his boots on the threshold, he stepped inside, bringing the fresh scent of salty cold air with him. "Whew, that was quite a workout," he said, handing Priscilla the bag. "And people wonder why we islanders don't need to go to the gym." He winked.

Priscilla laughed. "I know. It's a lot of work keeping up with the seasons." She looked inside the bag, then almost dropped it in surprise. Gerald had brought Candy's rosemary shortbread cookies, called "love cookies" by bakery customers. "These look great."

Gerald hung up his coat, took off his hat, and ran a hand through his rumpled hair. "I heard they were good. Hope you like them."

Did he know the meaning locals assigned to these cookies? They were an item people bought to signify special feelings. Priscilla clutched the bag. "Oh, I'm sure I will. Everything Candy bakes is superb."

She told Gerald to take a seat while she poured coffee and placed the cookies on a plate. After ferrying everything to the table, she slid into the chair opposite him. "Help yourself, milk and sugar are right here."

For a moment they were silent while they doctored their coffees and selected shortbread. Priscilla took a curious nibble of a cookie. The buttery crumbs practically melted in her mouth, releasing both savory and sweet flavors. "Wow. *Yum*." Then she blushed, hearing the echo of her fervent approval.

Gerald laughed. "I guess I made a good choice." His eyes lingered on hers. Then he cleared his throat and looked away, out the window at the snowy vista. "Supposed to snow again later."

"You know what would be real news?" she declared. "That it *isn't* going to snow."

"Too true. I haven't seen such a snowy winter for years." He sipped his coffee. "Good java. Hits the spot."

"Come by anytime." She blushed. Talk about brazen. And hadn't she already said something like that?

Again Gerald changed the subject, apparently more skilled at managing fledgling flirtations than she was. He reached for his wallet. "Want to see something cute?" He extracted a tiny photo of two children, his grandson Max, three and a half, and brand-new granddaughter Ava, born in January.

"They're precious," she said, studying the pride with which a grinning Max clasped his sister, whose bald head was adorned by a bow. "Do you see them often?"

"As often as I can." His lips quirked. "Sometimes Aggie lets me babysit."

Priscilla knew Gerald's divorce from his first wife hadn't been easy and relationships with his children had been somewhat strained as a result. But now, with the advent of a new generation, fences were being mended.

He glanced at his watch. "That reminds me. I'll be picking up Max for our lunch date at noon. We go out for burgers and ice cream as often as we can."

"That sounds nice," Priscilla said, feeling wistful. She and Rachel had gone out for special meals too, sandwiches and soup at the department store lunch counter. Was that department store even in business anymore? She didn't think so—

He scraped back his chair. "You hear that?"

She listened. "You mean that boat engine?" It was a pretty powerful one, but that wasn't so odd. All manner of commercial boats went by the lighthouse, from lobster boats to freighters to tankers.

"Excuse me for a minute." He got up and strode from the kitchen to a window with an ocean view.

Wondering what on earth was going on, she followed. She found him peering out into the bay with a pair of small binoculars he must have had in his pocket. She supposed a Coast Guard captain never went anywhere without them.

"Sorry," he said, still studying the water. "We've been watching for suspicious activity."

"Like what?" she blurted. She bit her tongue. He probably couldn't talk about it.

But he answered. "We've had a report of cigarette smugglers operating in these waters." He lowered the glasses. "Yes, cigarettes are smuggled, believe it or not. People try to get around the taxes. It makes them significantly cheaper. Almost a third of the cigarettes smoked in this state are smuggled in." He folded the binoculars and slipped them into his pants pocket. "That boat appeared to be legit, so no high alert this morning."

"That's good news." She gestured toward the kitchen. "Come finish your coffee."

Gerald stayed long enough to drink another cup and eat most of the cookies. Priscilla enjoyed his visit, reflecting on how nice it was to sit with a man and talk about nothing of great importance. One of life's simple pleasures.

After he left, she busied herself cleaning up the kitchen and making a grocery list. She liked to keep a well-stocked pantry on hand, especially now when the weather might make it difficult to get out to the store.

The telephone rang as she finished up her list. She hastily closed the refrigerator and answered.

"Um, is this Priscilla?" the caller asked. "This is Harper Jenson. Um, from the bakery?"

Priscilla was genuinely glad to hear from her new acquaintance. She'd been wondering if the young woman would actually call. So many people didn't follow through. "Hi there. How are you?"

"I'm good, thanks." A pause. "I hope you don't mind, I got your number from Candy. I was wondering when you might have time to help me do that research? If you still want to, that is."

Priscilla could practically feel the young woman's twitchy anxiety over the line. She pictured Harper holding her breath for the answer. "Of course I'll help you. I'm actually heading over to the museum in a few minutes. Maybe you can meet me there."

Harper's words flowed in a relieved rush. "Oh, I can do that, I just got off work. I'll see you there, then. Thanks so much." Another pause. "Um, what time?"

"Let's say half an hour. I have no idea what the roads are like."

"Not too great. But at least the plows are out. See ya."

Harper was right. Although most of the snow had been cleared, strong winds were causing drifting, the fine powder so thick in the air that at times it was like driving in a sandstorm. Or what Priscilla imagined a sandstorm was like.

Feeling as intrepid as any explorer or early settler, Priscilla navigated the route to the museum, arriving a few minutes before the appointed time she was to meet Harper. She went through the familiar ritual of leveraging her heavily clothed body out of the car while grabbing her tote and handbag.

Mildred watched her from the porch. Dressed in a long wool period coat, bonnet, and bright striped muffler, she looked like a woman on a Victorian postcard. But she leaned on a very modern plastic snow shovel. "Good morning, Priscilla. I didn't expect to see you two days in a row."

Priscilla climbed the stairs, thankful Mildred had cleared them of snow and ice. "I thought I'd get ahead of it all while we're more or less snowbound. In warmer weather, I won't feel like doing research."

Mildred pushed the shovel along the boards, scraping up the flakes filtering back through the spindles due to the wind. "I hear you. On days like this, it's hard to believe spring will ever come again."

That was something Priscilla had noticed too, how difficult it was to imagine another season while firmly experiencing its opposite. Sometimes she tried just for the refreshing mental break it gave her from hot or cold temperatures.

"Who's that?" Mildred had stopped shoveling and was gazing over Priscilla's shoulder. Priscilla turned to see Harper Jenson bolting down the street, heedless of the treacherous snow and ice covering the sidewalk. When she got closer, Priscilla saw that the young woman's pretty features were etched with fear.

CHAPTER FIVE

I wonder what's wrong," Mildred said. "She looks scared."

"I'm thinking the same thing." Priscilla walked down the steps and waved, hoping Harper would see her. "That's Harper Jenson. She's meeting me here to do some research."

Priscilla knew the moment Harper spotted her, because her expression smoothed out and the panic in her eyes was replaced by relief. Her steps slowed, and by the time she reached the museum, she was walking, one hand to her chest.

"Whew. I never thought I'd make it." Panting, Harper bent over, resting her hands on her thighs. Despite the cold and wind, she wore a skirt with thick tights, a pea coat, beret, gloves, and heavy black leather boots. A messenger bag was slung around her shoulder and chest.

"Come on in," Priscilla said. "It's freezing out here." On the porch, she introduced Harper to Mildred before opening the museum door to usher Harper inside.

"You two go ahead and get settled, and I'll be right in." Mildred's expression as she regarded Harper was curious, but she didn't pry. "I only have a little more to shovel." Another gust of wind cast a fresh layer of snow on the porch floor, and she set to work with a grumble.

In the entranceway, Priscilla showed Harper where to hang her coat and hat. She noticed that the young woman kept peering out the window while she was taking off her outwear. "Harper, is everything all right?"

Harper's gaze flew to the ornate staircase, up to the ceiling, down to the boots she still wore, anywhere but to Priscilla's face. Priscilla noticed her hands were trembling as she ran them across her skirt front.

"It's okay. We'll help you, if you need it." Priscilla spoke in the same reassuring tone she used on stray puppies and kittens.

Harper's big eyes met Priscilla's. "I might. I think. Maybe." Her face creased up like an upset child's. "I thought I saw someone I know drive by in a truck. It looked like he was following me...." The words trailed off, and she swallowed hard.

"Someone you want to avoid?" Tension twisted in Priscilla's midsection, and her pulse notched up. She had a good idea where this discussion was going. One of Priscilla's volunteer activities in Kansas had been helping out at a women's shelter. She knew that abusers rarely let their victims go without a battle.

Harper nodded, her gaze still fixed on Priscilla's face. After appearing to search for words, she said, "I left...my boyfriend when I came here. I think he might have followed me."

"All right. If he's dangerous, let's report that to the police." Priscilla kept her tone brisk yet warm. "They're very good out here, and I'm sure they'll find him if he's on the island." The front doorknob rattled, announcing Mildred's arrival. "We'll talk about it later," Priscilla whispered, wanting to preserve the young woman's privacy.

Harper nodded.

Once inside, Mildred stripped off her gloves and rubbed her hands together. "Wow. I'm frozen stiff. Why don't you two go up to the archives, and I'll join you in a few? I need to warm up first." She flexed her long fingers with a wince, then bent to unlace her tall leather boots.

"We'll do that," Priscilla said. She led Harper upstairs to the research room and set her tote and bag on her favorite table. "Have a seat, and we'll get started."

Harper ducked out of her messenger bag strap and placed the satchel on the table. "There sure is a lot of stuff in here. How do you find anything?"

"Believe me, Mildred has it all organized. But first we need to decide what we're looking for." Priscilla sat at the table and foraged for a notepad and pen in her tote. "Let's write down what you know about your mom, and then we can decide how to fill in the blanks."

"I brought the diary with me." Harper unfastened her bag and withdrew a small cream-colored book embossed with a flower and vine design. A metal latch held it closed. "Fortunately it wasn't locked. I found it in a box of old papers." For a long moment she held the book in both hands, as though reluctant to let go.

"It's precious, isn't it? A connection to your mother." Priscilla felt the same way about the items that once belonged to her relatives. They had touched, used, and in some cases, loved those objects.

With a look of surprise, Harper set the book on the table and opened it. "You get it. Now I know for sure you're the right person to help me." She spun the diary around so Priscilla could read the first page.

On the line for a name, *Megan* was written in a loopy, exuberant scrawl, giving Priscilla the impression of a vibrant personality. No last name was written.

"Do you know her maiden name?" Priscilla asked.

"Elliot was on my birth certificate, but my uncle said it wasn't her real last name."

How strange. Unfortunately Megan was not an uncommon first name, especially during the 1970s, when she figured Harper's mother was born. "How long ago did she pass away, and how old was she?" Priscilla asked.

"It was just last year, and she was forty-two," Harper said, which confirmed Priscilla's guess. She turned the book back around and began leafing through it. "This is where she mentioned the Vineyard. Before that, it was all about school and how much she hated it."

"'Summer is finally here,'" Priscilla read, "'and the Vineyard is as beautiful as ever. I can't wait to visit Big Rock, the Island, and Secret Cove. Robert and David and Zinnia came over to get me, and we went out in the motorboat and did some fishing. I caught the biggest one, which made them so mad—'" Priscilla stopped reading. "Does she ever give their full names?"

Harper thrust both hands into her hair and tugged with a growl. "No. And it's so frustrating."

"Well, I guess there's no reason for last names in a diary. She's writing only to herself, after all. Did she have any brothers or sisters?"

"No, none that I know of. It was just me, my mom, and my dad. And he died the winter I was three."

Poor child. She'd grown up without her father.

"And before you ask," Harper went on, "no one on his side knows anything. All he had was a brother, anyway. This is what Uncle Bob told me in an email." Harper scrolled through her phone, then read out loud, "'Your dad said your mom was the prettiest girl he'd ever seen, and he was right. But she also kept things really close to the vest. We all had the impression she was either an orphan or something terrible had happened to make her leave her family. Your dad told me Elliot wasn't her birth name, but he never did know her real one. Anyway, she never talked about her past or her family, and after a while we stopped asking. What does it matter? She was part of our clan. And you are too. Don't forget it while you're roaming around on your big adventure, okay?'"

"He sounds like a nice guy," Priscilla said.

"He is. But he's stationed in the Middle East. Not exactly next door. And my grandparents on that side are both gone." Harper set down her phone. "So what do we do now? How can we find Mom's family?"

Megan's mention of school had sparked something in Priscilla's mind. "I have an idea," she said. "Hold on a minute." She slid her chair back. "I'm going to ask Mildred something."

A few minutes later, Mildred entered the room and set a stack of colorful high school yearbooks in the center of the table. "Here you go. Good luck."

Seven books later, in a date range that she and Harper decided was the most promising, Priscilla was ready to concede defeat. She'd studied so many hopeful young faces that they were all blurring together. She'd been right—many girls born in the 1970s had been named Megan. Of that number, quite a few had dark hair and petite features, like Harper, but—

"None of them are Mom." Harper put her head down on her folded arms. "I want one of them to be, but..." She groaned.

Mildred poked her head around the doorjamb. "I've got hot tea in the kitchen if you want a break. You two look like you could use one. Bad case of research fatigue?"

"Bad case of a big fat dead end," Priscilla said. She slid back her chair. "I'd love a cup of tea. How about you, Harper?"

Harper raised her head. "Sure. That sounds good."

On the way downstairs, Harper touched Priscilla's arm. "About what I told you earlier, I might have been wrong. I didn't really see the guy's face."

Is she backtracking out of fear, or is she really uncertain that she saw him? Priscilla hesitated, not sure what to say. The last thing she wanted was to discourage Harper from confiding in her. "That's understandable. You were probably afraid it *was* him—what is his name?"

"Ollie Perkins," Harper whispered, as though she loathed verbalizing his name.

Priscilla filed that away for future reference and perhaps a bit of internet snooping. "Promise me one thing, okay? If you do see him or hear from him, please let me know." She attempted to inject the right note of friendly but not overbearing concern into her voice. "You're among friends here. Call me anytime, day or night."

The young woman nodded. "I will. Promise." She started walking down the stairs again. When they reached the entrance hall, she paused to say, "Today was a total bust, wasn't it? Do you ever think we'll find my mom's family?"

"I do," Priscilla said, though she had doubts about the likelihood of their success. "We've only just gotten started, so don't give up yet."

People talked about how hard it was to disappear and erase your identity. Megan had done a very good job of it, however, leaving only this lovely young woman as evidence that she had lived.

CHAPTER SIX

The throbbing sound of a boat engine woke Priscilla during the night. Not that she had never heard any before, but perhaps Gerald's visit had made her more alert. This one sounded especially low and grumbling. If it were a car, it would be a monster truck with huge tires.

It was very early on Sunday morning, two a.m., according to the clock on her bedside table. A very unusual hour for a tanker or fisherman or cargo ship. She slipped out of bed and went to the window. Jake, sleeping in his bed, lifted his head. "It's all right, Jake. Just a noise."

At the window, she pulled back the curtain and peered outside. *Maybe I should use a spyglass like my ancestors.* Now that she'd lived at the lighthouse awhile, she fully understood the desire to identify passing vessels.

The pearly half moon was sinking in the west, and the bay and sky were an inky expanse, broken only by the sweep of the lighthouse beam. No boat lights, yet the engine continued to thrum.

That was strange. Boats were required by marine law to engage navigation lights for safety at night. Priscilla made a note of the date and time and the direction the sound was coming from, although determining that was tricky. Sound echoed and bounced on the water. She did the best she could and crawled back into bed, grateful for the warm covers.

The next morning was clear and bright, Priscilla was glad to see, since she absolutely needed to go to church. Her hour in those hallowed walls was a sweet sanctuary, a time to recalibrate her life and her direction.

She made it on time despite the poor roads, joining the churchgoers streaming along the sidewalk to Faith Fellowship Church. She nodded hello to Tilly Snyder and Mildred, then stopped for a moment to speak to her cousin Gail, who had her father Hugh in tow. Gail took care of her elderly father, who lived with her.

"Isn't it a lovely morning?" Priscilla said. "I was starting to feel awfully housebound."

"Cabin fever get to you?" Hugh chuckled. He wore a striped wool hat so low over his balding head that it almost touched his bushy gray eyebrows. "You gotta be tough if you're going to make it living on the island. In the old days—"

"Pop." Gail's tone was reproving. "Don't tease Priscilla. You know you were fit to be tied yourself with all this bad weather." She was bundled up too, dressed in a practical down parka and duck boots made of leather with rubber soles.

Priscilla laughed. "I feel like I haven't seen you two for ages. Let's have breakfast tomorrow at the bakery."

"If we can make it out of the yard," Hugh grumbled.

"We'll make it." Gail sent her father a quelling glance. "I'll touch base with Trudy and Joan and invite them too."

"That sounds like a plan," Priscilla said. Her heart lifted at the prospect of spending time with her cousins and uncle. It would be a perfect way to start the week.

As the front door opened to let someone into the church, organ notes drifted out, a sure sign the service was about to begin. Priscilla glanced toward the door. "We'd better get inside."

In response, father and daughter turned and began trudging up the walk, Gail watching closely to ensure Hugh didn't slip and fall. Priscilla followed, chafing a little at the slow pace but not wanting to be rude and push past.

Gerald came trotting up the sidewalk. "Good morning, Priscilla. I see I'm not the only latecomer today."

"I wasn't late, but I got to talking." She slowed to let him catch up, and then they strolled along together. No one else was within earshot, so she said, "Remember the, uh, situation you mentioned the other morning? I heard something strange out in the bay last night."

He raised his brows, his keen eyes focusing with laser-like intensity. "Go on."

She described the boat engines, the lack of lights, and the time of night. He was so interested that he stopped and jotted notes in a small notebook he carried.

"Thanks, Priscilla. You've given me some really good intelligence. I'm glad you're so observant."

Warmth spread through her chest at the praise. "Well, I am descended from lighthouse keepers. I guess it's in my genes."

"That could be." He opened the tall front door for her. "After you."

They scooted into seats as the organist hit the first notes of the opening song. Sharing a covert smile with Gerald at squeaking in under the wire, Priscilla opened her hymnal to the correct page.

The service was lovely, and she was especially touched by the reading of Psalm 68, which continued to resonate in her heart and mind, especially verse six: "God sets the lonely in families."

All the way home, she meditated on that verse, thinking of Harper. If there was ever a young woman who needed a family, it was Harper. Poor brave soul, leaving all she knew to come to a strange place in search of relatives. And running away from a bad boyfriend to boot.

Priscilla said a prayer that the Lord would guide them to Harper's relatives and that they would welcome her with open arms and warm hearts. That the vulnerable young woman would be protected from harm and provided for in every way.

Invite her to church. The thought dropped into her mind like a pebble into a pond.

I will, Lord.

That wasn't all. As she drove past Rebekah's house, she felt a prompting to visit, not sometime in the future, but today. The feeling didn't disperse once she got home, so after taking off her outer clothes and greeting Jake, she picked up the phone and called. Maybe someday they'd be on a footing where she could pop in, but not yet. She needed to make sure it was a good time.

Maureen answered, as expected. "Alden residence."

"Good afternoon. This is your neighbor, Priscilla. How are you today? I'd like to bring over a tureen of..." She racked her brain, thinking about what she could make with what she had on hand. "Homemade pea soup and biscuits. Would later today be a good time? You can have my soup for supper, it's that hearty."

"Well...I suppose. What time you thinkin'?"

"How about three?" That would give her plenty of time to let the pea soup simmer. "Rebekah said she had some photographs she'd like me to see, and I was hoping to come over today. I'm putting together a museum here, you see—"

"Three o'clock will be fine. Maybe you can stay with Rebekah while we go out for a while. Me and Ed need to do some shopping."

All right, then. Despite a spurt of annoyance at the woman's presumption, Priscilla decided she'd actually prefer it if the caretakers were gone. Maybe she'd be able to better evaluate how well they were treating Rebekah. "That will be fine with me. I'll see you in a bit."

Priscilla dug out her mother's pea soup recipe. While some people preferred to soak the peas and others to simmer them for hours, she used the quick soak method, as her mother had done. The peas were brought to a boil for five minutes, then left, lid on, for an hour. While they were soaking, she made a fire, ate a quick sandwich, and read a book, thankful for the Sunday quiet.

After draining the peas of that starchy soaking water, she diced potatoes, carrots, onions, and celery, sautéing them lightly in olive oil before adding them to the peas, along with chicken broth. Last she added spices and diced ham for savory flavor and depth. A final stir, adjustment of heat, and she was done. Now on to the biscuits.

On the dot of three, Priscilla was ringing the doorbell at the Alden home. While waiting, she studied every detail of the classic New England house with interest. The front porch, while not large, had lattice screens on both ends and was lined with little benches. The multi-paned windows were big, the gray shingles in good repair, and the landscaping, what she could see of it under the snow, was tasteful.

Maureen answered, peeking through the crack as if afraid of who might be visiting. She held the door open wide. "Oh, it's you. Come on in."

"Thanks." Priscilla wiped her boots on the mat and stepped inside, first looking for a place to set the containers of food. "Here's the pea soup and biscuits."

"I'll take them." Hands full now, the caretaker jerked her chin toward a row of pegs. "Leave your things there. Rebekah is in the living room." Another chin jerk toward the doorway on the left.

Priscilla divested herself of coat and boots and entered the living room, her stocking feet sinking into plush Persian carpets. Like the exterior, the inside of this historic home spoke of good taste and careful maintenance. Her hostess was seated in a brocade wing-chair in front of a brick fireplace wide enough to roast a pig. The walls were paneled in authentic wide boards that spoke of their vintage.

Rebekah's face lit up like a candle behind fine linen. "Priscilla! I'm so glad you could visit." She shifted forward in her chair and indicated the matching chair across the hearth. "Please, have a seat." A small table at her elbow held a tea tray with a silver pot and fine china cups and saucers.

Priscilla settled in, wincing when she experienced the horsehair stuffing that made the seat rock hard. She found a small cushion behind her and used it make herself more comfortable.

Soft slippers on her feet, Maureen padded through the open arch to the dining room. "Is there anything else you need before we go out?"

"I don't think so," Rebekah said. "We've got our tea. And did I hear that you brought us a lovely meal, Priscilla?" Her blue eyes were lively and clear.

No confusion today. "Homemade split pea soup and biscuits."

Rebekah clapped her hands. "I adore pea soup. Perhaps you'll have a bowl with me later? I hate eating alone."

"I'd be happy to." Priscilla looked up at Maureen, who waited, stone-faced, hands clasped at her waist. "We'll eat when we're hungry, so no need to rush back."

Maureen made that chin-jerk nod again. "All right, I'll leave you to it then." She padded away as quietly as she'd entered.

"She's all right," Rebekah whispered once Maureen was out of earshot. "But not really my cup of tea." She winked. "Bradley hired them." Raising her voice to a normal volume, she said, "Speaking of which, would you like a cup?"

"Sure, that sounds perfect." Priscilla accepted a cup of what Rebekah assured her was the finest oolong, specially stocked for her at the local grocery store.

"Did you know that tea is good for your health?" Rebekah burbled on about the purported benefits of drinking tea several times a day while adding several sugar cubes to her brew, followed by a splash of milk.

Sipping what actually was a great cup of tea, Priscilla relaxed in front of the fire, listening to her hostess's chatter and noting the sounds of the Moodys leaving, their voices and a slamming door in the back of the house. Moments later, their truck passed by the side windows and exited the drive, turning toward town.

"Ah, alone at last." Rebekah nestled back in her chair and smiled. "I feel like I've always got someone hovering over me these days. They say they're taking care of me, but I feel like they're really waiting for me to croak."

Priscilla laughed in surprise, jerking her cup and making tea slop over the rim. "Surely not." She dabbed at the tea in her saucer with a napkin.

The older woman sighed. "Maybe not, but it feels that way. My husband was from a wealthy family, you see, and now that's all come to me. I appreciate living in comfort, of course, but it's really a burden. If only..." Gazing into the fire, she rubbed her forehead, lost in what appeared to be gloomy thoughts.

Priscilla shifted on the rock-hard chair, wondering how to respond. "Having your nephew around must be a comfort," she ventured. From her brief encounter with him, he didn't exactly seem the nurturing type, but she could be wrong.

Rebekah gave a bitter little chuckle. "You'd think that, wouldn't you?" She shook her head. "No, Bradley only cares about Bradley. He's been that way since he was a boy." She sighed, a gesture that heaved her bony chest. "I had a daughter but... she's gone."

CHAPTER SEVEN

Rebekah's words struck Priscilla, mother of a precious girl, like an arrow in the chest. She even put a hand to her heart. "I'm so sorry. What a terrible loss."

"It was. It still is." Rebekah picked up her cup and took a sip, then waved a hand. "Well, enough of my troubles. Why don't you tell me how you came up with the idea for your museum? I was glad to hear that something new was happening on this road. We're all very boring around here."

With an effort, Priscilla wrenched her mind away from Rebekah's loss and focused on the lighthouse project. "It all began with Misty Harbor Tours, run by Teresa Claybrook." Priscilla relayed how the lighthouse had become a popular stop. After learning more about her family and their role in island history and specifically the lighthouse operations, she'd decided to create an exhibit on the bottom floor for visitors to enjoy. "They can't go upstairs," she concluded, "or to where the light is housed, but at least they can satisfy their curiosity about the lighthouse and learn some history in the process."

"That's very public-spirited of you," Rebekah said. "I know some people were worried you'd cut off access altogether. That's happened with some lighthouses in private hands."

"I wouldn't feel right doing that," Priscilla said. "After all, it was a gift to me. As long as they don't barge into the cottage, I'm good." She held out her cup. "Is there any more tea?"

Rebekah felt the side of the pot. "Yes. It's still hot too." She refilled their cups. "As I mentioned the other day, I have some photographs you might like. I'll get the albums in a minute."

Priscilla's heart gave a little leap. She was becoming quite addicted to the thrill of the hunt when it came to historical research. "I'm excited to see them. Have you lived on the island all your life?"

"Heavens, no. This place was in Henry's family for generations, but we lived in New York City and used it as a summer place. I'm from Connecticut originally, and Henry and I met in the city when we were starting out in our careers. I worked in his ad agency." She pointed to a photograph on the mantel. "There we are, in our salad days."

Priscilla stood and examined the picture, which depicted a young and lovely Rebekah wearing a miniskirt and nestled close to a handsome man dressed in a T-shirt and bell-bottoms. Behind them was a park full of people lounging on the grass.

"A concert in Central Park. Don't you love our groovy outfits?"

"I remember them well." As a late '50s baby, Priscilla had come of age in the same era, although Rebekah had to be at least fifteen years older.

Priscilla smiled. "When did you begin living on the island full time?"

"Let me think. Has it been fifteen years? Yes, I think so. Henry died years ago now."

"I'm so sorry," Priscilla murmured, one widow to another. "I also lost my husband. Before I moved here."

"I'm sorry to hear that." Rebekah acknowledged their mutual situation with a sympathetic glance. "When Henry began to wind up his career in the city, he started buying commercial buildings on the island. That's how the family built their wealth in the first place, through real estate. Now Bradley manages the buildings for me."

Nice work if you can get it. Despite her reservations about Rebekah's nephew, she merely said, "It must be nice to have a family member manage your business enterprises."

"Better than a management company run by strangers. Would you like to see those albums?" Using both arms of her chair, Rebekah stood, then shuffled over to a long, low bookcase under the windows. She chose a couple of black leather books and brought them over to a round side table. "Let's look at them over here. It's easier to share."

The photographs were from the 1940s, '50s, and '60s, images of Henry's family and the island. They were mostly in black and white, fastened on the black paper pages with little triangles.

"Your relative Warren Latham was quite old by the time I met him, but Henry was full of stories about his adventures with him." Rebekah pointed to a man in a rowboat, a pipe held in his teeth.

By the tilt of his cap and the angle of his smile, Priscilla gathered her grandfather had quite a personality. Studying his face closely, she thought she saw a resemblance to her cousin Gail. "What kind of adventures?"

"Warren used to be a captain for hire. He'd take people out deep-sea fishing or to other islands for picnics and the like. He always claimed his fishing prowess was handed down from his mother, who was a descendent of the Wampanoag tribe. A Wampanoag was the harpooner in *Moby Dick*."

"I don't know much about them," Priscilla admitted.

"Their name means People of the Dawn, and at one time they lived all throughout eastern Massachusetts. They went through the same changes and assimilation as other Native Americans, but lately they've been working on reviving their language. They still have a reservation in Aquinnah."

"You're a fount of local lore. This is wonderful." Priscilla had pulled out a pad of paper and pen and made a note to look into the history of Native Americans on Martha's Vineyard, another fascinating facet of her new home.

Rebekah turned the album page. "Look at this. Henry caught a fifty-pound tuna when he was only twelve, thanks to Warren." A beaming boy stood on a dock, an enormous fish hanging beside him.

"That must have been a thrill." Priscilla wondered how many little cans of tuna a fish that size would make.

"Have you had fresh tuna? Or bluefish? I heartily recommend them both." Rebekah flipped the page again, then looked up. "You know what? I could use a bowl of your soup right now. I'm hungry."

"Want me to get it? Point me in the right direction."

They were scraping the last of the soup out of pottery bowls when a navy-blue luxury sedan pulled into the driveway and parked beside Priscilla's vehicle.

"Someone's here," Priscilla said, mildly curious. She set her spoon down and picked up the last half of biscuit. She was pleased with the way they'd turned out, tender and flaky.

To her surprise, Rebekah's shoulders hunched and her head lowered. "That's Bradley."

Priscilla was shocked at her demeanor. *Does he abuse her?* Anger flared, but she took a deep breath and tried to tamp it down. She was making assumptions. "Would you like me to tell him you're busy?" That was true, after all. They planned to look at more photographs after finishing their meal.

"You'd do that?" The older woman's eyes lit up. But then she sagged again. "But no, don't. He'll be mad. And it's not worth it to upset Bradley."

From her seat, Priscilla watched as Bradley exited his car, pausing to study hers as he pushed a button on his key fob to lock his vehicle. By the crease between his brows, she guessed he had no idea who was visiting his aunt.

A moment later, the front door opened, and Bradley entered, stamping his feet on the carpet to dislodge snow. From the hallway, he had a perfect view of them, and his frown deepened to a glare.

Priscilla gave it right back, and to her satisfaction, he dialed down his ill-humored expression from rage to mild concern. "Aunt

Rebekah. I had no idea you had company." The way he said it implied that the concept of visitors was outlandish and undesirable.

Rebekah huffed at his attitude, but she said in a pleasant tone, "Bradley, come in and meet my new friend, Priscilla Latham Grant. She's the owner of the lighthouse." The last was said with a smug lilt, as though to make the point that her guest was somebody when it came to island society.

Priscilla glanced at her, surprised at this unexpected bragging about knowing her, of all people. Rebekah winked, then picked up a biscuit to hide a smile.

"Hi, Bradley," Priscilla said. "Nice to meet you. I saw you at the museum a couple of days ago. Remember?"

He reddened. "Er, no. I don't recall. But nice to meet you. You own the lighthouse, huh? Taxes on that must be a pretty penny."

"They're enough." Priscilla refused to let him get under her skin. His refusal to admit to seeing her at the museum was decidedly odd. Maybe he didn't want his aunt to know he'd spoken to Mildred about her donation. Another point against him. She changed the subject. "Your aunt and I were looking at old photographs for my museum."

"Oh yeah?" He had moved to warm himself in front of the fire, standing in a position that blocked the heat from reaching them. "That sounds boring." He snickered.

"Bradley, would you like some pea soup?" Rebekah asked. "Priscilla made it, and it's very good."

He peered over at the table, tempting Priscilla to turn up her empty bowl for him to study. "Maybe. Oh, why not. I didn't eat lunch yet."

Rebekah began to rise, and Priscilla hurriedly said, "I'll go." She got up and cleared the table, stacking the bowls and bread plates to carry into the kitchen.

Bradley entered the kitchen as she was ladling soup into a bowl for him. He joined her at the six-burner gas stove, standing so close she could smell his spicy aftershave. She stepped sideways a hair, uncomfortable with his invasion of her space.

"That doesn't look too bad," he said.

"I'm glad. I made biscuits to go with it. One or two?" Her hand hovered over the basket, then selected two at his request. These she set on a plate.

Bradley cleared his throat. "This is, um, real nice, and I appreciate you taking the time to visit my aunt and bring her food...."

But? Priscilla turned to face him head on, hands resting on her hips, legs wide in what Gary had called the "she means business" stance.

He broke off a piece of biscuit, popped it into his mouth, and chewed. "But she's, ah, really delicate, and it's not good for her to have too many visitors. Or if anyone does come over, they shouldn't stay long. Understand what I'm saying?"

She crossed her arms. "I hear you, Bradley. Loud and clear."

CHAPTER EIGHT

Priscilla waited for Bradley to say something more, but he continued to munch on the biscuit, staring at her with those deep-set brown eyes. Finally she turned and went back to the living room, leaving him to handle his own meal.

She found Rebekah sliding several photographs into an envelope.

"I was thinking you could take these and have copies made for your exhibit. No rush in getting them back."

Priscilla was touched. She'd been planning to ask Rebekah if she could do that and had hoped she'd be trusted with the precious mementos. "Thank you so much. I'll mention in the write-ups that these photos came from your collection."

Rebekah colored with pleasure. "How nice. I'll make sure I come to your grand opening." She rose from the table, gathering the albums. "I've got others we can look through." Bradley sauntered into the room, carrying his soup, and her expression darkened. "Another time."

He sat in front of the fire in Priscilla's chair and proceeded to slurp up soup with a big spoon. He kept his eyes fastened on his aunt and Priscilla as though fascinated by their every move. "Nice to see you, Priscilla," he said. "Enjoy the rest of your Sunday. Aunt Rebekah and I have some business to attend to."

Dismissed. Feeling as slapped as a scolded child, Priscilla took her leave, giving her new friend a hug and a kiss on the cheek when Rebekah walked her out. "If you need anything, anything at all, I'm right next door," she whispered.

Rebekah returned the hug. "Thank you, dear. And thank you for the delicious soup." This last line was delivered in a loud voice with a wink.

"Yes, it's very good. Thank you," came the shouted reply from the living room.

"I know he's awful, but he's all I've got." Rebekah's face was sad as she opened the door for Priscilla. "Drive safe and take care."

"The whole thing was like something out of a gothic novel," Priscilla told her cousins the next morning at breakfast at the bakery. "The evil fortune-hunting nephew and the housebound elderly aunt." She picked up her crème horn and took a flaky bite. Still unsettled from yesterday, she had given herself permission to enjoy the treat.

"Not to mention the shady caretakers," Joan said. "They sound decidedly odd." She picked up a knife and cut her orange-cranberry muffin into quarters, finding the enormous pastry easier to eat that way.

Trudy had no such compunction. She picked up her peach praline muffin and crammed it into her mouth, taking a huge bite.

She chewed, started to speak, then finished chewing. "They're not islanders. I wonder where they came from." She wiped her lips with a napkin and dove in for another mouthful.

"Hired by Bradley, maybe? It can be hard to find good help." With a shrug, Gail broke off a piece of oatmeal raisin cookie and popped it into her mouth. As guardian of her elderly father, she was more pragmatic about the issues involved. Hugh had been feeling poorly that morning, so he had stayed home.

Priscilla thought the entire setup was sinister. Glancing around to be sure no other patrons were within earshot, and seeing only Jason bussing tables, she lowered her voice and said, "Bradley told Mildred that Rebekah wasn't going to make her annual contribution to the museum this year. I wonder if his aunt even knows he did that."

"Maybe she still thinks she gave it." Joan's tone was somber, but her meaning was clear.

Trudy gasped. "You think he stole it?" Her voice trailed off into a whisper.

Gail's brow furrowed. "Be careful, cousins. We don't know the facts. Or the challenges he might be facing with his aunt."

Priscilla could respect that point of view. *But still.* "You're right, Gail. We need to be discreet. But you weren't there when I discovered Rebekah running through the snow in her nightgown. Or when I witnessed the way Bradley was so . . . oh, I don't know, controlling? The whole thing smells bad."

"What smells bad?" The ladies turned to see Harper standing behind the table, coffeepot in hand. "Is everything okay?"

"Nothing from the bakery," Priscilla hastened to assure her. "We were talking about something else."

Harper looked relieved. "Oh, good." She moved closer and began refilling their mugs, starting with Priscilla. "I made the muffins today." Her smile was shy. "The peach praline is my recipe."

"Well, it's scrumptious," Trudy said, picking up the muffin in question and taking another bite.

"Harper, you haven't met Trudy and Gail, have you?" At the baker's headshake, Priscilla introduced her cousins.

"You're all related?" Harper's eyes traveled the circle, taking in their faces. "How nice. You're so lucky to have each other."

"We enjoy it," Trudy said. "Most days, that is." She burst into friendly laughter. Joan rolled her eyes, and Gail snorted. Priscilla just smiled.

"Priscilla is helping me find my family," Harper said. "My mom used to live here before I was born."

"I remember that from the other day," Joan said. "So you've started digging in to try to find them?" She held out her mug for more coffee.

"Yes, we met at the museum on Saturday," Priscilla said, relieved that Harper had raised the issue. Otherwise she wasn't going to discuss it with the others, except maybe Joan, who had heard her offer to help Harper. "Nothing so far, but we've only just begun." She gave Harper an encouraging smile.

"That sounds like a song," Trudy said. She sang out a bar or two of the popular Carpenters' song, simultaneously putting a hand over her cup to indicate she'd had enough.

"You are too corny for words," Gail said. She slid her mug closer to Harper. "I'll take some more coffee, please."

Harper poured steaming coffee into Gail's cup, and when she'd finished, she lingered. "Priscilla, remember the other thing we talked about? Well, something else happened." She lowered her voice. "A man was watching my house last night."

"A man was outside your house?" Trudy said at full volume. "Do you think he's stalking you?"

Crash. Jason bumped into the pan resting on a tray stand and knocked it to the floor. Dirty dishes, silverware, leftover food, and liquid went everywhere.

Harper sprang into action, setting the coffee carafe on an empty table nearby. "Jason, let me help you."

The dishwasher was already crouched down, picking up the broken dishes, his face deeply flushed. Even his scalp was pink, the tint showing through his thin blond hair. Harper fetched a mop and several dish towels from the kitchen. Other patrons retrieved glasses that had rolled their way or picked up chunks of baked goods that had flown across the room.

"How embarrassing," Trudy said. "It reminds me of the time I was waiting tables as a teen and dropped a tray of boiled lobsters and butter. Talk about a mess."

"I don't even know how you did it," Priscilla said. She'd seen wait staff hefting heavy trays overhead, keeping them in perfect balance.

"Hardly anyone does that now," Joan said.

"Wimps," Gail scoffed. "I used to carry hot plates up my arm. Both arms, if it was busy."

"Changing the subject," Joan said, "who has their outfit for the Valentine's dinner dance?" She pointed to herself. "I found the perfect red dress on sale."

Priscilla's heart gave a little leap at the mention of the dance. She scarcely dared to hope Gerald would invite her. "So it's a dressy event? That sounds fun."

"It's a blast," Trudy said. "Dan and I have the best time every year." Her lips curved in a mischievous smile. "It's the only time I can get him out on the dance floor."

Gail frowned, and Priscilla wondered if she was wishing Tommy would take her. But then Gail lifted her nose and sniffed. "Do you smell smoke?"

Trudy laughed. "Someone probably burned a tray of cookies."

With a grimace, Joan put a hand to her face. "That doesn't smell like food burning."

A shout from the kitchen rang out, and Candy burst through the swinging door. "Fire! Everyone out. Now." She pointed at Jason. "Go around back and turn off the power and gas, like I showed you." Jason scurried for the front door. Candy turned to Harper. "Check the restrooms." Harper hurried to obey.

Some patrons stood while others remained seated, confused. The bakery owner flapped her apron at them as if she were shooing a flock of reluctant chickens. "Go on, go." With amazing calm, she went to the register, removed the drawer, and ran for the front door. She held it open for her customers.

"I guess we better get out of here," Priscilla said, putting on her coat and grabbing her purse. Her cousins followed suit, and they joined the customers moving toward the door, all quite calm—until a thread of black smoke began to drift in from the kitchen. Then people panicked, pushing together in a crush.

Priscilla found herself jammed between Joan and a rotund man. Once outside the door, the pressure suddenly released, and she bounced back against the man's stomach.

"Easy, there," he said, steadying her. Gripping her arm, he moved her along the sidewalk out of harm's way.

"Sorry about that." Priscilla looked around for her cousins. There they were, standing in the street, tall Gail, blonde Trudy, and petite Joan. Face white with shock, Harper stood nearby, hands twisting in her apron. Jason tried to put his arm around her shoulders, but she moved away with a shrug.

Candy wasn't so reluctant to accept comfort from her fiancé, Beau. She cried in his arms while he stared grimly at the building. Up and down the street, other business owners and customers came out of their doors to watch.

Sirens wailed and fire trucks turned onto the street, followed by a police cruiser and an ambulance, standard protocol. The trucks pulled to a stop, and firefighters leaped out, a couple of them moving the crowd aside while others began pulling hoses toward the building. The fire chief went over to Candy, who began explaining what had happened. Priscilla moved closer so she could hear.

"Is everyone out of the building?" the chief asked.

"Yes, we got all the customers out," Candy said. "Although I sent Jason around back to shut off the power and gas." She scanned the crowd. "There he is."

"Take me through what happened," the chief said.

"It was getting hotter and hotter in the kitchen, and we started to smell something burning," Candy said. "Then the wall burst into flame, right next to a wooden cupboard. So then that caught."

"So it wasn't one of the ovens or a stove?" the chief asked.

"No, nothing was baking. We'd finished for the day." Candy bit her lip, staring at her building. Except for smoke leaking out when firemen went inside, everything looked normal.

The chief spoke into his handheld radio. "Check for electrical in the kitchen," he told his men inside.

"Roger that," came the reply. "We're in the kitchen now."

"I'll talk to you later, Miss Lane." The fire chief's nod was sympathetic. "Hang in there. We're getting it under control."

Candy gave the chief a half-hearted smile and thanked him, but as soon as he walked away, she burst into tears. "Oh, Beau! What am I going to do now? I can't afford to close the bakery. And who knows how long before I'm up and running again."

Beau put his arm around his fiancée's shoulders and pulled her close. "We'll get through it, honey. Maybe it won't be too bad. Don't panic until we know for sure."

Priscilla's heart hurt for Candy. She'd been hit with one challenge after another this winter. First a slowdown in business due to the weather and then a heating system problem. Now a fire. "We're here for you too, Candy," she said. "Whatever we can do to help." Her cousins, who had also been standing nearby, chimed in with their agreement.

Candy started to cry again. "You all are the best. I love my customers."

Beau handed her his handkerchief. "Honey, will you be all right for a minute? I want to make a circuit of the building and see what's happening out back."

"Of course." Candy dabbed at her eyes. "I'll be fine here."

Beau strode away, stopping to confer with a couple of firemen and a police officer on the scene. A tall, familiar figure made his way through the crowd, heading straight for Candy.

Bradley Alden pushed his way into their little circle, barely sparing a glance for Priscilla or her cousins. "Miss Lane? I'm Bradley Alden." His voice was deep and resonant, with a strength and confidence that made a person want to trust him.

Unless you had the misfortune to know him. Priscilla's hackles rose, and she stepped a little closer to Candy.

"I'm so sorry to hear about this disaster. If there's anything I can do to help, please let me know." He held out a crisp white business card. "Just give me a call."

Candy took the card numbly, not really seeming to absorb what Bradley was saying or even the fact that he was standing in front of her, all gleaming white teeth and handsome topcoat. "Thank you, you're so kind," she said, stumbling over the words.

With a nod, Bradley vanished back into the crowd.

"What was that about?" Joan asked. "Why is Bradley Alden interested in helping Candy Lane Confectionery?"

That is a very good question. And Priscilla was certain she wouldn't like the answer.

CHAPTER NINE

Outside the cottage, snow was falling, pretty flakes that looked more decorative than serious. In the living room, Priscilla studied the family tree poster she'd been drafting with satisfaction. Using a pen, she neatly wrote in "Warren Latham." Drawing lines above his name, she made spots for his mother and father, both of whom she needed to learn more about, since they weren't in the line of lighthouse keepers.

I especially want to learn about his mother. Rebekah's offhand comment that Priscilla's great-grandmother Lila was a descendant of the People of the Dawn was intriguing. Of course, if Priscilla wandered off researching cousins, second cousins, and cousins once removed, she might get lost for years.

A thought struck her like an arrow. *Harper.* She had begun to tell them about her stalker when Jason dropped the tray and fire broke out. She'd forgotten all about it. Priscilla hurried to the telephone and looked for Harper's number, written on a scrap of paper. She'd have to put that into her cell phone too.

Is it too late? The captain's clock on the wall reported it was just past eight o'clock. Early enough not to be rude, she hoped.

The phone rang a number of times and went to voice mail. Priscilla left a message. "Harper, this is Priscilla. With all the excitement today, we never heard the rest of your story. I hope everything is okay and please, don't hesitate to call, either this number or my cell." Priscilla recited her cell number, knowing that her home phone would show up on the caller display.

While she was replacing the receiver, the telephone rang, a shrill surprise that broke the evening quiet. Jake gave a sharp bark, rising from his spot on the hearth and coming over as though curious to find out who was calling. Priscilla snatched up the receiver. Maybe it was Harper calling back. Or news about Candy. She'd been worrying about Candy all evening. She hadn't heard a thing since she'd left the scene of the fire, so she had no idea how much damage the fire had caused or how long the bakery might be closed.

"Hi, Mom. How are you?" Rachel was on the line.

"I'm fine, dear. How about you?" Smiling, Priscilla reached down and scratched Jake's head. She retrieved her hot cocoa and sank down into a chair to chat, Jake at her feet.

Rachel sighed. "I'm good." The tone of her voice told her mother otherwise, reminding her of how she'd learned to read her daughter's mood through subtle cues. Interesting she could still pick them up through the telephone line when she had only Rachel's voice providing hints.

"What is it, Rach?" Priscilla deliberately softened her own tone so as not to sound as if she were prying or interrogating. Either tactic would make her daughter shut up faster than a startled clam.

"Oh, I don't know." From the background sounds, Priscilla surmised that Rachel was pacing around her townhouse. She heard the rattle of blinds closing, water running, the beep of the microwave. "You know Valentine's Day is next week." A pause. "I used to love the little projects we did together."

As a young mother, Priscilla enjoyed crafts, and she made it her mission to delight her daughter on holidays with joint projects. For Valentine's Day, they'd made strings of paper hearts and butterflies, designed original cards for family and friends, baked cookies, and even melted soap for molds.

"Me too. I came across some of the decorations we made when I was unpacking. I was thinking of putting them up." Priscilla had hoarded Rachel's childhood handiwork, and even moving thousands of miles couldn't convince her to throw any of it away.

Rachel laughed. "Really, Mom? That's awesome." The microwave beeped again. "Sorry. I'm making tea." Her tone was very casual when she added, "Mom, how did you know it was right with Dad?"

In the middle of a sip of cocoa, Priscilla almost choked. She hastily set the cup down and swallowed, thumping her chest and coughing.

"Are you there?" Rachel sounded puzzled. "Where'd you go?"

"Sorry. You surprised me and I choked." Priscilla took another sip to recover. "How did I know it was right? Well, for one thing I liked him." She laughed. "He wasn't just a handsome face. He was nice. And kind too."

"Really? That sounds a little, I don't know, boring?" Rachel's voice was laced with doubt. "I thought he swept you off your feet. Isn't that what's supposed to happen?"

"Oh, he did, that's for sure." Priscilla thought back to her first dates with Gary. She still remembered the moment when it all changed, when the man smiling at her became irresistible, the prince of her dreams. One moment he was Gary Grant, her friend. The next, her belly dropped, her heart turned over, and she was in love.

But it was different than other times she'd been infatuated. Those men had disappointed her, let her down, even betrayed her trust. Being with Gary felt...safe, like she was finally coming home. How could she convey that to Rachel?

Priscilla took a deep breath. "Falling in love is mysterious. It kind of just happens. But when it's with someone who is good for you, who cherishes you above all others, then you know it's right. You don't doubt that he'll be there for you no matter what. And you'll do the same for him. Nothing on earth can separate you." She found herself twining two fingers in demonstration, although Rachel couldn't see that.

"Oh, Mom, that's beautiful. You and Dad had that, didn't you?" Rachel sounded breathless, almost teary.

"We did." Now Priscilla was tearing up too. At the same time, she was grateful she'd had such a good marriage. Not everyone did. Then an idea dropped into her mind with the compelling clang of a bell. "Have you met someone special?" She waited with held breath for the answer.

Rachel laughed. "No, Mom, not yet. What gave you that idea?"

Only this discussion. "Just wondering. And hoping. I'd like that for you, a happy marriage." It'd long been a mainstay of her prayers.

"You know, I've been thinking about that." A huge sigh. "Work just isn't enough. I want that happy ending."

Hallelujah. Priscilla felt a grin stretching across her face. "And God will help you find the one, my darling. Pray and believe."

Priscilla had barely said goodbye to Rachel when the phone rang again. *Who now?* "I'm as surprised as you are, Jake," she told the dog staring up at her with inquiring eyes. "Hello?"

"Hi, Priscilla. It's Joan. Candy got the verdict on the bakery."

"Already? That was fast. How bad is it?" She cringed, waiting for the answer.

Joan laughed. "Get this. It's not bad at all. The damage was confined to one wall. All the equipment is still functional, and although there's a lot of cleanup, she'll only need to be closed a couple of days."

Priscilla sagged against the back of the chair. "I am so relieved. I was worried this would put her out of business. Did they find out what caused it?"

"Looks like it was electrical. That building is pretty old, so something overheated and caught fire. She's going to have the wiring replaced too."

Priscilla stretched out her legs and flexed her toes. "Poor Candy. She's had one problem after another."

"I know. We'll have to buy extra treats to make up for it." Joan laughed. "Like that's a hardship for us."

"Count me in. And let me know if there's anything I can do."

Joan promised she would and signed off. Priscilla hung up and stared at Jake. "How about a walk before bed? I could use some fresh air." His leaping dance told her all she needed to know.

The evening air was still, the snowflakes drifting down and melting on Priscilla's face and clothing. Jake romped toward the shore, his tail waving like a joyous flag. Priscilla took the risk of sliding after him, allowing the drifts to carry her to the beach. She stood in knee-deep snow, watching while he ran along the shore, darting toward the surf, then retreating when it licked at his paws.

She loved being outside, spending time soaking in the beauty of God's world. The clouds hid the stars, but overhead the lighthouse beam made its rotation, illuminating the ever-changing ocean with every pass. On the mainland, lights glittered like jeweled necklaces draped around a woman's neck. Far out to sea, a tanker passed, moving slowly up the coast.

As was Priscilla's habit, she mentally went through her day, releasing every situation and person to the Lord with a prayer. Like many women, she tended to carry the weight of the world on her shoulders when it came to her family and friends and their concerns. The farm, too, had been a source of worry in times of drought or flood, blight or pestilence.

Through the trees, Rebekah's lights twinkled. During the summer, they weren't visible due to the thick band of trees between the properties. Now, with the leaves gone, she could see the Alden home and several others. It was comforting to know that if she had a need or trouble struck, she could go to any of them. That was what neighbors were for. She hoped they felt the same way about her. "Love thy neighbor." A good precept to live by.

Harper called back the next morning while Priscilla was eating breakfast by the light of a pale but welcome winter sun. "Hope it's not too early to call," the young woman greeted her.

"No, of course not. With Jake around, I'm up early every day." Priscilla took a bite of toast and marmalade. "How are you?"

"Fine, thanks." Harper blew a puff of air into the receiver. "Except for my workplace being shut down. I'm going over later to help clean."

Priscilla felt a tightening in her chest. She wanted to ask Harper about the stalker, but at the same time she didn't want to raise a difficult subject. She'd let Harper set the pace on that discussion.

"I know you're probably busy, but I wanted to tell you about a couple of clues I found in the diary. First, I think Mom had a crush on David, whoever he was. She practically swoons over their first kiss in Secret Cove."

"Sounds like a crush to me," Priscilla said with a laugh.

"Oh, and she mentioned going to the West Tisbury Centennial. Can we use that to do some research?"

"Oh yes. We can look that up in the newspaper archives. Who knows? Maybe we could get lucky and she could show up in a crowd photo. You never know what you'll learn."

"Where do we find old newspapers? At the museum?"

"The library is a better bet. How about we meet over there at ten? They're open this morning."

Harper gave a squeak of excitement. "You're the best. I'll see you then." She paused. "And I'm taking you out to lunch. Don't even try to say no."

Priscilla laughed. "I won't, then. See you in a while." She ate the rest of her breakfast in good cheer, glad they were making progress on the mystery of Harper's mother.

Clara Lopez looked up from her station behind the front desk and smiled at Priscilla. "Good morning. Cold one, isn't it?" Today she wore her soft black hair up in a bun, and rose-red lipstick flattered her walnut complexion.

"It sure is." Priscilla almost gasped in relief at reaching the warm sanctuary of the historic library. "How are you, Clara? And how are the children?"

"I'm fine, thank you. I wanted to tell you, Raymundo loves his therapist." Clara beamed. "I'm so relieved." Her bright, lively son struggled with ADHD and associated learning disabilities.

"That's good news, Clara. I'm really happy to hear it." Priscilla headed toward a spot at the carousel desk near the local history section. As she walked past the desk, she smiled at the portrait of Llewelyn Latham, his wife Elodie, and his mother Priscilla hanging above Clara's desk. How wonderful that her ancestors had cared so much about literacy and education that they had donated generously to the library.

Priscilla took a seat and shrugged out of her jacket. She slung it over her chair, then sat to log in to the computer. She then logged in to the one next to it, figuring she and Harper could both search the newspaper archives.

The tall front door squeaked open, and Harper entered the library, looking around as though lost in the lofty room. Priscilla raised her arm in a wave, and Harper veered in her direction, her boot heels clacking on the polished wood floor. She gave Clara a friendly smile as she passed by the desk.

"You beat me," Harper said, unwinding a scarf from around her neck. "Even though I live closer." The scent of fresh cold air clung to her clothing.

"I just got here," Priscilla said. She kept her voice low so as not to disturb the elderly man reading a newspaper a short distance away. "I've logged us both in to computers, and after we decide where to focus, I'll show you how to access the database."

Harper hung her coat on her chair and placed her bag on the table. "I'm so excited. I really feel like we're closing in." She sat down and unlatched her bag, then reached inside to pull out the diary. A slip of paper peeked out from the top partway through.

"Me too," Priscilla said. She held a pen poised to write down the information Harper had found.

After flipping the book open to the marked page, Harper read her mother's entry about the fun she and her friends had at the West Tisbury Centennial Agricultural Fair.

"That's a great place to start," Priscilla said with excitement. She looked at the date at the top of the page Harper had read from August, 1992. She scooted her chair over to Harper's monitor. "Let's get you started with the *Vineyard Gazette*."

Priscilla logged in to another local paper, the *Martha's Vineyard Times,* and searched for the relevant year. "I'm going to start with June," she told Harper, "since we know for sure your mom was on the island that summer. Look for pictures or headlines that might include someone her age. She would have been, what? About eighteen, I think."

"Yes, that's right," Harper said. I'll start with June too." Her fingers flew over the keys as she entered dates in the search bar.

As the first issue of the paper appeared on the screen, Priscilla reflected on how much easier this was. Using rolls of microfilm frankly made her nauseated, with the way the film flew by and the odor of the acetate. She'd given a silent *hurray* when she'd learned the library had moved the archives to digital files.

Priscilla scrolled through the pages, enjoying a glimpse of a 1990s Martha's Vineyard. Internet was new to the island, a television smaller than hers cost twice as much, and the theater was showing *Sister Act*, still a favorite.

She flipped to another issue, scanning the front page. Then she stopped, her eye caught by a headline.

"Tisbury Teen Rescued in Storm, Boat Lost."

CHAPTER TEN

That's right, Bradley sank his uncle's boat. Priscilla scanned the article and saw that yes, this was the report of Bradley's misadventure. She read how the teen had set sail off the island and was caught in an afternoon thunderstorm. A Coast Guard officer was quoted as saying that he should have checked the weather forecast, because the incident could have been prevented. There had been a small craft warning posted.

The boat ran aground on a shoal and was almost totally underwater by the time Bradley was rescued. Also according to the officer, the lack of life jackets on the boat meant he probably would have drowned once hypothermia set in, which affected sailors year-round due to cold ocean temperatures.

None of this had anything to do with finding Harper's mother, and Priscilla was ready to move on when she saw something interesting at the bottom. According to the article, witnesses originally thought there might be two young men on the boat. But according to Bradley, he had gone out alone. His friend, David Castonguay, stopped by the dock to say goodbye, as he was leaving the island that day.

David. The David from the diary? The boy Megan was sweet on? Of course the name David was a very common one, and there was no real reason to believe this David had anything to do with Harper's mother. But a tingle down her spine told Priscilla that this article was significant in some way to Harper's quest. She must have made a sound, because Harper looked over.

"What is it? Did you find something?" Harper asked too loudly. The elderly man rustled his paper and glared. She gave him a little "I'm sorry" wave.

Priscilla ran a hand through her hair and sighed. "I'm not sure. Nothing? Something?" She swung the monitor around so Harper could read the article. "I was thinking about the David in the diary. It's just a shot in the dark."

"Let me see. David Castonguay. Hmm." Harper squinted, peering at the page. "What date is that paper?" When Priscilla told her, she picked up the diary and turned to the end. The page she held up to Priscilla was blank.

"What am I looking at?" Priscilla said with a laugh.

"That's the end of the book." Harper flipped back a page. "Look, this is the last entry. The day before Bradley had his boating accident and David left the island."

The pair absorbed the implications of this. "Let's look for David Castonguay," Priscilla said. "Maybe he can help us." She printed a copy of the newspaper article for future reference, then opened an internet browser.

There were very few people in the United States with that last name, which was of French origin, and only around twenty David Castonguays. Priscilla saved the search and sent it to her own computer by email. "It will take a while to sort through these," she told Harper. "I'll look for men who are the right age."

Harper's eyes were hopeful. "Wouldn't it be great if we could find him?" Then her mouth turned down. "But it could totally be a wild goose chase. What are the chances he knew my mom? The guy in the diary could have been a thousand other Davids."

"I know. I had the same thought. But I like to follow every lead that presents itself, no matter how slim." That approach had led Priscilla to solve a number of mysteries.

"What about the guy who sank the boat–Bradley Alden?" Harper asked. "Is he still around, do you know?"

Is he ever. Priscilla shivered with distaste at the idea of questioning him about David. From their brief encounters, she had the feeling he only helped people when it was to his own advantage. "Yes, Bradley still lives here. I don't know if you noticed, but he approached Candy the day of the fire. He manages real estate around town."

Harper whistled, earning a harrumph from the elderly reader. "Seriously? Small world. Let's go talk to him."

What would it hurt to try? "Let me talk to him first." At Harper's exclamation, Priscilla held up a hand. "From what I've seen of Bradley Alden, he's not the most helpful person. In fact, he's a jerk. I'll try to smooth the path before I introduce you, okay?" The last thing she wanted to witness was Bradley Alden demolishing Harper's fragile heart. "And if he tells me anything important, I'll call you immediately, I promise."

Swallowing back further objections, Harper finally nodded. "All right. If you think that's the way to approach Bradley, I'll let you handle it."

Priscilla patted Harper's arm. "Hang in there. We're making progress." She remembered the stalker. "So tell me, what's this about someone watching your apartment?"

Harper plucked at her lower lip, her eyes fixed on the bookcases across the room. "Yeah. The other night I noticed someone standing across the street from my place. Just out of range of the streetlight, of course, so I couldn't get a good look. When he saw me looking out the window, he took off."

"You're sure it was a man?" Priscilla felt she should ask, although there weren't that many women stalkers, statistically speaking.

"Yep. He was tall, with broad shoulders. I could see that much." She demonstrated with gestures. "And I could tell by the way he walked that it was a guy. You know what I mean." Harper chewed on a thumbnail. "I just hope it wasn't Ollie."

Priscilla resolved to do some checking up on Ollie Perkins. "Be careful, okay? Don't go anywhere alone at night. And if you see that man hanging around again, please promise you'll call the cops. And me. I want to know."

Harper smiled. "Okay, *Mother*. I promise." She gave Priscilla a brief hug. "Honestly, I appreciate that. And you, for caring." She slid the diary into her bag. "Are you ready for lunch?"

Priscilla closed the browser. "I sure am. Where should we go?"

"I was thinking the Colonial Inn. I heard the food is stellar." Harper stood and put on her coat. "It's close too, so we can walk."

"The food there is great, and yes, I can use the exercise." Priscilla patted her belly. She gathered her belongings and donned her outerwear. "I'm ready when you are."

It was several blocks to the inn, and the brisk walk was invigorating. Heaps of fresh snow framed the historic buildings, and the sky was pure blue. The Colonial Inn was near the water, so they enjoyed a view of the harbor the last block or so. It was quiet except for fishing boats and other working vessels. The slips along the docks and moorings were empty, since sailboats and motor boats were stored on land for the winter.

"This is so beautiful," Harper said. She tilted her head back to watch a gull circling above with its distinctive cries. She took a deep breath. "I never get tired of salty air."

"Me neither. I could close my eyes and know where I am just by the aroma." Priscilla demonstrated. "Yes, we're next to the ocean."

The gull squawked again, and Harper said, "And by the sound."

They both laughed. "There's the inn," Priscilla said, pointing out the tall, elegant building with its wraparound porch. This time of year, the usual hanging flower baskets weren't on the porch, but Tilly Snyder, the owner, had decorated with vine wreaths and garlands of cranberries, evergreen boughs, and pine cones.

"It's so pretty," Harper said. "I wonder if my mother ever came here."

Priscilla preceded her friend up the steps to the front door. "It's been around for over a century, so perhaps she did."

They stepped into a front hall characterized by carved wood paneling and a lovely staircase rising upward. To the right stood the front desk, vacant at the moment. Priscilla led the way to the dining room on the right, a long room filled with tables and booths. Half of them were occupied, including Gerald O'Bannon's favorite spot by the window. And he was in it, spooning up what looked like chowder.

He glanced up and saw them, then gestured them over. "Priscilla, how nice to see you." He smiled at Harper. "Who's your friend?"

"Gerald, this is Harper Jenson, who works at the bakery. Gerald is a Coast Guard captain."

His brow furrowed, then he shook a finger at Harper. "That's right. I thought you looked familiar."

"I remember you." Harper glanced between Priscilla and Gerald, her eyes sly. "Didn't you buy rosemary shortbread cookies last week?"

To Priscilla's bemusement, Gerald blushed, a red tide moving up his neck. He cleared his throat. "I might have." He nodded at the other side of the booth. "Why don't you two join me?"

Priscilla looked at Harper to see what she thought, and when the young woman nodded, she slid into the booth. Harper sat next to her.

Gerald waved to Hilda, the waitress, who hurried over with glasses of water and two menus. "Can I bring you ladies something to drink?" she asked.

"I'll have coffee, please," Priscilla said. She wanted something warm to drink.

"A Coke, with lots of ice, please." Harper smirked, as though guessing what the others thought. She opened the menu. "What's good here?"

Priscilla and Gerald said at the same time, "Everything." They laughed.

"Do you know what you want?" Hilda asked, pad and pen poised.

"I'm not sure," Harper said.

"I recommend the shrimp salad," Priscilla said. "They serve it all year round." The shrimp salad was the best she'd ever eaten, and with the main ingredient coming from the docks, it couldn't get any more local.

"I'll try that," Harper said. "With a side of bread." She folded the menu and grinned. "Gotta check out the competition."

Priscilla echoed the order and added a cup of clam chowder. Harper added that to her order as well.

"Are you a bread baker?" Gerald asked Harper after Hilda left.

Priscilla realized she knew very little about her new friend and awaited Harper's response with interest.

"I am." Harper picked up her glass of ice water and spun the cubes, then took a sip. "I've been baking bread since I was a kid, and when I found out you could make money doing it, I decided to make it my career. I've taken all kinds of pro classes."

"Candy doesn't do much bread," Priscilla noted.

"I'm hoping to change that," Harper said. "In the meantime I'm having fun with the quick breads."

Hilda brought over the drinks, chowder, and a bread board with a mini loaf and a dish of butter. "Here you are. The bread is fresh out of the oven. Your lunch will be right out." She bustled away, stopping to check on other customers and take a dessert order.

"What an excellent waitress," Priscilla said. "She's amazing." She took a taste of chowder. The broth was creamy rich, and the clams were succulent. Delicious.

"Hilda has been here forever," Gerald said. "You can really see the contrast between her and the rookie high school and college girls Tilly hires every summer."

"I can imagine," Priscilla said. She tilted her head at Gerald. "Isn't this your sack lunch day? Monday is your Colonial Inn day. What got you out of your routine?"

Gerald laughed. "You caught me, fair and square. I just didn't feel like it was a banana and peanut butter sandwich kind of day. And my instincts must've been right, because here I am at lunch with two lovely ladies."

Priscilla felt her face grow warm, and she ducked her head to take another bite of soup.

Harper was slicing the loaf of bread. She stopped, holding the bread knife midair. "I just had a thought."

Gerald chuckled. "Do you always announce them this way?"

The young woman began sawing through the loaf again. "No, seriously. My mother was a waitress before she got the manager job at the dress shop. I wonder if she worked somewhere here on the island."

Gerald opened his mouth to ask the obvious question, and Priscilla jumped in. "Harper lost her mother recently, and she just learned that she lived here on the island as a teen."

"So we're retracing her footsteps." Harper pushed the bread board closer to Gerald. "Have a piece." She put a slice on her bread plate and buttered it, then took a bite. "Not bad. The crust is tender and the inside fluffy. I'd give it a strong B+."

Gerald was still stuck on Harper's mother. "When did she live here? I've been on the island a good long while."

"Almost twenty-five years ago," Priscilla said. "We were scouring old newspapers at the library this morning."

"Do you think you met her?" Harper's face was heartbreakingly eager. "Her name was Megan and people say she looked like me."

"Megan Jenson?" Gerald asked. He shook his head. "Doesn't ring a bell."

"Not Jenson." Harper blew out a gust of air in frustration. "I don't know her maiden name. Not her real one, anyway. The one on my birth certificate was a dead end." She ate a spoonful of chowder as calmly as if such situations were commonplace.

Gerald's brows rose. "Really. What was she, a runaway?"

"I think she must have been," Priscilla said. "And not a resident. We already checked the school yearbooks, and she doesn't show up."

"A summer person, then." Gerald looked up as Hilda appeared with their lunches.

She placed shrimp salad plates in front of Priscilla and Harper and served Gerald a fish sandwich with fries. "Is there anything else I can get you?"

"No, this all looks super," Harper said. Taking a deep breath, she asked Hilda if someone named Megan had worked at the inn during the summer of 1992. She explained she was trying to learn more about her deceased mother, which got a groan of sympathy from the kindhearted waitress.

Tucking the tray under her arm, Hilda tapped her foot. "Gosh, not that I remember right offhand. That's a pretty common name, you know. Lots of Megans have worked here over the years."

"Yeah, you're probably right." Harper looked deflated.

Hilda took pity on her. "Listen, we take a staff photo every summer, so why don't I dig out the one for that year? We'll see if your mom is there."

Harper leaped to her feet and embraced the startled waitress, who laughed. Harper plopped back down, somewhat abashed, her cheeks flaming. "Sorry, I got a little excited. Everyone here has been so helpful."

"Honey, I'd rather get a hug than a plugged nickel." Hilda winked and scurried off toward the kitchen.

Priscilla put her drink down. "If you were living here back then, Gerald, you must remember Bradley Alden's boating accident."

Gerald finished chewing a bite of sandwich and wiped his mouth. "I certainly do. I was pretty low on the totem pole back then, but I was sent out on the rescue boat. We barely reached him in time. The boat was slipping into the drink with him clinging on."

"Wow, that sounds intense." Harper stabbed a shrimp. "And you were right, Priscilla. This salad is awesome."

"I'm glad Bradley was okay," Priscilla said. "But what I'm really wondering about is David Castonguay. We think he might have known Harper's mom."

Harper smiled at her. "Thanks for bringing that up. I was too busy chowing down to think of it."

A thoughtful expression passed over Gerald's face. "That was a strange one. Someone told us two boys were on that boat, so when we saw Bradley by himself, we thought we'd lost David. That was a bad moment, the first of more tragedies than I like to think about. But Bradley denied taking David out. He said David left before he set sail."

"Did David leave the island?" Priscilla asked. "The newspaper article I read said he did."

"He must have," Gerald said. "He was seen buying a ferry ticket that morning, so it was assumed he left. Unless a family member files a report or there is evidence of foul play, the police aren't likely to investigate. But as far as I know, no one on Martha's Vineyard ever saw him again."

CHAPTER ELEVEN

Trudy called while Priscilla was cleaning the cottage. After lunch, she'd gone home and changed the bed, started laundry, and mopped the kitchen floor. All the while, Gerald's words haunted her. *No one ever saw him again.* Did David actually leave the island, or had he been on that sailboat? Perhaps Bradley had been afraid to tell people his friend had drowned, worried he might be blamed or even charged with a crime.

Trudy's call was a welcome relief, both to Priscilla's spinning thoughts and her list of chores. She stripped off her rubber gloves and dashed for the phone.

"Girlfriend, you are on a painting crew," Trudy sang. "Nine a.m. tomorrow at the bakery. Be there or be square."

Priscilla felt her spirits lift at the silliness. "Okay, I can do that. I'd be happy to help Candy get up and running. I'm missing those muffins and crème horns. Not to mention Tisbury Tizzy cake."

"Me too. I think I've lost a couple of pounds already. So are you in?"

"I'm in. See you then." Priscilla hung up, warmed to the core by her cousin's contagious good nature. She'd also been jolted out of her ruminations. Maybe David had left and was living a happy life somewhere. *There's only one way to find out.* After she finished cleaning, she decided, she had a date with her laptop and the internet. If David Castonguay was out there, she would find him.

And hopefully he would bring them closer to solving the mystery of Megan's identity.

Priscilla heated up a bowl of leftover turkey meatball soup for dinner and settled down to research. Jake lay under the table, hoping for a dropped treat, brushing her legs with his feathery tail every once in a while to remind her he was there. If a few stray bread crumbs were dropped accidentally now and then, and if a happy dog happened to gobble them up, who was the wiser?

She started with a White Pages program to see if she got any viable candidates. As she'd noted before, there were very few people with that particular name. If he were named John Smith, the task would have been impossible. Thankfully it was much easier than that, although still limited by the possibility that David didn't have an online presence. To conduct a search beyond the internet would require a private investigator.

Priscilla scrolled through the list, eliminating the men who were too young or too old. That left her exactly three candidates—one each in Massachusetts, Connecticut, and Utah. The site provided phone numbers and street addresses, which was rather frightening. Stalking was a whole lot easier with the internet. The Massachusetts man had only a cell phone number, and that was grayed out, available only under the premium service.

Jake thrust his nose into her knee.

"Want to go out?" She pushed back her chair. "I could use some fresh air too." Priscilla knew she was stalling on making the calls, but she quickly reframed that as gathering her thoughts. It wasn't wise to be hasty. Maybe David had a reason to leave the island and wouldn't appreciate hearing from her. There was that point to consider.

After fifteen minutes outside, she returned to the cottage with a renewed sense of purpose—and a tentative script in her mind. She gave Jake one of his treats and sat down to place the calls.

She dialed the Connecticut number first, since Utah was two hours behind and that David was probably just getting home from work. The phone rang a few times, and Priscilla got ready to leave a message. So many people screened calls these days to fend off telemarketers.

"Hello?" a cultured male voice answered. "David speaking."

Priscilla took a deep breath. "Hi, David. My name is Priscilla Latham Grant, and I'm calling from one of Martha's Vineyard's lighthouses." She figured that might give someone pause for a few seconds.

He laughed. "What can I do for you, Ms. Grant from the lighthouse?" His tone sharpened. "You're not selling vacation packages are you?"

Now Priscilla laughed. "Far from it, though I encourage you to visit the island." The call was veering off script a little, but maybe that was to her advantage.

"I'd like to someday. I've never been. Nantucket, yes, but not the Vineyard."

Disappointment panged. *Not the right David.* "That's too bad. You see, I'm looking for a David Castonguay who stayed on Martha's Vineyard about twenty-five years ago. He's connected to, er, a history I'm working on." Since he wasn't going to be able to help, she decided not to disclose details of Harper's situation.

"Sounds intriguing, but I'm not he. Perhaps I'll see you out there next summer."

They exchanged goodbyes and hung up.

One down. Without pausing to think and perhaps lose her courage, she dialed the Utah number. She got voice mail, thought about leaving a message, but hung up. If David had bad feelings about the island, he might not return the call. She needed to speak to him.

If he's the right person, that is. A sense of futility tried to creep in, something she battled during every investigation. It took courage and hope and faith to push through obstacles and find answers.

Priscilla spent the rest of the evening puttering with her family tree and designing possible exhibits. This reminded her that she ought to call Rebekah tomorrow and see if there were any more photographs she could borrow. She also needed to take the ones Rebekah had lent her to the photo shop to have copies made. She might even get extras of the one of Warren and give them to her cousins. It was such a great picture.

Around ten, she headed to bed with a book and Jake jingling along behind. The temperatures weren't quite as frigid as they had been, but she still enjoyed snuggling up under the comforter.

The telephone rang around midnight. Priscilla had dozed off, the book still open on her chest. She reached for the bedside receiver, almost knocking over her glass of water, and picked it up, her heart kicking into gear. Late night calls were rarely good news. "Hello?" Even she could hear the fear in her voice.

"You called me." The voice was abrupt. "What'd you want?"

Priscilla pulled the phone back from her ear and squinted at the number. *Utah.* "Uh, I'm doing a research project, and a David Castonguay may have some information for me. He was on Martha's Vineyard about twenty-five years ago."

"That wasn't me, lady." A note of finality in his voice gave credence to the words. *Click.* He hung up.

Number two down. Her heart still racing, Priscilla replaced the receiver and lay down. She took deep breaths, willing her nerves to settle so she could go back to sleep. She switched off the light and stared at the ceiling, almost wishing for streetlights to break the inky dark.

Out in the harbor, engines thrummed. She held her breath and listened. Hoisting herself out of bed, she went to the window. No lights were visible.

She grabbed the receiver again, this time to place a call to the Coast Guard.

Priscilla had a fitful night, not made any more restful by a bad dream involving a shipwreck. In the dream, she was on the deck, attempting to hold on while ocean water sloshed over her and the boat tilted bow up, ready to slide under.

She woke up, her heart pounding. And as she'd learned to do, she started praying, asking God to take all her thoughts captive and then laying her concerns before Him.

To her delight, sunshine greeted her in the morning, making it the second nice day in a row. Temperatures had soared into the thirties, and icicles on the eaves were dripping as they melted.

Priscilla opened the door to let Jake out, and relatively warm air gusted in, a foretaste of spring. Not bothering to dress, she threw boots and a coat on over her flannel pajamas and ventured out.

"Better enjoy it while we can," she muttered. A glance at the local weather online had shown a sharp reversal by nightfall, with the mercury plummeting and another storm moving in the next day.

Jake cavorted down the shore, then up along the bottom of a small cliff, sniffing away. Priscilla called for him to come back, but he kept going and disappeared around a boulder thrusting out into the encroaching tide. The water wasn't deep right now, but in a few minutes it would be. Ugh. She'd better go get him before he was stranded.

Priscilla ran through the snow as fast as she could, hoping the burning sensation in her muscles translated into firmer legs. She splashed around the boulder to another inlet, where Jake was busy nosing something red and white.

"Come on, you naughty boy. We need to get out of here now."

At her voice, he raised his head and gave a woof. Then he picked up the object in his mouth and carried it to her, tail wagging. He dropped it proudly at her feet, looking up as though to say, "See what I brought you, Mom?"

Not wanting to leave litter on the beach, Priscilla picked up the mangled cardboard cigarette packet, noticing it was still unopened and full. The tax stamp on the bottom read, "Virginia."

CHAPTER TWELVE

Perhaps a fisherman had dropped the pack overboard and it had floated to shore. *Perhaps.* But something told Priscilla that it was part of a smuggling load. A pack with a Virginia stamp found in Massachusetts? It had to be. She didn't know much about cigarettes, never having smoked, but she did know that every state marked packs before putting them out for sale. That was proof the tax had been paid.

Priscilla tucked the soggy pack in her jacket pocket. She'd show it to Gerald and let him decide if it was important. If not, well, she'd toss it. She started back along the beach, whistling for Jake, who was cavorting about. His head jerked up at her call, a piece of seaweed draped over his neck.

"Come on, you silly goose. We'd better get back. The tide is coming in." Sometimes the movement of the water seemed so slight it was barely visible. But near high tide, it moved inches or feet within minutes.

He flung off the weed with a toss of his head and galloped over. The big rock was only a short distance away, but by the time they reached it, the water was lapping at its base. When it receded a moment later, only a tiny strip of sand was exposed.

"Jake, we're going to have to run for it," she told the dog. They'd still get wet but not as soaked as they would wading through water up to their knees. Or higher.

But when the moment came, the dog balked. He dug his paws into the sand, looking back at her.

"Come on, Jake." Priscilla turned to study the cliff. It was mostly loose sand and rocks and had an overhanging slant to it besides. She'd never be able to climb up it. There was no exit on the other end of the cove either, since huge jumbled rocks blocked the way. Even if she could climb over them, the breaking waves might wash her off into the surf.

They had to make a run for it, there was no choice. Priscilla watched closely as the water flowed in, reaching even farther than the time before. Then it pulled back.

"Let's go, Jakey. Now." She grabbed his collar and tugged, pulling him along the sand by brute force fueled by panic.

After a moment, he stopped resisting and seemed to finally understand what she wanted. He pushed past her legs, almost making her fall. She was forced to grip the coarse granite to maintain her balance, and in the process let go of his collar. He bolted ahead to safety. She followed too slowly, however, and another wave washed in and soaked her, right up to the thighs.

Priscilla gasped at the cold force of the water pushing her against the rock face. As the wave receded, the undertow tugged the sand from beneath her feet. She leaned against the boulder, clinging for dear life. At last the bottom stabilized, and she was able to slosh the rest of the way to safety.

Jake came to greet her, panting, and pushed his nose into her hand. *No hard feelings, right?* She knuckled his furry head, grateful they'd both made it. "Let's go get dry. And I could sure could use another cup of coffee."

Inside the side door, she peeled off her boots and pajama bottoms. Her feet and legs were icy cold and clammy. Shower first, then coffee. She took the cigarette pack out of her jacket pocket and placed it in the middle of the kitchen table. That would have to wait until she was warm and dry again.

Gerald didn't pick up when she called after her shower. Glancing at the clock, she saw it was time to go to the bakery. Rather than leave a message, she took a picture of the pack's tax stamp and sent him a text.

Guess what I found this morning on the beach? Going to the bakery to help paint.

Dressed in old jeans and a long-sleeved T-shirt and carrying ancient sneakers, Priscilla jumped in the car and headed to town. The temperatures were so balmy that she rode with the window cracked open, enjoying the fresh cool air. The roads were wet with melting snow, the tall banks almost visibly shrinking.

A truck approached from the other direction, and Priscilla slowed so they could edge past each other. She recognized the vehicle as belonging to Maureen and Ed Moody, Rebekah's caretakers. As the pickup crept by, she looked up at the driver. She hadn't gotten a close look at Ed before, and she was curious.

He glanced down at her, and she saw he had heavy features and a square, stubbled jaw. He appeared burly, his shoulders thick in a plaid lumberman's jacket. He wore a matching hat pulled low over his brow.

She lifted a hand in a wave, but he didn't return the gesture. Instead his head snapped around so that he faced out the windshield.

"Friendly sort," she murmured. But maybe he hadn't recognized her as his neighbor. Better to give the benefit of the doubt rather than take offense.

The rest of the drive was uneventful, except more people seemed to be out and about, taking advantage of the nice day. Priscilla found a place down the street from the bakery and parked, then gathered her sneakers. Candy was going to provide all the paint and tools, so nothing was needed besides willing hands.

She met Trudy at the front door. "Isn't it a great day? It feels like spring."

"Don't get used to it," Trudy said, cynical, as most hardened islanders were. "Another storm is roaring in later today."

They stepped into the alcove between the plate glass windows, and Trudy reached for the front door handle. Then she frowned and pointed down at her feet. "What's that?"

A trail of water was leaking under the door and trickling toward the street.

"Uh-oh. Looks like a flood." Priscilla splashed through—what was this compared to what she'd dealt with earlier?—and cupped both hands around her eyes so she could see through the glass door.

The front room floor was covered with a sheet of water.

Priscilla jumped back. "It's definitely a flood. Where's Candy?" She'd expected the bakery owner to be there already.

"I don't know. She was supposed to meet us here." Trudy took out her cell phone. "Let me give her a buzz." After a minute she said, "Candy, it's Trudy. Priscilla and I are down at the bakery. And listen, hon, you've got a problem. Yes, another one. Something's leaking inside."

Beau's pickup screeched to a stop in front of the bakery a few minutes later. By then Joan and Gail had arrived, along with Harper and Jason the dishwasher, making up the rest of the painting and cleaning crew.

Candy leaped out of the truck, leaving the passenger door open. "What's going on? Sorry I'm late." She waved toward Beau, who was getting out of the driver's seat. "We went out to breakfast and got hung up with one of his customers." She dashed to the front door, keys jingling. She inserted the key, tap dancing around when her boots splashed into the river exiting the building. "Wow, this isn't good."

Beau joined her, helping push the door open against the tide. Water gushed out, forcing everyone to stand to one side or the other. "Come on Jason, let's figure this out."

Jason detached himself from the crowd and followed, calling back over his shoulder, "We'll get it fixed in no time, ladies." The two men disappeared into the bakery.

The others stood in a group, discussing the situation. "I can't even begin to take this in," Joan said. "A flood on top of a fire? If this was fiction, no one would believe it."

"And she had furnace trouble before that," Priscilla recalled. Something niggled. Joan was right, the string of disasters was implausible if they were random mishaps. *But if someone were causing them?* Was it malicious mischief or something more sinister?

Beau returned to the front door within a couple of minutes. "We found the problem. One of the pipes in the sink behind the bakery case is leaking. Jason is shutting off the main and we'll get it fixed in a jiffy, after we run to the hardware store." He opened the door wide and propped it with a wedge. "You can start cleaning if you want."

"Thanks, honey," Candy said. She gave a huge sigh. "I guess we'd better get to work. Let's mop the floor, and then if we have any steam left, we can start painting."

While a couple of people moved tables and stacked chairs, the others mopped up the flood, squeezing dirty water into large buckets. The final drying was done on hands and knees with rags.

"This floor hasn't been this clean in ages," Candy said, wiping an arm across her forehead. She hefted the cloth mop into the wringer bucket and pulled the lever to squeeze out the rinse water.

"At least it's a warmer day so we can let the place air out," Gail noted, following behind Candy with a rag. "That will help the floor dry."

Despite the fresh air blowing in through open doors and windows, all of them had worked up a sweat, Priscilla included. She tossed her rags into a bucket, pulled a chair off a table, and sat. "Whew. That was hard work."

"So my back and knees tell me," Joan said with a laugh. She joined Priscilla at the table, followed by Gail and Harper.

"Pipe's all set," Beau called from behind the counter. "What would you like me to do next?"

"How about go get lunch for everyone at Walt's?" Candy handed Beau some money. "Burgers, fries, and milkshakes. Then maybe I can twist everyone's arm into staying and painting."

"We'll stay," Priscilla said. "I'll be all set after a rest." The others chimed in, voicing agreement.

"We'll be right back, then," Beau said. He settled his cap on his head. "Coming, Jason?"

"Those two are becoming quite the team," Joan said when the men had slipped out the front door, which was still propped open.

"Jason's all right," Candy said. "He's willing to put his hand to whatever needs doing, I'll give him that. He helped Beau rip out the damaged wall in the kitchen and rebuild it."

Sitting next to Priscilla, Harper had been pretty quiet, seemingly absorbed in something she was writing. She lifted her head. "Candy, I have an idea how you can make a lot more money and even out your sales all year round."

Everyone looked at Candy for her reaction. She was silent for a moment, then she laughed. "I'm all ears. Like I've been saying, this winter's been tough, and my little problems are eating up my nest egg. So go ahead, shoot."

Harper shifted in her chair, sitting up straight, shoulders back. "Okay." She reminded Priscilla of a youngster giving a report in school. A little nervous but hopeful and excited too. "This may sound a little strange, but bear with me. Take out your phones and look up Café Du Pain on the Maine coast."

Along with her cousins and Candy, Priscilla dug out her phone and searched for the site. It was beautifully done, with stunning pictures of gorgeous baked goods and claims of using locally grown fruit. "What am I looking for?" she asked.

"Check the top bar," Harper said. "You can order these baked goods and have them shipped to you all year round. I think Candy can do the same for very little money or effort." She lifted up the paper she'd been writing on. "I came up with a budget and a basic design for a website."

"'Taste o' Maine goodness, even in the dead of winter,'" Joan read. "That's their tagline."

"You mean mail my muffins or Tisbury Tizzy to people?" Candy bit her lower lip, considering the idea. "You think they'd want them?"

Everyone erupted in cries of affirmation. "The best part," Priscilla said, warming to the idea, "is that every single person who comes here during the summer is a potential winter customer."

"And you don't have to offer everything online," Joan said. "Just the best sellers."

Gail had been staring off into space, and now she proclaimed, "A taste of Vineyard summer, delivered right to your door." She looked sheepish. "I kind of stole that 'taste' part from the Maine bakery."

"No, that's an excellent tagline," Priscilla said. "Especially if Candy sells treats baked with Vineyard-grown cranberries, blue-berries, and apples. That would definitely make them stand out."

"I could do that." Now Candy sounded excited. "I buy fresh fruit from local farmers all the time. This could help them too."

Other ideas began to fly around the room, and by the time Beau's truck pulled up in front, a full-blown plan and timeline for the website roll-out had been developed. Joan offered to photograph the baked goods, and Priscilla said she'd write the descriptions—while eating samples for inspiration, of course. Gail said she'd find out how other businesses on the island gathered email addresses and contact information from customers.

Beau and Jason strolled in, their arms full of paper bags emitting delicious aromas. "What's going on in here? Did you start the party without us?" Beau grinned.

Candy flew off her chair and ran to kiss his cheek. "Harper figured out how to help me save the bakery. And my friends are going to help. So yes, you could say I'm celebrating."

As the men set down the bags, everyone started talking at once, trying to bring Beau up to speed. But in the general merriment, Priscilla noticed someone who didn't participate. Jason stood off to one side, his pale-blue eyes studying each face in turn.

CHAPTER THIRTEEN

D o you want a hamburger or a cheeseburger?" Beau asked Priscilla. He held the paper bag open, prepared to reach inside.

"Cheeseburger, please." In the resulting flurry of settling down to eat, Priscilla forgot about the strange expression she'd seen on Jason's face. When she glanced at him again, he was seated between Harper and Gail, laughing at a joke.

Beau had selected sweet potato fries and vanilla milkshakes, so Priscilla found herself eating a much larger lunch than usual. She told herself she'd burn it off painting the kitchen that afternoon. And she'd have a small dinner to set off the caloric intake.

"Knock, knock." Everyone swiveled to see Gerald standing in the front doorway. Priscilla's heart gave a leap when their eyes met. He smiled and touched his hat in a salute.

Candy rose to her feet. "I'm sorry, we're still closed, Gerald," she said. "But we've got plenty of hamburgers and fries if you want to join us."

"I packed my lunch today, but thank you for the offer." He stepped inside, taking off his hat. "I'm actually here to talk to Priscilla."

A hoot burst from Trudy. She quickly covered her mouth and pretended to cough. But she didn't bother to hide the teasing expression she turned Priscilla's way, complete with fluttering eye-lashes and raised brows. Gail threw her an elbow and a scowl. "We're not in grade school, you ninny," she whispered.

Priscilla stood. She had an idea why Gerald had sought her out, and she wasn't under the illusion that it was for her company. "Sure thing, Gerald. Shall we step outside?" She turned to others. "I'll be right back."

"Take your time. Don't hurry on our account," Trudy called. "Ouch. What'd you do that for?"

Looking over her shoulder, Priscilla saw Trudy rubbing her shin while Gail glared. Smiling at the tomfoolery, she fell into step with Gerald and exited the bakery.

"Cleaning up?" he asked. "I saw all the mops and buckets."

"We were supposed to paint the kitchen this morning, but there was a flood when we got here," she explained.

Gerald shook his head. "Poor Candy. She can't win for losing. I'll check in with her later and see if there's anything I can do."

"That'd be wonderful. I love the way everyone here helps each other. It makes it a real community, you know?" A sea breeze lifted her hair, and she breathed in the briny air with pleasure. Her small town in Kansas had been tightknit, and she was happy to find that closeness on the island too.

"That's why I've stuck around." He gave her a crooked grin. "I could be working in Florida right now."

"And miss all this?" She waved at the grimy snowbanks and closed seasonal businesses. Shifting gears, she said, "You're here about the cigarette pack, aren't you?"

He pressed his lips into a thin line. "I am. Good work, Priscilla. Can you tell me where you found it? And how?"

She ran a hand through her hair. "Well, Jake and I were outside enjoying the sunshine this morning when he took off." She took him through the sequence of events, leaving out how she and the dog had almost been stranded by the tide. She knew Gerald well enough to guess that he would give her a friendly scolding.

He'd been gazing at the harbor, listening intently as she talked. He turned toward her. "Where's the pack now?"

"On my kitchen table. I saved it for you."

"Good. How about I swing by later and pick it up?" He glanced at his watch. "When do you think you'll be done here?"

"By dinnertime, I hope. We're behind, thanks to having to clean up the leak, but we should be able to knock it out in a few hours."

"You're going to be tired after working so hard all day." He paused. "How about I bring over dinner? I'm no cook, but I can pick up one of those rotisserie chickens and some side dishes."

Priscilla's heart thudded. She was already a sweaty mess, and how much worse would she look after painting all afternoon? "That sounds really nice. Let's make it seven, okay? I'll need time to clean up."

"Seven, it is. See you then." With another salute and a smile, he strode away.

A weary Priscilla arrived home just after five. She let Jake out for a necessary run, then shed her paint-spattered clothing and hopped in the shower. She had white paint under her nails, on her nose, and even in her hair, the last thanks to Trudy's vigorous efforts with a paint roller. While scrubbing up, she smiled at the humorous memories she had gathered that day working with her cousins. And tonight she had dinner with Gerald to look forward to. She burst into song, startling Jake, who rocketed to his feet from a prone position on the bathroom floor. She laughed. "Sorry, Jake. I guess I haven't sung in the shower for a while."

After the shower, she dried her hair and sprayed perfume on her neck. Not wanting to look as if she'd tried too hard, she selected a flattering pale-green cashmere pullover and her favorite dark jeans to wear. A pair of soft moccasins and tiny hoop earrings completed the outfit.

Gerald was bringing the meal, so all she had to do was set the table. After moving the cigarette pack to a safe place on the counter, she laid out dishes and silverware on quilted cranberry and green place mats. Then she added a couple of candles and a bouquet of flowers she'd picked up at the grocery store.

The phone rang, and she hurried to answer, hoping it wasn't Gerald canceling. She'd be very disappointed if so, she realized.

"Is this Priscilla Latham Grant?" a familiar voice inquired.

Priscilla smiled at the greeting. "Rebekah. How are you?" Catching her reflection in the plate glass window, she flicked her hair into place.

"I'm very well, thank you. I was wondering if you might be free tomorrow to look at pictures again?" She cleared her throat. "My keepers are going out for the afternoon."

Rebekah's remark startled a laugh out of Priscilla. *No flies on that one.* Again she wondered at Rebekah's bouts of confusion. Was that normal?

"I'd be glad to come over, Rebekah. What time is good for you?" She'd have to dash out to the photo shop in the morning and get reproductions made of the borrowed photos. That way she could return the originals. They settled on two o'clock.

Next Priscilla built a fire and lit candles on the mantel. Soft classical music on the stereo also set a pleasant mood. Preparations complete, she peeked out the curtains at the night, the booming surf discernible even through the glass. High tide, which arrived every twelve hours without fail. A crescent moon and diamond stars decorated the sky. How beautiful. She allowed herself to pause and savor the beauty of God's creation, knowing that such moments were like precious jewels amid life's struggles and heartaches.

The doorbell rang on the dot of seven. Smiling at Gerald's punctuality, Priscilla went to the door. "Come on in," she said with a wide smile.

He was clutching two large paper sacks. "I had to ring the doorbell with my elbow." He stepped inside. "Brr. The temperature's dropping like a rock out there."

"That's what they said would happen. Too bad they were right for once." Priscilla reached for the sacks of food. "Give me those so you can take off your things." She carried them to the kitchen while Gerald took off his coat and boots and greeted a tail-wagging Jake.

He entered the kitchen in his stocking feet, the dog trailing him. "I hope you like what I brought."

She unpacked a lemon peppercorn chicken, a container of garlic mashed potatoes, a broccoli cheese cranberry salad, dinner rolls, and a small carrot cake. "This all looks fabulous." Her belly gurgled. Perhaps she wouldn't have a light dinner after all.

"Not as good as homemade, but tasty all the same. The deli does a good job." He spotted the cigarette pack on the counter. "Is that the one you found?"

"Yes, it is. I think it's still soggy, so watch out." She turned on the oven. She'd heat up the chicken, potatoes, and rolls. The salad went in the fridge to wait, and the cake on the counter for later. "Would you like iced tea or water?" she asked. "I also have soft drinks."

"Ice water would be great, thanks." Gerald was busy studying the pack, handling it with a pair of latex gloves he'd brought.

"I'm sure my prints are all over it," Priscilla said. "When I first saw it, I thought it was just litter either dropped or washed up on shore."

"No worries. The water probably washed off whatever was there, if anything, but I like to be careful just in case. What probably happened is a carton opened up, and this spilled out." He pulled a plastic bag out of his pocket and inserted the pack, then sealed it. "This should be very useful in helping us trace the rest of the load."

"I'm glad I could be of help," Priscilla said lightly. "Even if it was accidental."

"Keep your eyes peeled for more packs washing up on shore, okay? And if you hear those engines again, call me, any time day or night." He held up the evidence bag. "I'm going to tuck this into my glove compartment. Be right back."

Priscilla opened the oven and checked the progress of the meal. Almost ready. She scooped the broccoli salad into a bowl and set it on the table, then lit the candles.

Gerald returned within a couple of minutes, shedding his outer garments again. "I swear the temperature dropped another five degrees already."

"Let's check." Priscilla pulled back the curtain over the sink and checked the thermometer attached to the window casing outside. "It's fifteen degrees."

Gerald rubbed his hands together. "Wow. A twenty-degree drop since this afternoon." He glanced around the kitchen. "Need some help?"

"Sure." She slid her hands into mitts and pulled the chicken out of the oven. "How are you at carving chicken?" She lifted it with utensils onto a platter, then reached for a carving knife and fork.

"That's one of my many talents." He stood at the counter and began to cut the breast into even, succulent slices.

Her husband had always carved the chickens and turkeys too. Bemused by a sense of déjà vu, yet knowing that this situation was entirely new, Priscilla pulled the rolls and mashed potatoes out of the oven. The hot rolls she popped into a napkin-lined basket. The potatoes in their casserole dish received a serving spoon and were set on a trivet on the table. She poured fresh glasses of ice water, gave the table a final check, and pulled a dish of cranberry sauce out of the refrigerator. Gerald carried over the platter of chicken, and they were ready to eat.

"Shall I say grace?" Gerald asked, flipping open a napkin and settling it on his lap.

"Please." She hid a smile. Gary had said grace most nights also.

After a short but heartfelt prayer, Gerald smiled at Priscilla. "Thank you. This is really nice."

"It was your idea," she said, taking a slice of breast off the platter and passing it along. "And you brought all the food."

"But you provided the lovely atmosphere to enjoy it." He served himself chicken and a big scoop of potatoes, then passed those to Priscilla. She swapped potatoes for broccoli salad and, last, reached for the breadbasket. Hot rolls and butter. *Yum.*

They ate for a few minutes, accompanied by soft classical music and the clink and clatter of silverware against china. She was about to ask about his grandchildren when he cleared his throat and said, "Uh, Priscilla?"

"Yes, Gerald?" For no reason at all, her heart began to thump. Feeling suddenly shy, she kept her eyes on her plate, dipping her fork into her potatoes and then into the cranberry sauce.

"Have you heard about the Share a Little Love event?"

"I have. It sounds like a wonderful benefit."

Another throat clearing. "I was wondering..."

Spit it out, please! She was so keyed up that she was almost levitating out of her chair. "Yes?"

"Will you go with me?" His words fell one by one into Priscilla's ears.

She jerked up her head, and their eyes met. She opened her mouth. Hesitated. Then said, "Yes, I'd love to go with you."

CHAPTER FOURTEEN

Gerald's cell phone broke the silence. He grimaced. "Sorry, but I've got to get this. Two of my guys are out sick with flu." He pushed back from the table and strode out of the room, fishing his phone out of his pocket.

The low murmur of his deep voice drifted in from the other room. Priscilla sat staring into the candlelight, tingling with shock and excitement. Had she just agreed to go on a date with Gerald? *Yes.* Objections and guilt and fears tried to crowd in, but she mentally held up a hand. It was all right. They were good friends, that was all.

"Priscilla. I'm sorry, but I've got to go." He stood in the doorway, his expression apologetic.

She stood. "Is it the smugglers?" She reached for the platter of meat. She might as well pack it up for him to take home or to the station.

"No, a distress call." He entered the kitchen, his eyes falling on the carrot cake. "We didn't even get to have dessert."

"You can take it with you. I'll never eat all that." She set the platter of meat on the counter and opened a drawer to grab some plastic bags.

"Keep some," he said, bringing over the vegetables. He set the bowls on the table, then stood, shifting foot to foot. "I'm so sorry.

This is exactly what used to happen with Cathy." Cathy was his ex-wife. Without warning, she had taken the children to Texas when they were eight and ten. His daughter at least had moved back, married now and the mother of his adorable grandchildren.

Priscilla waved off his concern. "Don't worry about it. It's your job." She sent him a teasing grin. "We need you and the others out there guarding our shores."

His expression relaxed. "Yes, ma'am." He lowered his voice into a John Wayne growl. "But you better believe I'm making sure there is plenty of coverage next week."

The night of Share a Little Love. Her heart skipped a beat. "You'd better, mister. I'm not getting dressed up for nothing."

Now he grinned. "I can't wait to see that. You all fancy."

"Yeah, well, I should take off these long johns once in a while. Wash them, you know." They both laughed.

A few minutes later, she sent him off with a packet of chicken and half the cake. There weren't enough vegetables or rolls left to bother splitting. The rest of the cake she'd take over to Rebekah's the next day. They could have it with tea.

The house felt empty without him, and she had the letdown feeling that comes after a party ends. "I feel like a deflated balloon," she told Jake as she poked the living room fire into life. But then irrepressible excitement sparked. She had a big social event on Valentine's Day to look forward to—with a date. The thought of calling Joan to share crossed her mind, but instead she sat in front of the fire, Jake at her feet. She wanted to keep this news to herself for a while and savor it, like the sweet dessert they didn't have a chance to eat.

Gusts of wind and heavy snowfall greeted Priscilla the next morning when she peeked outside. She almost crawled back into bed, but then she remembered she had to visit the camera shop to get Rebekah's photos reproduced.

"Where are the fifty-degree temperatures I heard the island got last year?" she grumbled to Jake. "This is like January in February."

He lifted his head and regarded her with liquid brown eyes, not offering any wisdom but loads of sympathy. Then he gave a heart-wrenching sigh and put his head back on his paws.

"I guess you don't like it either. Well, you've got to go out and do your business before I leave. There's no way around it." She tugged open a bureau drawer and hunted for a fresh pair of long johns. Despite her joke with Gerald, she had several pairs she rotated—and washed.

Gerald. We're going to the charity event together. A thrill ran through her at the thought. She'd have to confide in Joan about the invitation, since she had no idea what to wear. She couldn't even remember the last time she'd gotten dressed up for an evening out. She and Gary rarely did that kind of thing, preferring the comfort of casual occasions like cookouts or potluck suppers.

Jake cooperated during a brief outing, and Priscilla reentered the house with relief. It wasn't a day to linger and look at the view. She made a breakfast of poached eggs on toast and then got ready to go into town. First she dressed in winter gear, and then she waddled out to warm up the car. The plow truck hadn't come to do her driveway yet, but only a couple of inches had fallen so far. She'd be able to make it out to the road without a problem.

She'd stop at the grocery store, she decided. Then if the weather got worse and she was stranded for a few days, she'd have enough supplies on hand.

What was it like in times past, she mused, before people had cars and the roads were plowed? How long had they been cooped up in the lighthouse at a stretch? She pictured the basement shelves full of provisions that had to last weeks, if not months. She stared up at the lighthouse framed by blowing snow, imagining how it was on this spot a hundred years ago. She shuddered at the bleak loneliness that descended over her spirit. There had been nothing out here but wind, water, and the eternal light guiding sailors home.

Jake barked inside the house, breaking the spell gripping her. With a laugh, she threw the brush back in the car and went to see what the fuss was about.

The answering machine light was blinking. "I do hope you're still coming today," Rebekah said in the message. "I've been so looking forward to your visit."

Priscilla grabbed her handbag and then, still dressed in her coat and boots, called Rebekah back. She was looking forward to their time together too.

Her first stop was the camera store, where she arranged to have the photos scanned and printed. The young clerk with dark spiky bed head and an earring promised to have them in an hour. "We're not exactly jamming today," he said with a cheeky grin. He leafed through the photos again. "Cool pics. Vintage, huh?"

"They are. I'm going to include them in my museum at the lighthouse."

His thick brows skyrocketed. "You're putting a museum in the lighthouse? Way cool. I'll be sending people over. They're gonna love that."

"I hope so. See you in a while." Priscilla pushed open the plate glass door, wincing at the wind and snow that greeted her. An hour wait meant she had time to get groceries, although the store's location meant backtracking the way she'd come. Oh well. With the bakery closed, she didn't have a place to wait.

The Stop&Shop parking lot was half empty, something that would never happen in the summer. During that season, hapless shoppers sometimes had to lurk in the parking lot, stalking those exiting to get a parking spot.

As she walked inside, Priscilla searched for her list and found it in her coat pocket, then scanned it, making sure she had everything written down. Still thinking about meals, she absentmindedly grabbed a cart and pushed it into the produce section. She grabbed the basics—lettuce, bananas, carrots, winter squash, onions, and potatoes—then splurged on hothouse tomatoes and a cucumber.

Next she headed for the canned goods. As she turned the corner of the aisle, she heard a woman say in a low, furious voice, "What are you doing here? Leave me alone."

Priscilla halted but not soon enough. Ida Lee Jones stood nose to nose with Jason, the dishwasher from the bakery. He worked at the diner too, she remembered, as did Ida.

"I'm going to tell Randy, and he'll—" Ida Lee broke off when she saw Jason's eyes dart over her shoulder to Priscilla. She whirled around, her mouth dropping open.

Jason took advantage of the distraction. He pivoted on his thick rubber boots and barreled down the aisle the other way.

"Was he bothering you, Ida?" Priscilla asked. There really was no other explanation as far as she could see, and she felt her hackles rise on Ida's behalf.

Ida stubbed a toe of her duck boot into the glossy tile floor. "Yeah, well, kind of. Not that he's done anything criminal, but he always seems to be wherever I am." She shrugged one slim shoulder. "It's bugging the heck out of me."

"Maybe you should tell Randy. That will scare him off." Randy was a nice guy, but Priscilla guessed he'd be formidable if anyone was bothering his wife.

"I might." Ida consulted a piece of paper. "Now where was I? Oh yes, canned beets. I'm going to make red flannel hash with some leftover roast beef."

"I love hash," Priscilla said. "Maybe I'll do that too. Of course I need to make roast beef first." *Does Gerald like red flannel hash?* The thought flitted through her mind, and she firmly pushed it away instead of letting it take root. It was far too soon to make him the centerpiece of her plans.

Ida nodded, obviously distracted, so Priscilla wandered off and continued browsing. While she selected groceries, her mind kept returning to Jason's odd behavior. Should she warn Candy? But maybe that wouldn't be fair to the young man. He was probably more of a pest than anything else.

The snow was coming down even thicker and faster by the time Priscilla left the store. She had a terrible time pushing the cart across the rutted lot, so she gave up and lugged the bags two by two to the car.

Out on the main road, things weren't much better. The plows weren't able to keep up, and the streets were covered with slippery slop. She considered going straight home but, thinking of Rebekah, went back to the camera shop and retrieved the photographs. She didn't even look at the copies, just thanked the friendly clerk and dashed back outside.

The ride home was slow going, with Priscilla gripping the wheel and praying she wouldn't go off the road or hit someone—and that they wouldn't hit her. Some people refused to let a little thing like treacherous driving conditions force them to slow down.

At the cottage, Priscilla unloaded the groceries, put them away, and ate a quick sandwich. She'd walk over to Rebekah's, she decided. It wasn't far, and she could use the exercise. She sealed the photographs in a plastic bag and zipped them into the pocket of her backpack so they wouldn't get wet. The cake was already in a plastic container, so she slid that inside too. A pad of paper and a pen followed for notes.

Then, feeling like an Arctic explorer, she set off into the storm. Within a few steps, whirling ice pellets mixed with snow enclosed her as though in a cocoon. The silence was total, except for the hiss of sleet. She trudged past huge old maples, so magnificent in summer and fall, now standing with branches lifted in supplication, enduring another winter.

Lights from the Alden house winked through the snow, a beacon guiding her up the driveway. Fresh tire tracks revealed that the Moodys were gone, as Rebekah had said. Priscilla chose to walk in one of them rather than wade.

Rebekah answered the bell immediately. "Oh, do come in, Priscilla." She peered outside. "Isn't this snowfall gorgeous? I love the feeling of being snug inside during a storm."

Priscilla laughed. "Me too. But I enjoyed the walk. It was so peaceful."

"You walked over? Oh my. You'd better come warm up." Rebekah took Priscilla's pack and watched anxiously while her guest removed her boots, coat, and mittens.

"I brought your photographs back." Priscilla dug a tissue out of her pants pocket and wiped her running nose. "And there's carrot cake to have with our tea."

"Carrot cake? My favorite." Rebekah leaned close, her eyes mischievous. "Actually it's the cream cheese frosting I like."

"Me too," Priscilla said. "The cake is just the delivery mechanism." She hoped that when she was in her seventies, she'd have the childlike joy Rebekah possessed so abundantly.

After drinking hot tea and enjoying the cake, which received Rebekah's seal of approval, they sat at the table to browse through the photographs. Rebekah had several more from the early twentieth century to share, and Priscilla found a few depicting a picnic at the lighthouse she wanted to have copied. Women and girls wore long white dresses and either big hats or floppy bows on their heads. The men wore suits, handsome and surely very hot in the summer sun.

Rebekah opened another album, this one appearing to be much more recent in vintage. "Remember I told you about my daughter, Sally?" Her voice was almost a whisper.

Priscilla studied the photograph Rebekah was pointing to, a family portrait. Rebekah appeared to be in her forties, with only a few threads of gray in her light-brown hair. Tall and wiry, Henry had a long, clever face and keen eyes. Sally was a combination of her parents, with her mother's fine-featured beauty and her father's air of watchful intelligence. Sally's hair was thick and blonde like his too.

"She's lovely," Priscilla said. Her heart twisted in sorrow for her friend. How tragic to lose a child—unthinkable, really. With trepidation, but sensing Rebekah wanted to talk about Sally, she asked, "What happened?"

Rebekah's eyes filled with tears. "She ran away. And I've never heard from her again. I don't know if she's alive or—"

CHAPTER FIFTEEN

Dead. Priscilla's mind filled in the word Rebekah couldn't bring herself to utter. And who could blame her? She tried to put herself in her friend's shoes. What would she have done if Rachel had run away and was never heard from again? What terrible imaginings must fill Rebekah's mind.

"Oh, we looked. Even hired a detective to look for her and . . . a friend she might have been with. He didn't find either of them." Rebekah's smile was wry. "She's certainly her father's daughter. Smart as a whip." She turned the page. "Here she is with some of her friends."

A gang of young people lounged about the lawn in front of this house. Priscilla spotted Sally sitting right in the middle, laughing at Bradley's posturing. He was definitely recognizable, although his hair was longer and he had a ridiculously furry moustache. A shirtless boy wearing a large ornate cross and a petite girl with a long red ponytail watched Bradley, smiling.

"I know Bradley. Who are the others?" Priscilla asked, making conversation.

Rebekah turned the page with a snort. "What does it matter? I don't remember anyway." Her lips were set in a thin line.

Priscilla didn't pry further. Most children had reasons that seemed valid to them when they ran away, even if it was only an overblown reaction to something their parents said or did. What had caused Sally to leave and never get in touch with her parents again? How cruel. *Unless she couldn't.* That was an even worse thought.

Her hostess had moved on. "Here's a picture of the lighthouse when your aunt was still living." The shot showed Aunt Marjorie weeding the flower beds, a hand to her forehead to shade her eyes from the sun. She was smiling. "I loved your aunt. She was a good woman."

"She was indeed." Not that Priscilla had known her well. In fact, she regretted that she hadn't visited the island more frequently. The long-standing feud between her mother and Aunt Marjorie reminded her uncomfortably of Rebekah's situation with her daughter. Priscilla's mother hadn't spoken to Marjorie for decades, and now both were gone. "I'm doing my best to honor her legacy and take care of the place."

Rebekah tilted her head, regarding Priscilla steadily. "You're committed to it, I can see that. You're a Latham through and through. Honest, forthright, steadfast."

Priscilla found herself blushing. "I don't know about that. I just do my best."

"And from what I see, that is very good indeed." Rebekah closed the album. "I'll let you take this if you want. There are quite a few shots of the lighthouse and your relatives. Make whatever copies you need." She added another album. "This one too."

"Thanks, Rebekah. I really appreciate it." She took a deep breath. Should she? Why not? "If you want, I'll look for Sally. It's amazing what you can find online nowadays."

The expression on her friend's face was like dawn over the ocean. "Would you?" She put a hand on Priscilla's arm. "I've heard about you, that you're good at solving mysteries. I was hesitant to ask. I know you're really busy."

"Not too busy for you, Rebekah." Priscilla's heart twisted in sympathy for her new friend. She deeply empathized, both as a mother and a daughter. She couldn't—no, didn't—want to imagine being estranged from either Charlotte or Rachel. "I'll do what I can to help you find your Sally."

Rebekah clasped her hands together. "Oh, I pray you can find her." Her face sagged in sorrow. "You see, it was all my fault. I'm the reason she ran away." She bowed her head, her voice a whisper. "What I wouldn't give to take it all back."

Her neighbor's words haunted Priscilla all the way home, a laborious effort, due to the continuing storm. To lose a child—and believe it was your fault. She couldn't think of anything more dreadful. She stopped under one of the magnificent maples and said a heartfelt prayer for Rebekah and for Sally, should she still be living.

The first thing she did after making it back to the cottage— once Jake was fed and let out briefly—was call her daughter.

"Mom, you know I'm still at work," Rachel said. "Is everything all right?"

"I'm sorry, darling. I just wanted to hear your voice." Priscilla bubbled over with joy. What a blessing it was to call Rachel whenever she wanted, even if it annoyed her.

Rachel sighed. "Hang on." After a minute or so, she came back on the line. "Hey. I'm in the break room, and we can chat." There was the sound of a microwave door shutting and several beeps.

"Making tea?" Priscilla decided to do the same. They could drink tea together even though physically many miles apart. She took the shortcut of using the microwave too and picked out a tea bag while she waited.

Over the airwaves, a refrigerator door opened and shut, then Priscilla heard the scraping of a chair. "Okay, I'm ready. How's the weather?"

Priscilla burst out laughing at such a mundane question. "Terrible. We have snow up to our armpits. And it's still coming down." She tugged aside the kitchen curtain to check. Yes, it was.

"Wow. Are you going to tie something to Jake's tail so you can find him in the snowdrifts?"

"Good idea. You should see him when he ventures into snow that's over his head. He tries to swim through it."

They went on discussing the small happenings of daily life, then Priscilla said, "I was visiting my neighbor again today, Rebekah Alden. I think I told you about her. She's older and lives alone."

"Yes, I remember you mentioning her," Rachel said.

"I learned today that her daughter ran away when she was a teenager." Even verbalizing this was upsetting, and Priscilla had to stop and take a few deep breaths. "She's never heard from her since."

"Oh, Mom. That's awful. What do you suppose—oh, what are the chances she's alive and well somewhere?"

"Slim to none, I imagine. Rebekah asked me to look for her. Sally Alden, that's her name." She pictured the pretty young woman with curly blonde hair. What would she look like now, if she were alive?

"And you said yes. Well, if you learn something, even if it's not good, at least it will put her mind at rest."

Priscilla shifted in her kitchen chair. "I suppose. If only I could help her find a happy ending."

"Aw, Mom. You're the best. Hang on, I'm going to reheat my tea."

While Rachel was busy, Priscilla's thoughts went to the invitation from Gerald. Should she tell her daughter? What if she didn't and Rachel found out some other way? Priscilla had no idea how that could happen, but with her luck it would and then Rachel would be hurt.

"Uh, Rachel? I have some good news to share." At least she hoped her daughter would perceive it that way. "Gerald asked me to Share a Little Love."

Tea spluttered. "Uh, what?"

Priscilla realized what she had said and burst out laughing. "No, I didn't mean that. Well, I did, but Share a Little Love is a charity event on Valentine's Day. It's going to benefit the homeless shelter at my church and also an animal shelter."

Rachel chuckled. "After that lead-in, I'll be relieved if you go to a charity ball with Gerald every week, if that's all you do." She snorted. "You had me going there for a second."

"I know. I'm sorry." Priscilla's body still hummed with merriment. Laughter was the best medicine, right? It certainly felt good to enjoy a belly laugh.

"I'm going out on Valentine's too, you'll be glad to know. But with a group, not a date." Rachel laughed. "It's a step in the right direction. If I'm ever going to find someone, I have to get out of the house and have a social life."

"That's great, Rachel. I'm glad." Priscilla knew Valentine's Day could be an occasion fraught with emotion for those who were single and alone. It sometimes felt like the rest of the world was in happy couples except for the lonely one. "So what do you think I should wear?"

For the rest of the call, Rachel happily discussed various outfit options with Priscilla, even offering to send photographs of clothes she thought would look good. When they finally hung up, with promises to speak soon, Priscilla's heart was full of gratitude and love. If she could help others reconnect with their loved ones, then that would surely be a worthwhile pursuit.

"I'm the luckiest woman in the world," she told Jake. He thumped his tail as though to say he felt pretty lucky too. She crouched down to give him a thorough petting. "What shall I make for dinner, old boy?"

The idea of lasagna floated into her mind. A hearty baked pasta dish was perfect on a night like this. The recipe made a full-sized pan, but it froze well. Perhaps she should have a small dinner gathering with the cousins. They hadn't done that for a while. People tended to hunker down in the winter and didn't socialize as much. "Would you like to have a party, Jake?" He gave a yip, then unfolded himself to follow her into the kitchen.

While mentally planning the dinner party, she made a batch of homemade sauce, thanks to a lesson from an Italian neighbor in Kansas. She began by sautéing onion, garlic, and celery in olive oil, then browned sweet sausage in the same pan. She added spices, a splash of red cooking wine, and crushed tomatoes, then left it to simmer. A big bowl of ricotta cheese mixed with eggs, a touch of parsley, and grated Parmesan was next.

The phone rang while she was pouring sauce over the last layer of pasta. She finished spooning out sauce, then grabbed the receiver.

"Priscilla? It's Harper." The young woman took a quivering breath. "The stalker is back."

CHAPTER SIXTEEN

W hat's he doing?" Priscilla heard the sharp note of alarm in her tone. "He can't get in, can he?"

"No, the outside door to the building is locked. He's standing across the street, staring up at my window. How did he find out where I live?" Her words rose on a note of desperation.

"Harper, call the police right now and report a prowler." Priscilla hesitated, a prompting to do the right thing warring with her desire to stay in her cozy home. "I'll be right over."

"Are you sure?" Relief softened Harper's voice. "But it's awful out there," she added. "I don't blame you if you want to stay put."

"No. I can't let you face this alone. I'll be there as soon as I can." Priscilla got the address and hung up. After placing slices of mozzarella cheese on top of the casserole, she put the pan into the fridge. She could bake it later.

"Want to go for a ride, Jakey?" she asked the dog. It wouldn't hurt to have a dog along if she ran into the stalker.

Once again she went out into the storm. Thankfully the plow truck had come and gone, leaving her driveway passable. The crest of snow left at the end was the tough part, but if she left now, she'd be able to break through. Coming home, well, she'd cross that bridge—er, snowbank—when she had to.

The road into town was slick, so she crawled along, planning ahead for when she'd have to stop by slowing even more. It was the injudicious use of brakes that sent people off the road or into a skid. She wanted to avoid both situations.

Harper lived on a side street of homes converted into apartments. Priscilla easily identified the right one thanks to the police cruiser sitting out front. She parked behind it, the street clear due to the parking ban. As long as she didn't stay here overnight, she'd be fine.

Priscilla grabbed a flashlight before getting out of the car, Jake at her heels. Before she went to the house, she wanted to check the spot where Harper said the stalker had been standing.

Harper was right. The street was deserted, but an area of snow freshly trampled by boots was clearly visible in the flashlight's beam. The hollows were rapidly filling with snow, but they were still visible. A line of footprints led to the nearest corner, and she followed them to where they turned down another side street. So it hadn't been someone who lived in one of the houses opposite, outside smoking a cigarette or waiting for a ride.

"Let's go see Harper, Jake," she told her faithful mutt. They returned to the house and climbed granite steps to the small front porch. A line of mailboxes hung there, along with a row of buzzers. She pressed the one for number three, Harper's apartment.

A loudspeaker crackled. "Who is it?" Harper's voice.

"Priscilla." A buzzer sounded, and the front door unlatched. She headed up the steep flight in the entryway, which had sensible linoleum floors and brown wainscoting. A two-bulb brass pan fixture spoke to the age of the house.

Upstairs, a door at the front of the house stood slightly open, voices drifting from the apartment beyond. Priscilla knocked.

"Priscilla. I'm so glad you're here." Harper opened the door onto a large, sparsely furnished room. "Your dog is so cute! What's his name?"

"Jake," Priscilla said, noticing Officer April Brown perched on a brown tweed sofa near the double front windows. Synthetic fabric drapes were pulled tightly against the view of the street. Good. That meant April hadn't seen her snooping around the footsteps. "Officer Brown," she said with a nod.

"Mrs. Grant." April rose to shake her hand. "Ms. Jenson said you'd be coming by."

Harper was still fussing over Jake, who was lapping up the love. "Priscilla is the one who told me to call the police."

April returned to the sofa, and Priscilla took the matching armchair opposite. "That was wise advice," the officer said, "although we can't do much unless we catch him in the act. Or you can clearly identify him. Then you can get a restraining order."

Harper ducked her head, still focused on the dog. "I'm not sure who it is."

Priscilla traded a look with April, who raised one brow. The officer probably saw this all the time, the refusal to take matters further when it came to ex-boyfriends or husbands. "If you see him again, call. And if things escalate in any way, with verbal contact or phone calls or emails, let us know immediately. We want to protect you, Harper. Help us do that."

The young woman nodded, still not making eye contact with the officer or Priscilla.

April sighed and stood. "I'll move along now. I've got the information, and I'll start a file." She pulled out a card and set it on the coffee table. "Call me anytime, day or night."

Priscilla walked Officer Brown to the door, then followed her into the hallway. "I'll keep an eye on her," she told April. The urge to tell the officer about Ollie Perkins rose to her lips, but she hated to betray Harper's confidence.

"I'm glad she has you to lean on," April said. "A young woman alone needs friends." She pulled out another card and pressed it into Priscilla's hand. "You can call me too." Her eyes sent Priscilla a message. *If you learn something, I need to know.* "We take women's safety very seriously on the island."

"I'm glad to hear that. Good night." Priscilla watched as the officer headed down the stairs. A moment later, the front door opened and shut.

Harper looked up when Priscilla returned to the apartment. "She seemed nice."

Priscilla sat on the armchair. "She is. Very competent too."

The young woman gave Jake a final pat and rose to her feet. She crossed to the front window and peered out the curtain, an action that Priscilla guessed had become a habit. She dropped the curtain. "Phew. He hasn't come back."

"I think the police car probably scared him off." Priscilla was dreading the drive home and wanted nothing more than to be safe and snug at the cottage. But she hated to leave Harper alone. Even if the man didn't return, she'd be on edge. At least that was how Priscilla would feel, if it had happened to her.

An idea drifted into her mind. Without giving herself time to examine it too closely, she blurted, "Do you want to come home with me?" The peace sweeping over her informed her that this was the right thing to do, take the young woman away from the apartment. Conventional wisdom might argue that she barely knew Harper, and what if Ollie followed her to the cottage? *Then we'll deal with it.*

She said, "I'm making homemade lasagna for dinner. And besides, Jake would like it." She smiled at the dog, who hadn't taken his eyes off Harper since they'd arrived.

Harper flitted over to the sofa and perched. "Really? I've been wanting to see the lighthouse." She glanced around the room with a shudder. "And I'd like to get out of here for a night. I've been feeling like I'm living in a horror movie, waiting for the bad guy to show up."

"How many times have you seen him out there?"

Again the head drop. Harper chewed on a thumbnail, her gaze on the threadbare carpet. "Three times." She jumped back up and went to her trash. "Oh yeah. I found these in my mailbox yesterday." She showed Priscilla a withered bunch of flowers wrapped in the cellophane used by grocery stores.

"Oh, Harper. You should have told Officer Brown about these."

Harper sighed. "I suppose you're right. But I thought maybe someone else left them." She wrinkled her nose. "That kid Jason at work, for one. He's a little too friendly."

Priscilla set the flowers on the coffee table, careful not to touch the wrapper. "There might be fingerprints on the cellophane. If Ollie left them, we can find out."

"No, he's too smart for that. If he did leave them, he'd wear gloves." She pointed at the red carnations in the bouquet. "Besides, Ollie knows I hate carnations. I don't like their smell. Why would he buy them for me?"

That was a good point. Priscilla switched gears. "What's going on with Jason?" The dishwasher was also harassing Ida, she recalled.

Harper was back at the window, peeking out. She made a scoffing sound. "He's a real weirdo. Every time I turn around at the bakery, he's standing right there, grinning at me."

Jason had been at the grocery store, but that was today, not yesterday, when these flowers were dropped off. *Hmm.* Priscilla resolved to have a word with Candy. "Let's drop these flowers off at the police station." At Harper's protest, she added, "You never know what's important in an investigation. You should save every clue, just in case."

Harper quickly threw a change of clothes and toiletries into a small backpack, and they left the apartment. She helped Priscilla clean off the car, and they set off for the cottage, first detouring to the station. "I'll run in," Priscilla said when she parked in front of the building. "Want to stay here with Jake?" Harper readily agreed.

Inside, Priscilla handed the shopping bag with the dead bouquet to the desk sergeant. "I'm dropping this off for Officer Brown."

He peered inside and made a face. "That's an odd gift."

Priscilla repressed a laugh. "It's for a case. Harper Jenson. Her stalker left those in her mailbox yesterday." When he still looked confused, she added, "Officer Brown was at Harper's apartment tonight. I found out about these after she left."

"Okay." Still looking skeptical, he set the bag behind the desk. "I'll give them to her when she reports in. She's on patrol tonight."

Rather than point out that she knew April was on patrol since she'd seen her only a few minutes before, Priscilla thanked him and left. Hopefully he would pass the bouquet along and not just toss it.

Although they were driving to the lighthouse in a snowstorm at night, Harper was enthralled by this glimpse of the countryside. "I haven't had a chance to really explore the island yet, since I don't have a car. But I can't wait to get out and roam around."

"It's a gorgeous place, that's for sure." Priscilla was glad her companion was enjoying the ride, but she was literally marking off milestones as they progressed, eager to get home again. The roads were atrocious. As she turned into her driveway, she noticed with gratitude that the plow truck had made another pass while she was gone.

"Can I go inside?" Harper stared up at the lighthouse, its faithful beam shining through the murk. "I've never been in a lighthouse."

Priscilla parked the car and then dug out her house keys. "Sure. It's cold in there, but we can take a peek." They headed for the cottage first, where Priscilla unlocked the door and stood back. Jake pushed past both Harper and Priscilla in his quest to be first.

"This is where you'll be," she said, showing Harper the spare bedroom. "You can leave your bag here."

Harper took in the quilted bedspread, antique furniture, and gingham curtains. "It's so cute. I love it."

"Me too." Priscilla smiled at her guest's enthusiasm. Not everyone appreciated historic and simply furnished rooms. "Let me turn on the oven, and I'll be right back." She gave Harper a tour of the rest of the cottage and then put the lasagna in the preheated oven. Her last task was to poke the dormant fire into life. "We'll need this when we come back in."

Wearing coats and gloves, they pushed their way through the snow to the lighthouse and entered the first floor, which was circular and ringed by a thick wooden rail. A set of metal spiral stairs led up to the watch room and the light itself.

"I'm going to put a small museum in here," Priscilla said. "Designing the exhibits is my winter project. My family has lived here since the mid-1800s, so I've got a lot to work with."

"The mid-1800s? Wow, that's so cool, to be in the same place your ancestors lived." Harper sounded wistful.

"It really is. I know how fortunate I am. Most families don't have such an intact legacy."

"Some of us don't have any history at all." Harper gave a self-deprecating laugh. She paced farther into the room, gazing around as though envisioning the museum. "I'll help you design a website and social media pages if you want. Then people who can't visit can still enjoy it."

Priscilla hadn't even thought about a website. "That'd be super. I'm sure the tour company would like to link to it too. We're going to be a stop on the itinerary next summer."

Harper had reached the bottom of the stairs. "Can we go up?"

"Certainly. Go ahead." Priscilla followed, moving a little more slowly than the energetic young woman. "This is the watch room," she said when they reached the second floor, which was ringed by evenly spaced windows. "The keeper would stay up here and watch the horizon for ships, then note them in a log." She showed Harper the remaining items left from days past—light bulbs, wick trimmers, and other tools.

"I can just picture it, the keeper up here staring at the water with his spyglass." Harper demonstrated. "A little boring, but probably really peaceful."

"Yes, until something dramatic happened, like a shipwreck or big storm." Priscilla felt the cold seeping through her garments. "Let's go in. How does some of that lasagna sound?"

"Awesome." Harper left the windows where she'd been staring out into the night. Then she stopped, cocking her head. Her brow wrinkled. "What's that noise?"

Priscilla heard it too, the grumbling of low engines. She turned off the lamp illuminating the room and went to the closest window overlooking the water. She wasn't surprised to see that there weren't any boat lights visible. Of course, it was snowing, but still, if they were that close to shore, something should show.

"I think the smugglers are back," Priscilla said. "Come on, I've got to call the Coast Guard."

CHAPTER SEVENTEEN

All the way back to the cottage, Harper chattered about smugglers. "It sounds like something out of a book. People really still smuggle things by boat these days?"

"Oh yes," Priscilla told her, regretting what she'd already said. "All kinds of things." She put her hand on the young woman's arm. "Harper, please don't say anything to anyone, okay? The Coast Guard is in the middle of an investigation, and I'd hate to have my loose lips sink it." Gerald had confided in her, and it would be terrible if the smugglers were warned somehow. Not that Harper would do anything on purpose, but even casual discussion might reach the wrong ears.

Harper nodded. "I get it. I won't say a word to anyone, promise."

In the living room, Priscilla settled Harper by the fire with Jake. "I'll be right back." She nipped into her bedroom to place the call on her cell phone. Gerald didn't answer, so she left a message. Maybe they were already in pursuit of the mysterious boat.

"Can we toast marshmallows over the fire after we eat?" Harper called from the living room.

Priscilla thought about it. Why not? "Sure, but we need a couple of sticks. There's a bush outside that would work. Oh, and Jake would probably like to go out." While Priscilla served plates of bubbling lasagna topped with golden melted cheese, Harper and the dog found two long sticks that were perfect for roasting.

The two women sat cross-legged on the hearth rug, eating the pasta. "I like how you used a lot of ricotta cheese," Harper said. "Some people skimp, and to me it's the best part."

"I love it too," Priscilla said. "Another favorite recipe of mine is ricotta cheesecake. An Italian friend in Kansas gave me her family recipe. This sauce is also her recipe."

Harper cut off another large mouthful. "It's great." She chewed and considered. "I like to experiment with different fresh herbs when I make sauce."

The two of them traded favorite cooking tips while they ate, then Priscilla made cocoa to drink while they toasted fluffy white marshmallows. Harper liked hers charred and on fire. She pulled the gooey mess off the stick with a laugh and ate the whole thing in one bite. "Burned sugar, yum."

Priscilla smiled at Harper's childlike enjoyment of simple pleasures. Her mother had done a great job raising her. "So your mother never mentioned any relatives?" she asked, hoping for further clues to Harper's heritage.

Harper shook her head. She slid another marshmallow on her stick. "Nope. When I asked about my grandparents, she said they were dead. Maybe there isn't anyone else, but I can't help hoping, you know?" She held the marshmallow above the glowing coals. "Whenever I read about big happy families when I was a kid, I was always jealous. But I suppose big families have their drawbacks too."

Harper's words struck a chord with Priscilla. "I was an only child, and so was my husband. And we had only one daughter. I used to wish I had a big family too. Then I moved here and found three cousins. They're like sisters to me." Where was she going with this? The Scripture she'd heard in church popped into her mind. "'God sets the lonely in families.' I always loved that verse, especially after my husband died." Priscilla's words seemed to resonate in the quiet room.

Although Harper kept her gaze on her marshmallow, which burst into flame, Priscilla sensed the words had sunk in. She also remembered another resolution she'd made regarding Harper. "Would you like to go to church with me?" she asked.

Harper blew on her marshmallow. "Sorry, had to save it. Yes, I'd love to go to church. Thanks for asking me." Her grin was heartfelt.

"I'll pick you up Sunday morning," Priscilla offered.

After an hour by the fireside, Harper's head was drooping.

"Why don't you go to bed?" Priscilla said. "You must be exhausted." She knew from experience that personal trauma was very draining, and seeing the stalker again was firmly in that category.

The young woman didn't need to be told twice. She made her way to the spare room, Jake at her heels, and soon everything was quiet. Priscilla wasn't quite ready for bed, although it had been a long day full of intense experiences. She thought about Rebekah's confession that her daughter had run away and that she was to blame. *How painful.* Next her mind skipped to Harper's problems, including her mysterious stalker. Was it Jason from the bakery? Or her ex-boyfriend, Ollie? Thinking of Ollie, she decided to do a little online sleuthing.

She got her laptop and opened a search engine. She started off with his name and the state, hoping there weren't a lot of men named Ollie Perkins in Massachusetts.

The first hit made her heart sink. Ollie Perkins, 24, of New Bedford, had been arrested for disorderly conduct for getting into a fight in a tavern. The article also referenced other charges he'd had in the past—nothing major, but enough to imply that Ollie wasn't exactly an upstanding citizen. The photograph of him in court showed a burly young man with a shaved head. He wasn't bad looking, but his glare was belligerent. His occupation was given as crew on a fishing boat.

Maybe Priscilla was jumping to conclusions. She didn't know for sure that Harper had lived in New Bedford, since she'd never said. She entered Harper Jenson into the search bar, feeling a little like a stalker herself.

Soon she discovered her intuition was correct. Harper had lived in New Bedford, and there was a photograph of her with Ollie. In the picture, the duo were clowning around, and Priscilla could see why Ollie was attractive to Harper. His grin was boyish and charming. But knowing what she did, was his arm around her a little too tight, his gaze a shade too possessive?

At least now she knew what he looked like, so if he were hanging around the island, Priscilla would recognize him. Her fingers lingered over the keyboard. If Harper were her daughter, she'd send April Brown the picture. But, since doing so would be intrusive, she bookmarked it instead. Maybe she could convince Harper to report Ollie to the police and provide identifying information.

The brass captain's clock chimed eleven. *Time for bed.* Priscilla made her rounds of the cottage, ensuring the doors and windows were locked. She peeked outside and saw that the snow had stopped. That was good news.

Sunshine and the aroma of fresh coffee woke Priscilla the next day. Someone knocked tentatively on her door. "Priscilla? May I come in?"

"Of course." Priscilla pushed herself to a seated position, noticing that Jake was conspicuously absent. *Traitor.* Good thing she wasn't the jealous type.

Harper opened the door and sidled through, carrying a tray, Jake behind her. "I hope you don't mind, but I really did make myself at home." She set the tray on Priscilla's lap.

In addition to a steaming cup of java, there was a plate holding two eggs, crispy home fries, and two slices of what had to be homemade bread.

"Oh my, this looks wonderful," Priscilla said. "Did you really bake bread this morning?"

Harper's smile was shy yet proud. "I did. I'm used to getting up early, so I went ahead and made my signature loaf. It's inspired by the Portuguese farm bread I used to buy in New Bedford."

Ding. Without even trying, Priscilla had confirmed her theory from last night. She picked up a slice of bread and took a bite. Yeasty, chewy, and delicious. "This is incredible." She dipped a corner into an egg yolk and took another bite.

"I'm glad you like it." Harper headed for the door. "I'll let you enjoy your breakfast in peace."

Jake sat at Priscilla's bedside, tongue hanging out while he monitored her every move. "'In peace,' really?" Priscilla asked, tongue in cheek. They both laughed. "What are your plans today, Harper?"

"Candy is picking me up on the way to the bakery in an hour. We're going to get ready for our reopening tomorrow."

"That's wonderful. I've missed going to the bakery. And I'm sure a lot of other people have too."

Harper paused, her hand on the doorknob. "So I hear. If you need anything, just holler. I'll be in the kitchen, cleaning up."

Priscilla leaned back against the pillows and did as Harper suggested, enjoying her breakfast. *How thoughtful she is.* And what delicious bread. She fed Jake a corner, and he gobbled it down. Priscilla wondered if Candy would start offering Harper's bread in the bakery. It would be a hit, she knew that much.

Her cell phone rang, and she reached for it.

"Good morning," Joan said. "How would you like to go off-island with me? I want to do some shopping in Falmouth."

Priscilla considered her plans, which weren't pressing. "Count me in." She paused. "I need to buy an outfit for Share a Little Love."

"Oh, you *are* going to the event? That's great."

Excitement blossomed in Priscilla's chest, and she hurried to say, "Guess what? I have a date. Gerald is taking me."

Her cousin gave a whoop, something that was more in character for Trudy than the more reserved Joan. "That's fabulous, Priscilla. When did he ask you?"

Priscilla found herself giving Joan the play-by-play of the event, feeling almost as giddy as a girl in high school. "I feel really good about it," she concluded. "It will be my first date since..." She didn't have to finish the sentence.

"I know, hon." Joan's voice was sympathetic. She was a widow too. "Take it one step at a time. It's a dinner, not a proposal of marriage."

"That's what I'm doing, taking it slow." Priscilla took a deep breath, releasing her keyed-up excitement. She remembered the dinner party she wanted to have. "Are you free for Sunday night supper? I made my signature lasagna dish."

"Sure, that sounds delicious."

Priscilla and Joan weren't the only ones heading off-island on this relatively nice day. They waited in a line of cars for their turn to board the ferry and then parked on the lower deck. Leaving the car, they went upstairs to the waiting room with the other passengers to buy cups of coffee and take in the view.

"One thing about being housebound in this weather, I've gotten a lot of painting done," Joan said. Her lips quirked in a sly smile. "Featuring *winter* bouquets of course. With lots of berries and evergreens."

"They sound lovely." Priscilla sipped her coffee. "I've been making good progress on the museum exhibit too. It's easier when you don't have the temptation of spending time outdoors as we do the rest of the year. If it wasn't for Jake's needs, I might go days without setting foot outside the house."

A familiar figure walked their way, holding a similar to-go cup. "Good morning, ladies." After a minute of dislocation at seeing the woman outside her usual element, Priscilla recognized Hilda, the waitress from the Colonial Inn.

They exchanged pleasantries, Priscilla sliding down the bench to make room for Hilda. "Heading over for some shopping?" Priscilla asked.

"Sure am. Need to buy a new dress for the Valentine's event." Hilda smiled. "We don't get many chances to dress up, so I take advantage of each and every one."

"Us too," Joan said. "Plus I have a whole list of things to buy that are hard to find on the island."

Hilda's presence put the kibosh on anything more than talking about general light topics. As the ferry engines throttled down to make the approach to the dock, the waitress stood. "Remember I thought I had photos of our staff from each year?" she said to Priscilla. "I found some pictures that your young friend might want to see."

"I'm sure she'll be interested," Priscilla said. "What's the best way to get in touch with you?"

"I'll bring them to the Inn, so come over any shift I'm working." Hilda waved. "I'd better get to my car. I'm near the front of the line for a change. Have a good day."

In the hubbub of returning to their own vehicle and then driving off the ferry, Joan had to wait until they had left the terminal to ask, "What was Hilda talking about?"

"Harper and I were at the Inn having lunch when she got the idea to see if maybe her mom had worked there as a teenager. She was a waitress before she started her career, apparently. Hilda offered to look for photos of summer staff for the relevant years. And I guess she found some." Priscilla mentally crossed her fingers, hoping that Harper's hunch was correct and Megan had worked at the Colonial Inn.

"What have you learned so far?" Joan asked. "I remember you saying you were going to the museum with Harper."

"Not a whole lot. We didn't see Megan in the high school yearbooks." Priscilla watched the passing scenery and traffic from the passenger seat, noting how much more hectic the mainland was than the island. Although Falmouth wasn't urban by anyone's standards, the pace of life was much faster here. "That's why I hope Hilda comes through. Of course, Harper still might not have any family here. Her mother said her parents were dead, and there weren't any siblings. So it's probably a long shot." Sadness dampened her spirits.

"Then we'll help her find a new family," Joan said stoutly, coming up with the perfect thing to say, as always.

"Getting to know you and Trudy and Gail has been a blessing to me," Priscilla said. "I guess I want other people to find the same connection and caring."

Joan reached over and patted Priscilla's knee. "Your kind heart does you credit. We're thrilled you're here with us after all these years." She returned her hand to the wheel. "Tell me, what kind of outfit do you want to buy?"

Priscilla scrolled through her messages. Rachel had sent ideas as promised. "How dressy is this event?"

"Not too. A nice dress or pantsuit will work, maybe with a little bling. I wore a red sequined headband last year with black velvet pants and a flowing white silk blouse."

"That sounds nice." Priscilla wanted to be comfortable as well as pretty.

"I know the perfect boutique. It's not too pricey, either." Joan threw Priscilla a smile. "And let's get manicures and pedicures. My treat."

"Thank you. I haven't had a pedicure in ages, and I love them." Growing up without a sister, Priscilla rarely experienced a girls' day out. This was going to be fun.

CHAPTER EIGHTEEN

Two hours later, Priscilla was sitting in a vibrating chair, leafing through a beauty magazine and having her toenails painted bright red. Nestled beside the chair were two bags, one holding a long, deep-red velvet skirt and brocade jacket, the other a pair of metallic gold flats.

Joan looked over from the adjacent chair, where her toenails were receiving a coat of pearly pink. "Want to have lunch after? I know a great little café around the corner. They make wonderful chowder."

"That sounds perfect," Priscilla said. "I'd forgotten how much energy shopping takes. I'm starving."

Having Joan along had been a godsend. With her unerring good taste, she'd helped Priscilla choose a stunning outfit. And since there were two pieces, she could wear the skirt or the jacket with other tops or bottoms. The velvet skirt especially was going to be a favorite. She would wear it on holidays or when lounging on a cold winter night by the fire.

The pedicure area of the salon gave a good view of the street, and in addition to browsing the magazine, Priscilla watched people strolling along the sidewalk. Three young men stopped in front of the plate glass window outside, talking and laughing. She glanced idly over, then stared in disbelief. The man wearing a red and black plaid jacket strongly resembled Ollie Perkins. The other two were dressed in olive green and navy blue.

The young man wearing the olive-green coat opened the salon door and entered, his friends trailing along. *He's coming inside.* Priscilla ducked her head and pretended great interest in a magazine article about a new diet consisting of leafy greens and meat.

"Hey, Monica," the one in the green coat called. "Got time to give me a haircut?" He pulled off a knit cap and rubbed a hand over his already short hair. "We're heading out to fish tonight, and I won't be back for a week."

One of the hairdressers, a tiny blonde with fluffy highlighted hair, turned off a blow dryer. "Give me five minutes. Have a seat, and I'll be right with you." She turned back to her client.

The three men settled in the waiting area and continued to josh each other, thankfully lowering their voices to whispers. Priscilla sharpened her ears, hoping to hear something that would confirm that the one in the plaid coat really was Ollie—or not.

Priscilla's manicurist finished painting her toes and placed toe separators on her feet. "Be careful until they dry," she said. She nestled Priscilla's feet into small dryer units. Joan was receiving the same treatment from her attendant.

Monica finished her client's hair and rang up the sale. After the woman left, she sauntered over to talk to the men. She ruffled the haircut requester's hair with a grin, the gesture clearly expressing that they were well acquainted. "Hey, Ollie," she asked, turning to the young man in the red and black coat. "Heard from Harper? I still can't believe she ran out on you like that."

Priscilla couldn't help it—she gasped. Joan looked over, and worse, Ollie noticed, his brow furrowing. "Do you believe this story?" Priscilla said to Joan, holding out the magazine, pretending she was shocked at something she had read. "Who could live on greens and meat?"

Joan frowned in confusion but, to Priscilla's relief, played along. "I know. It's crazy the things people do to lose weight."

Ollie merely shook his head in response to Monica, and the man in navy blue said, "He doesn't talk about it."

Monica shrugged. "Come on, handsome. Let's buzz your head. I got another appointment in fifteen minutes."

The rest of their time at the salon, Priscilla was a bundle of nerves. Every time she glanced over at Ollie, who was slouched in the waiting area, holding a magazine, she caught him staring at her.

Outside, Priscilla rolled her shoulders, shedding the stress. "I thought we'd never get out of there."

Joan looked hurt. "I thought you were enjoying yourself." She pointed down the street. "The Captain's Table Café is this way."

"I didn't mean the pedicure." Priscilla fell into step. "I loved every minute of it, until Ollie Perkins came in. He gives me the creeps."

"How do you know him? I thought something was up when you were so shocked. That diet you showed me wasn't that extreme." Joan stopped at the car and pulled out her keys. "Let's put our shopping bags in here."

They stowed the bags in the trunk and continued down the sidewalk. On the way to the cozy restaurant tucked between a bookstore and an antiques shop, Priscilla told Joan what she knew about Ollie. "There's someone stalking Harper, and I think it must be him. She's seen someone watching her apartment several times. I was over there with the police last night." Wanting to keep their outing lighthearted, Priscilla had deliberately not told Joan yet about the incident the previous evening. But Ollie showing up had changed that decision.

Joan held the café door open for Priscilla. "At least we know what he looks like and can keep an eye out for him."

"That's a good way to think about it." Priscilla stepped inside the small space with wooden walls and fishnets and buoys hanging from the ceiling. "This is cute."

Joan steered her to an empty booth. "I always eat here when I come to town." She sat on one side, Priscilla the other. "I recommend the fish chowder or the shrimp burger."

Priscilla studied the menu. "I want both. A cup of chowder and the sandwich without fries."

"The fries are awfully good," Joan tempted her. "How about we split an order?"

"All right. If you're going to twist my arm." She smiled.

They placed the order, including mugs of coffee, and sat back to wait. Wanting to change the subject, Priscilla shared the story of how she and Jake were almost stranded by the tide coming in. Funny, she hadn't told Gerald that detail, and now she didn't mention the cigarette pack to Joan. Information about the smugglers wasn't hers to share, and while she trusted Joan implicitly, she wanted to show respect for Gerald's work.

Their cups of chowder and sandwiches arrived, the serving of fries placed in the middle where both could reach. Joan picked up a fry and dipped it in ketchup. "You're making me want a dog. After Champ died, I couldn't face getting another one, but now I'm starting to think about it."

"You should," Priscilla said. "Jake is such a great companion. And so funny." She shared a couple other anecdotes about him while they ate. The food was scrumptious as promised, and Priscilla was groaning by the time she ate the last bite of crispy shrimp burger adorned with cocktail sauce. "I hope my skirt still fits me after that."

"I think you burn more calories in the winter." Joan smiled. "Another reason to get a dog—to take it on walks and get more exercise."

"Or more often." Priscilla pulled out her wallet, ready to pay half the bill. "By the way, Trudy, Dan, Gail, and Uncle Hugh will be joining us for dinner tomorrow night."

"That sounds fun. I'll bring a dessert." Joan selected some bills and laid them on the check. "I'm looking forward to it. You're a great cook."

The fact that her cousin thought so warmed Priscilla's heart. "Well, I can't claim credit for this recipe. A friend taught me how to make the best lasagna I've ever had."

She slid into her coat and followed Joan to the door. They had a little more shopping to do, and then they'd head back to the ferry terminal.

"We'll need to drive to the next stores," Joan said. "I'm picking up some groceries."

They trudged along the sidewalk back to her car. In some places, they had to walk single file due to the snow. As Priscilla navigated her way along an icy stretch, someone darted out of an opening between two buildings.

"Hey, lady." Her heart jolted when she saw it was Ollie.

She kept walking. She had nothing to say to him, nor any duty to respond to such a rude greeting.

Thankfully he didn't follow her and contented himself by yelling, "Mind your own business, lady. Okay? I could tell by the way you were giving me the stink eye that your nose is all up in mine."

Cringing inside, Priscilla kept her gaze fixed straight ahead. By an effort of will she kept her shoulders up, but she felt like curling into a ball, she was so embarrassed.

Joan was standing by the car, her phone out. "That was pleasant. What a jerk, accosting you that way."

"Are you calling the police?" Priscilla risked a glance over her shoulder. Ollie was gone. She put a hand on the roof of the car and took a few deep breaths. He had scared her.

"Not unless you want me to. But I did get a picture." She showed it to Priscilla, a great shot of Ollie mid-yell, his fists clenched at his side. "No wonder Harper wanted to get away from him. He's not a nice guy at all."

By the time they reached the supermarket, Priscilla had calmed down. Her encounter with Ollie seemed like an aberration in an otherwise wonderful day. And hadn't his friend said they were headed out to sea? With any luck, she'd never set eyes on him again.

She even enjoyed trawling the aisles of the grocery store, something she'd regarded as a chore in Kansas. But with the understandably limited choices on the island, she reveled in the variety offered in the larger supermarket.

Only once did she think of Ollie again, when she went through the flower area of the store. They sold bouquets of flowers, and she wondered if the one Harper had received came from here. Or was it purchased on-island? Hopefully April Brown would be able to find out. If she thought Harper's case was worth pursuing. With limited resources, threats and stalking often didn't get the same attention as other crimes.

After Joan made it through her list of errands, they returned to the ferry and headed for home. Early winter dusk was falling, casting land, water, and sky in a blue-gray light. The sun was a yellow orb in the west, sinking with great fanfare into the mainland.

"Another storm coming," Joan said, checking her phone. She sighed deeply. "It feels like winter will never end."

Priscilla shifted on the bench so she could look at the islands in the bay. "It does seem never-ending. But just as that sun will rise tomorrow, spring *will* come." And so would answers to prayers, she reminded herself. No matter how bleak things looked, God always came through. Her heart soared with gratitude, much like the seagulls following the ferry, their white wings touched with gold.

By the time Joan dropped Priscilla at the cottage, it was full dark. "Thanks again for a wonderful day," Priscilla said. "Let's do it again before much time passes. It's easy to get into a rut."

Joan smiled. "I totally agree. We will, and maybe we can drag Trudy and Gail along. On another note, I can't wait to see you in that outfit next week."

"I can't believe it. That event sure is coming up fast." Priscilla gulped. "I hope I'm ready." Trepidation churned in her belly. Gerald was taking her on a date!

"It will be so much fun." Joan gave her a quick hug. "See you soon. Maybe at the bakery?"

"Oh yes, the bakery. They're opening up tomorrow. I can't wait to have a crème horn again." Priscilla gathered her purchases and somehow made it to the door, her arms full. Joan waited until she had stepped inside, then turned around and drove out of the drive with a toot.

Jake barreled out the door before she had a chance to fully get inside. "I don't blame you, boy. Go ahead." She let him take off into the yard while she carried her shopping into the house. She unloaded the food into the cupboards and then took her clothing bags into the bedroom.

She loved her new clothes at home as much as she had in the store. She held up the jacket, then the skirt in front of herself in the mirror. What fun, to buy a pretty new outfit. She carefully hung them up in the closet and set the flats on the carpet underneath.

Jake was scratching at the door, so she let him in and fed him, then foraged for something light to have for dinner. That hearty lunch had stayed with her all afternoon. As she built a roaring fire in the living room, a thought struck. Why not invite Rebekah to come with her to the bakery? Before she could talk herself out of it, she dialed the number.

A man answered. "Bradley Alden."

Did she have the right number? Yes, that was Rebekah's house number. "Um, this is Priscilla Grant, your aunt's neighbor. May I speak to her, please?"

Bradley was silent. Why did she feel like she was doing something wrong? He had the ability to infuse silence with intense disapproval. Finally he spoke. "She's retired for the night. May I take a message?"

Should she? Oh, why not. "I called to see if Rebekah would like to come with me to Candy Lane Confectionery tomorrow. They're reopening, and I thought she'd enjoy it."

"The bakery is open again?" His voice sharpened. Then it modulated into creamy tones. "Are you good friends with Ms. Lane, by chance?"

Where is this going? Priscilla frowned. "I helped her clean up the bakery after the fire and the flood, so if that makes us good friends, I suppose we are."

"The flood? I didn't hear about that. Is the building all right?"

"It's fine. It was only a pipe in the bakery area itself. We got to the leak in time."

Bradley sighed. "Good. So, Mrs. Grant, if I allow Rebekah to go with you, perhaps you'd consider a little quid pro quo in return."

CHAPTER NINETEEN

Anger rushed up the back of Priscilla's neck, setting her scalp on fire. He wanted to barter with her, using his dear old aunt as a bargaining chip. With huge effort, she held her tongue. If she told him what she thought of him, she'd never see Rebekah again, she was certain of it.

"What do you mean?" To her relief, she sounded normal, even blasé.

Bradley chuckled. "Well, I've been wanting to buy that building for a while. I'd still let Candy rent but I—we—own most of that block already. It would complete my portfolio in that section of town."

"I'm still not clear. What are you asking me to do?"

He coughed. "Merely put in a good word for me. I'm extremely fair and would pay her above market rate." Then he spoiled his generous offer. "Maybe. I need to get in there and check out the building, so leave that part out, about the premium price."

Priscilla felt very uncomfortable with this development. It was none of her business, and in any case, she wasn't going to become a go-between for Bradley Alden. Something about him set her teeth on edge. "I'll mention your interest to her." That was all she'd do. "And I'd like to pick up your aunt around nine. Will that work for her?"

"I don't see why not. I'll tell Maureen to have her ready."

Again anger flashed, this time at Bradley's manner toward his aunt. He spoke of her as if she were a child. She counted to ten. "That would be great. I'll see her then."

Once she hung up, she was tempted to wash her hands. *Breathe, Priscilla, breathe.* It wasn't wise to rush to judgment. At the same time, discernment was important.

Something was wrong in the Alden household, she was certain of that much.

Maureen answered the bell the next morning, the bright sunlight not doing her frazzled appearance any favors. She squinted up at Priscilla. "Come on in. She's putting her boots on."

Rebekah was seated in the hall, wearing a fur coat and struggling with her boots. When she smiled, Priscilla noticed she was wearing lipstick. The perfume she wore revealed how important this little outing was for her. Priscilla was touched.

"Let me do that for you." Maureen knelt down and pushed the boots onto Rebekah's feet, muttering the whole while.

Priscilla pretended great interest in the house although she'd been there before, not wanting to witness what surely had to be a humiliating experience for her friend.

"There we go." Maureen hoisted Rebekah to her feet and pulled her forward. "She's all yours. We'll be going out, so if you're home first, Rebekah has the key." She put her face close to her employer's and spoke loudly in slow syllables. "You do have your key, right?"

"Yes, I do." Rebekah's eyes flashed. Then she sank into confusion, unlatching her old-fashioned pocketbook and searching through the contents. "I think I do."

Priscilla spotted the key ring and pointed to it. "There it is. We're all set." She favored Maureen with a sweet smile. "If we were locked out, I would be happy to have Rebekah as my guest, so please don't worry about her."

"Bradley might not like that," Maureen mumbled. "So make sure she's back here, okay?"

"Of course." Priscilla took Rebekah's arm and gently assisted her through the door. "We'll see you later."

Outside, Priscilla took a deep breath of frosty air, feeling as though she'd been released from some kind of captivity. She glanced sidelong at her friend, who was beaming in delight at the sun sparkling on the snow and water like diamonds. "It's a gorgeous day, if cold."

Rebekah's smile grew even wider. "I don't care how frigid it is. I'd rather be out here than in there." She jerked a thumb back at the house.

All right, then. "Let's go. The crème horns await. Or you might like Tisbury Tizzy. It's Candy's own recipe for hummingbird cake."

The older woman's laughter rang out. "Tisbury Tizzy? It sounds like us girls in the old days, when we were falling in love."

"I'll have to tell Candy that." Once they were settled in the car, Priscilla turned it around and headed out of the driveway. "Have you met Candy Lane? She's the bakery owner."

"No, dear, I haven't. I don't get out much anymore."

We're going to change that. The depth of compassion she felt for her neighbor surprised her. How hard would it be for Bradley or the Moodys to take her places? It wasn't like she was in a wheelchair, and even that wouldn't be an excuse. No, it was lazy selfishness.

Careful, Priscilla. She sighed. She needed to pay attention to her own faults and flaws, not focus on those of others.

The bakery was humming, the steaming hiss of the cappuccino maker punctuating the cheerful chatter and clatter of dishes. Almost every table was full.

"This is nice," Rebekah said, looking around. "It smells good too."

Priscilla spotted her cousins sitting at a big round table in the corner. "I have some people I want you to meet. But first let's go order."

Rebekah was impressed by the contents of the bakery case. "I hardly know what to choose. The cakes are so lovely. And the pastries look as good as anything in the city."

"Thanks, I guess," Candy said with a laugh. She stood waiting, a plastic glove on her hand. "Everything is made fresh daily, right here. I use local ingredients when I can get them."

"Marvelous, just marvelous." Rebekah clasped her hands together, continuing to survey the choices. "I think I'll try that Tisbury Tizzy. Oh, and a crème horn too. Both came highly recommended."

Priscilla raised a brow. "Both? You put me to shame. I'll have a crème horn too, please. I've been missing them while you were closed. Everything is back to normal now?"

"Yes, thank goodness," Candy said as she pulled their treats out of the case. "Better than ever, actually. I had new wiring done, and the fresh paint in the kitchen is much more cheerful."

"I'm glad to hear it. The cousins and I were saying how much we missed coming in here."

"Everyone is saying that. It's awesome to know you're loved." Candy winked. "Two coffees?"

"I want one." Priscilla turned to Rebekah to see what she wanted to drink and found her looking at the other customers.

"Sally. She looks like Sally," Rebekah said.

"What was that?" Priscilla wasn't sure she'd heard correctly. She looked around at the packed room. Harper and another helper were refilling coffee and clearing tables. A young blonde woman in the corner had curly hair worn like Sally's. Could Rebekah have been talking about her?

"Yes, she does," she said, to be agreeable. "What would you like, Rebekah? Coffee or tea?"

Rebekah turned to study the blackboard listing the beverages. "I want a cup of chai tea, please. I love chai."

"Coming right up," Candy said. She bustled around the service area, making Rebekah's tea and pouring Priscilla's coffee. Their meal went on a tray, and Priscilla picked it up after paying despite Rebekah's protests.

"What a nice woman," Rebekah said. "I'll have to come in here more often."

"Yes, you will." Priscilla ushered her toward the table where the cousins were sitting and made the introductions.

"The Tisbury Tizzy is amazing," Rebekah said a few minutes later. She used her fork to slice off another mouthful of the creamy, cranberry-studded cake. "It's the best thing I've had to eat in ages. It's far better than bran cereal, my usual breakfast."

Everyone laughed. "Wait until you try the crème horn," Priscilla said.

"Speaking of which, here comes another crème horn aficionado," Joan said. "Mildred Pearson is in the building." She waved to the museum director.

"Mildred is a very good friend of mine," Rebekah said. "I was on the museum board for years."

"Let's ask her to sit with us, then," Gail said. She peered into her mug. "I could use a refill. Be right back."

"Where's Uncle Hugh?" Priscilla asked once Gail had left the table. Usually Gail had her dad in tow wherever she went.

"He's still under the weather," Trudy said, her mouth turning down. "A cold he can't shake."

"Are you speaking of Hugh Latham?" Rebekah asked. "I haven't seen him for ages."

Priscilla supposed she shouldn't be surprised that Rebekah knew Hugh. They had both been on the island for a long time—Hugh, all his life—and were of the same generation. "He's usually right here, chowing down on Tisbury Tizzy."

"I always thought Hugh was a smart man," Rebekah said in her dry way, making the others laugh again. She popped the last bite of cake into her mouth.

When Gail returned to the table, Priscilla said, "I understand your dad's not well. Perhaps I can come by and visit."

"He'd like that," Gail said. "So would I. It'd give me a break. He's a bear when he's sick."

"Aren't most men?" Rebekah said. "My Henry was a royal pain whenever he had a hangnail." She held her big mug of tea in both hands and sipped.

Mildred appeared at the table, and Trudy and Gail made room for her while Joan pulled up another chair. Mildred nodded to the group at large. "Good to see you all." Then she noticed Rebekah. "Why, Rebekah Alden! I haven't seen you in ages."

"That's true, Mildred, I'm sorry to say," Rebekah replied. "I've been more or less housebound during the bad weather. Thank goodness Priscilla dragged me out of the house to this delightful place."

"It is wonderful, isn't it?" Mildred picked up her crème horn and took a huge bite, sending flakes of pastry raining down onto her plate. "Yum, yum, yum," she said after chewing the mouthful. She turned to Rebekah again. "You know, we were really disappointed that you weren't able to continue on as a patron this year. We've always greatly appreciated your support of the museum."

Trudy raised her brows, expressing the surprise Priscilla felt at Mildred's blunt statement, although the museum director was known for her strong opinions and forthright nature. Gail pretended great interest in her coffee, while Joan slipped off to the restroom.

Rebekah's pale, delicate skin flushed, bringing a look of youth to her cheeks. "I have no idea what you're talking about, Mildred. You know I always make a gift every year. Perhaps my check was lost in the mail."

CHAPTER TWENTY

Priscilla squirmed in her chair. Rebekah thought she had given the museum $10,000, but her nephew said she had decided not to make the gift. *Where is the money, then?*

Mildred was equally stunned. Usually never at a loss for words, her mouth flapped open and shut a few times. Then she straightened her shoulders in resolve. "Rebekah, I had a conversation with your nephew. He told me you had changed your mind about giving this year."

Rebekah looked confused. "Bradley told you that?" At Mildred's nod, the flush on the older woman's face deepened, and a steely glint came into her eyes. She pushed back her chair, waving at her half-eaten crème horn. "I've lost my appetite, Priscilla. Can we go home, please?"

"Of course." Priscilla wrapped the remains of her crème horn in her napkin. "Let's go." She told Gail and Trudy she'd be in touch.

"No problem," Trudy said. "We'll see you later." Gail nodded assent.

"Nice to meet you all," Rebekah said. "Tell Joan that for me, please. And remember me to Hugh." She slipped into her fur coat and gloves, every inch an elegant and dignified lady.

Outside the bakery, Rebekah's proud façade crumbled. She leaned heavily on Priscilla's arm. "What was that all about? Oh, Priscilla, I'm so upset."

Priscilla put her arm around Rebekah's narrow shoulders. "Let's get in the car, and we can talk about it." The wind whipping off the water wasn't conducive to remaining outside for longer than a minute or two.

Once on the road, Priscilla said, "Do you want to come to the cottage and visit a while and stay for lunch? Or should I take you straight home?"

Rebekah twisted her hands together. "I'm not sure...Maureen is expecting me home shortly." She seemed to hear herself, and a glint of humor lightened her expression. "But she's not my keeper, is she? Let's go to the cottage. I want to see that darling Jake again."

"The cottage it is." Emboldened by Rebekah's comment about Maureen, she asked, "Have the Moodys worked for you long?"

Her passenger was studying the passing landscape. "A couple of years. Bradley thought I was getting too forgetful to live on my own. He travels too much on business to make a home with me, so he hired them." She shrugged. "They're not who I would have chosen, but they treat me well. In fact, I've decided to leave them a bequest for their service."

"That's generous of you." Priscilla considered what Rebekah had said. She wondered if the Moodys knew Rebekah had left them money in her will. That was a reason to turn a blind eye when she wandered off in the dead of winter. Her thoughts returned to Bradley. If he was truly concerned for Rebekah's welfare, why did he keep them on? If someone had messed up like that even once with her mother, they would have been fired. And the disconnect regarding the museum gift was troubling. She hoped he wasn't skimming money out of Rebekah's accounts.

As if she had been thinking along parallel lines, Rebekah said, "I'm going to take a peek at my checkbook when I get home. I'm pretty sure I wrote a check to the museum." She drew herself up. "I'm still sharp enough to handle my own money, I'll have you know, even though Bradley keeps offering to take over."

I'll bet he does. Priscilla bit her tongue.

Rebekah went on. "This situation with Mildred and Bradley must be a misunderstanding. I'm sure she misheard what he said."

Priscilla knew Mildred hadn't been mistaken, since Priscilla had been right there listening when he said it, but she decided not to press the issue. It was between Rebekah and her nephew. On the other hand, she was going to keep her eyes open in case something *was* wrong. Someone had to look out for Rebekah.

Changing the subject she asked, "How does chicken soup sound? We can have some of Harper's bread with it. Harper works for Candy, and she's a great baker, I've just learned."

"That sounds lovely. A perfect meal on a cold day like this."

At the cottage, Priscilla settled Rebekah and Jake in the living room next to the fireplace where they all had a nice long chat, then went to the kitchen to make soup. A quart of broth made from Gerald's chicken, diced chicken leftovers, frozen diced vegetables, and dry noodles went into a pot. She sliced bread for toast and set two trays. They could eat in front of the fire today. She also put the kettle on for tea.

"Lunch will be ready in a few minutes," Priscilla said when she brought Rebekah a mug of hot tea, doctored the way she liked it.

Rebekah smiled up at her, her hands busy petting Jake's ears. "Thank you, dear. Jake and I have been having a nice time visiting. I'm quite over my little upset, thanks to him."

"I'm glad to hear it." Priscilla moved a coaster and set the mug on the end table where Rebekah could reach it. "Jake has a way of cheering everyone up, including me." She smiled at her pet. "You're everyone's best friend, aren't you, boy?" He thumped his tail in response.

"May I use the phone?" Rebekah asked. "I'm going to call Maureen and tell her where I am. It's only polite." Priscilla brought her the phone, and Rebekah punched in the numbers. "Maureen? I'm having lunch at the lighthouse. I'll see you sometime later this afternoon. No, I'm not sure what time. Does it matter?" She smiled in satisfaction as she set the receiver down. "That surprised her. Maureen hasn't met the independent Rebekah Alden. And it's high time she made a reappearance." She gave Jake a pat. "And she has the courage now, thanks to her new friends."

They were halfway through lunch when Priscilla's cell phone rang. "Excuse me," she said to her guest, picking it up to check. Her pulse began to hammer when she saw it was Gerald calling. Bemused by her reaction, she hesitated, not wanting to be rude to her guest by picking it up.

"Go ahead and take it, please," Rebekah urged. "It might be important."

Or not. But it was Gerald, so it was a call she wanted to answer regardless. She pushed the Answer icon before it went to voice mail.

"Good afternoon, Priscilla. I hope I'm not interrupting anything," Gerald said. He cleared this throat. "I was thinking of stopping by this afternoon. The bakery is open again, and I bought some treats for you."

What a lovely excuse for him to visit. "Please do come over, Gerald." At Priscilla's words, Rebekah's eyebrows went up and she smiled. "Right now I'm having lunch at home with a friend. What time were you thinking?"

"In about an hour or so, if that's okay." He hesitated. "We're making progress on our case thanks to that clue you found. The boys were impressed."

"I'm glad. And it will be good to see you." Priscilla felt a huge smile break over her face as she hung up. "Sorry about that. Thanks for understanding."

"Someone special, was it?" Rebekah's face was innocent, but her eyes danced with merriment. "Not that I want to pry."

"You're not prying. That was Gerald O'Bannon. He's a Coast Guard captain here on the island. He's become a...um, a good friend. We're going to an event together next week."

"I dated a few times after Henry passed," Rebekah said, surprising Priscilla. "It was fun. Sometimes you need to kick up your heels and have a plain old good time."

As a recent widow of almost sixty, the prospect of dating after losing a spouse and at an advanced age was new to Priscilla. She'd thought most widows and widowers retired from the field when they lost loved ones but was learning that wasn't always the case.

"It doesn't diminish the love you had for your husband in the least," Rebekah continued. "But at first it can feel awfully disloyal."

"You understand," Priscilla said, struck by the depth of Rebekah's insight. "This is the first time since Gary's death that I've even considered going out with another man." Mingled guilt and sorrow and sheer disbelief at her situation began to churn in Priscilla's belly. Maybe she should nip this whole thing in the bud. She wasn't ready—

"If the situation were reversed and Gary had lost you, what would you think about him dating?"

More emotion—a flash of possessiveness and jealousy, then the realization that she'd want him to be happy, not miserable and alone. Or not for long, at least. Hopefully he would have missed her. That was what love was about, right? She thought of 1 Corinthians, Chapter 13. *Love is patient, love is kind. It does not envy, it does not boast, it is not proud.*

"I'd want him to be happy," Priscilla said. "If that meant he found another woman, even got remarried, then I'd want that for him."

Rebekah's smile was smug. "And I'm sure he feels the same about you. And I say it that way because I believe in heaven, where loved ones have gone to join our Lord."

"Me too." Priscilla could firmly agree with that assertion. "It's such a comfort." And she had to confess, sometimes the belief that she would see Gary again had been all she had to hang on to in the wilderness of devastating loneliness and grief she experienced right after he died.

Rebekah ran her spoon around the bottom of her bowl and came up with only a smidgen of broth. "I enjoyed every last drop of soup, literally," she said. "Thank you again for lunch."

"Thanks for joining me." *And for the sage advice and wisdom.* "A refill on the tea?" Priscilla rose from her chair to collect the trays.

"Sure. And then I suppose I should be going." Rebekah winked. "Captain O'Bannon will be here soon."

The doorbell rang while Priscilla was refilling the teapot with boiling water. Her first thought was that Gerald was early, so on her way to the door, she stopped at the hall mirror to check her hair.

Bradley Alden stood on the porch. "I understand my aunt is here."

Priscilla experienced a brief moment of disorientation when she saw Bradley instead of Gerald. The welcoming smile dropped from her face and she blinked a couple of times. "Um, yes she is. I was going to run her home soon."

He stepped inside without invitation, forcing Priscilla to move back. "I'll take her home right now."

"But we were going to have another cup of tea." Irritation at his high-handed behavior began to simmer. Once again he was treating his aunt like a child. "Surely deciding when to leave is up to her."

He showed his teeth in an unpleasant grin. "You don't understand, Priscilla," he said in a low voice. "My aunt isn't well." He waved away her protest. "She may look fine, but she isn't." He tapped his temple with a forefinger and grimaced. "Too much stimulation tires her out. And we're the ones who have to deal with it."

To Priscilla's horror, Rebekah appeared in the doorway. How much had she overheard?

"What's all this about?" Hands on her hips, Rebekah eyed her nephew up and down with a frown. "What are you doing here, Bradley?"

"Auntie, I'm here to take you home. It's past time for your afternoon rest." Bradley reached out a hand. "Come, let's get your coat on."

"And what if I say no?" Rebekah stepped back a pace. "And another thing. I have a bone to pick with you, Bradley Alden. Does the museum donation ring a bell?"

Bradley's eyes darted around, and when they met Priscilla's, she thought she saw fear. "Ah, actually, yes. We decided not to give to them this year."

Rebekah's arms folded across her chest. "We? I don't recall that discussion."

"Excuse me," Priscilla murmured. She retreated to the kitchen to allow them privacy to hash out this issue.

There was a mutter of low, furious voices, then the front door slammed shut. Priscilla hurried to the window in time to see Bradley bundling his aunt into the passenger seat of his luxury sedan. He hurried around to the driver's side and slid in. The engine started with a roar, and he backed up, hitting a snowbank with a crunch, then rocketed forward and out the driveway.

Well, that was interesting. Priscilla shook her head and went to the living room to clear away the tea things. *Poor Rebekah.* It was almost like Bradley didn't want her to have friends.

She stopped short, the tray of dishes rattling. Jake stared up at her in surprise. That was exactly right. Bradley was isolating his aunt. Despite Priscilla's attempts to give him the benefit of the doubt, this truth sank like a stone into her belly.

The doorbell rang again, and she rushed to set the tray down and answer, guessing this time it was Gerald.

"Bradley Alden almost ran me off the road." Gerald hung his coat on a peg, then ran a hand through his hair. "He was driving far too fast for the conditions."

"That was probably my fault," Priscilla said, leading him to the kitchen. "Would you like a cup of coffee? I can put on a fresh pot."

"Coffee sounds great, thanks." He pulled out a chair and sat with a sigh. "It's been a busy day. I just now stopped running."

"Same here," she said, turning on the faucet to fill the carafe. "I took Rebekah Alden to the bakery, and then we had lunch here."

"Is that what you meant when you said it's your fault Bradley was driving like a maniac?" Gerald asked. He leaned back in the chair, arms folded across his chest. Jake jingled into the room and plopped under the table right beside Gerald's feet. He reached down and gave the dog a pat.

Priscilla measured coffee into the filter cup. "He came to pick up his aunt, no doubt thinking she'd been gone long enough. They had an argument, and he forced her out the door, then tore out of here." She barked a laugh. "I'm a bad influence, don't you know? They didn't even say goodbye. I'm sure she wanted to, of course. Rebekah is a dear. And a lady."

Gerald considered this. "Sounds like he's treating her more like a child than an adult."

"Exactly." She whirled around. "I was thinking that very thing. Not that I want to interfere in other people's family lives, but I'm disturbed." She remembered the coffee and flicked the switch to turn it on. She grabbed mugs and spoons and brought them to the table. "I think he might be abusing her."

Gerald frowned. "Physically? We need to report that then."

Priscilla shook her head. "No, I don't mean that. I think mentally. And financially." She perched on a chair, propping her elbows on the table and her head in her hands. She put her hands over her eyes. "I don't have proof, but that's the picture I'm getting. I keep telling myself it's none of my business...."

She felt a gentle hand on her shoulder and opened her eyes to see Gerald peering down at her, his eyes dark with sympathy. "Priscilla, you can tell me about it. I'll keep it confidential. If he's really doing all that, we'll bring in the authorities, okay?"

While they drank coffee, she told him everything about her encounters with Rebekah and Bradley. It felt good to get it off her chest. He was a wonderful listener, allowing her room to ramble on but also interjecting insights or observations.

"I've been wondering about Bradley Alden for a while," he said. He gave a brief smile. "Now it's my turn to confide in you."

Priscilla mimed the zipping of lips. "Go on."

"Nothing substantial, but there have been rumors of financial trouble. His little empire is as shaky as a house of cards." He took a sip of coffee. "I've come across his name when investigating some, shall we say, shady characters."

"Known associates, you mean?" Priscilla felt a stab of pride at knowing the lingo.

He pointed a finger at her. "That's right. Known associates. Not that I've found any definite ties or indication that he's actively involved in something criminal, but his name comes up where it normally wouldn't. Or shouldn't."

"That could explain the diversion of funds from his aunt's bank account," Priscilla said. "She thought she gave the museum money. But I heard him tell Mildred that she'd changed her mind." She'd mentioned this to Gerald earlier, but it continued to rankle. The sheer nerve of the man.

"Keep an eye on her, okay? Even if he doesn't like it." Gerald's phone rang, and with a grimace of apology, he checked it. His eyes widened. "It's Aggie."

"Please take it." Priscilla firmly believed family calls were always a priority, especially when offspring became adults and their communication with parents was spotty, to say the least.

He listened, his brow furrowing. A knot formed in Priscilla's chest. Hopefully something wasn't wrong with the baby or the three-year-old. When he hung up, she waited with held breath.

"It's Nick. He has to go to the hospital. They think he has appendicitis." He tucked his phone in his pocket. "Want to help me babysit?"

CHAPTER TWENTY-ONE

Gerald took the snowy back roads at a good clip, anxious to get to his daughter's house. Aggie's husband had already gone to the hospital by ambulance, but she couldn't leave because of the children. In the passenger seat of the SUV, Priscilla discreetly held on, trusting Gerald's driving but a little nervous all the same.

Aggie and her family lived in a modest, newly built Cape Cod in a neighborhood of similar homes. Priscilla saw swing sets and trampolines in backyards, buried in snow now but evidence that this street was home to families with young children.

Gerald pulled into the driveway and parked to one side so Aggie could pull out of the garage. He hopped out and headed for the open bay, where a small sedan sat amid the usual garage clutter. He gave the door to the house a brief knock and walked in, Priscilla behind him.

The kitchen was small, cute, and in chaos, with dishes, clothing, and children's toys everywhere. A small boy knelt on a chair at the table, coloring, while his mother frantically straightened the counters, tossing dishes into the dishwasher or the sink.

"Dad, I'm so glad you're here." Aggie pushed wavy dark hair off her face in a gesture that echoed her father's. Her gaze went behind him to Priscilla. "Hello."

Gerald tugged Priscilla forward. "Aggie, this is Priscilla, a friend of mine. We were having coffee when you called, and she graciously agreed to help."

"Hi." Priscilla gave a small wave. "Nice to meet you."

"Nice to meet you too." Aggie eyed her with reserve, her arms crossed.

Max had no such compunction. He jumped down from the table and barreled toward his grandfather. "Papa, pick me up."

"Priscilla made that beautiful quilt I gave you for Ava," Gerald said. He hoisted the boy with a grunt. "You're getting big, bucko."

Aggie's wary expression dissolved into delight. "You did? Oh, it's gorgeous. Thank you so much." She darted forward and gave Priscilla a hug, tentative but sincere.

Max rocked back and forth in Gerald's arms, making his grandfather grunt again. "I'm a big brother now." He poked Gerald in the nose. "Do you want to go see Ava?"

"Ava's sleeping," Aggie said, her shoulders slumping. "Finally. That's why I'm not taking her to the hospital."

"What is she?" Priscilla asked. "Three weeks old?" She well remembered those days, a blur of feeding, changing, rocking, and praying the baby would sleep and let you rest.

Aggie must have picked up on the note of empathy in Priscilla's voice, because she cracked a small smile. She was very pretty behind the fatigue, with Gerald's eyes and to-die-for cheekbones and jawline. "Three weeks and a day. And I've been awake almost every minute of them."

"We'll be fine, Aggie," Gerald said, still jostling Max, who giggled in glee. "Show us where her milk is."

Aggie opened the refrigerator to display a group of filled bottles ready to go. "We've got fish sticks and fries for Max's dinner, and for the adults, there's a container of leftover spaghetti and meatballs."

"Your meatballs? What a treat." Gerald set Max down. "Aggie is a great cook," he told Priscilla.

That compliment earned another smile from Aggie. She put on her coat and boots, then picked up a handbag. "I'd better go. They don't like you to use your cell phone in the hospital, but I'll call you with an update when I can."

"Please do that. Give Nick our love." Gerald opened the door for his daughter. "We'll be praying for him."

Max flung himself at his mother's knees. "Bye, Mom. I'll be a good boy, I promise."

She bent, kissed his head, and ruffled his hair. "I'm sure you will. Show Papa where the diapers are, okay? I'll be home later tonight."

Gerald made a comical face. "Diapers? I didn't know that was part of the deal."

Aggie hit him on the shoulder. "Cut it out. You told me you were a diaper-changing expert."

"I lied," Gerald said. Everyone laughed.

Aggie kissed him on the cheek and then slipped out the garage door. A moment later, the sedan started up, and she pulled away.

Max bounced toward his grandfather. "Want to play with me, Papa?"

Simultaneously, a cry sounded from upstairs.

Gerald looked torn, so Priscilla said, "I'll go get her."

Thankful she'd kept her hand in, so to speak, by helping with friends' grandchildren, she climbed the staircase to the second story. Following the cries, she found Ava in a small bedroom painted pale lavender. The quilt she had made held pride of place, folded over the end of the white crib where the baby lay. Ava was adorable, with a tuft of dark hair and a perfectly round face, now scrunched up in full-fledged distress.

Cooing, Priscilla lifted the precious bundle out of the crib and carried her to the matching changing station. She changed her tiny diaper and put on a dry onesie. "Let's go get you something to eat," she said, holding the child against her shoulder. She rubbed her gently on the upper back. The wails diminished, as if the baby sensed a meal was on the way.

Downstairs, after descending carefully, she discovered Gerald had thoughtfully heated the milk. She sat in a rocking chair to feed the baby, watching Gerald and Max play on the living room floor. They had strewn a container of connecting blocks over the floor and were building a skyscraper.

The baby attacked the bottle's nipple with such gusto that everyone laughed. "She's got a big appetite," Gerald said. "It runs in the family." He reached out and tickled Max. "Isn't that right, Max?"

Max hopped up and down on his knees. "I'm hungry too, Papa. Can I have some chips?" He favored his grandfather with a winning smile.

Gerald glanced at Priscilla. "It's almost dinnertime," she told Max. "And we're having fish sticks and french fries. Can you wait for that?"

"French fries? With ketchup?" His eyes grew big. "Okay. I can wait." He picked up another block and placed it on the stack, making motor sounds with his lips.

"Deflect and distract," Priscilla said in response to Gerald's dropped jaw. "Works most of the time."

The baby stayed awake for a short while after her feeding, then drifted off to sleep again, this time in her rocking seat. While they were eating dinner, Aggie called. Gerald put his phone on speaker so Priscilla and Max could hear.

"Nick made it through surgery fine," she said, her voice filled with relief. "I'm going to stay here awhile, and then I'll head home. How are the kids?"

"I'm good, Mama," Max bellowed. "Papa made me french fries."

Aggie laughed. "Be a good boy for Papa and Priscilla, okay? How's the baby?"

Priscilla gave her a report, including how many ounces the baby had swallowed. "She's sleeping right now."

"Perfect. She'll probably want to eat again soon." Aggie sighed. "She's still on the every-two-hours schedule."

"Ava has a big appetite," Max said. "It runs in the family." He picked up a fish stick and crammed it in his mouth as though in illustration, making loud chewing sounds.

Gerald gently reproved him. "The spaghetti is awesome, Aggie. I'm on my second helping."

"Eat as much as you want. I have another container of sauce in the freezer, so there's plenty." Aggie signed off with a final admonition to Max to listen to Papa.

The three-year-old did quite well, brushing his teeth and hopping into bed without argument. Gerald read him a couple of stories, and Max was fast asleep by the time he finished the second. As Gerald backed out of the room and switched off the light, he said, "I'm loving this. It's like a do-over."

Priscilla regarded the sleeping boy, illuminated by the hall light. His thick lashes lay like fans on his cherubic cheeks. "Having them is a blessing, that's for sure." The baby wailed, and she laughed. "There's my cue."

This time she settled Gerald on the couch and had him feed Ava. The sight of his big hands cradling the fragile infant made her heart hurt, it was so beautiful.

She pulled out her phone and took a picture. "I'm going to send this to you. You can show all the guys down at the station."

Gerald beamed. "I sure will. I'm already driving them crazy with pictures and stories about the kids. I guess I'm trying to get the young officers to see that family is more important than anything." He looked into Ava's eyes, and she gazed back, still sucking away. "Maybe they can learn from my mistakes."

"God can redeem and use anything," Priscilla said softly.

"I sure hope so." He continued to drink in Ava's every detail. "What a gorgeous little girl. Looks just like her mama did at this age."

"Aggie is still gorgeous," Priscilla said. "I'm glad I had a chance to meet her, even though it wasn't under the best of circumstances."

"We'll visit again," Gerald said. "Or I'll have them over for a meal at my house." He pulled the bottle away. "Looks like she's out again."

Priscilla marveled at Gerald's matter-of-fact statements about her involvement in his life. It felt natural, and she liked that it did.

While the children slept, Priscilla and Gerald watched a nature show on television featuring whales and sharks in the Atlantic. Priscilla was both fascinated and appalled that such huge creatures lurked in the waters off the island. Thinking about the ocean reminded her of the encounter with the fisherman Ollie the day before.

"I'm concerned about Harper," she blurted. "Remember her? She and I had lunch with you at the Inn."

Gerald muted the show. "Of course I do. She's a nice young woman. What's going on?"

With a sigh of relief, Priscilla unloaded the saga, from Harper's first mention of a possible stalker to seeing Ollie outside the beauty salon in Falmouth. "I checked him out online, and he's got a few priors. I'm really concerned about what he might do."

Gerald's brows lifted at the word *priors,* but he didn't comment on that. He did zero in on possible danger to Priscilla. "Did he threaten you?"

"Not exactly. He told me to mind my own business." She thought back to when she was getting her pedicure. "I recognized him when he came into the salon from a picture I'd seen online. Even though I didn't say anything to him he knew I knew who he was, because I overreacted when he mentioned Harper's name."

Gerald rubbed his chin. "Ollie Perkins. I'll do some checking of my own. He's a fisherman, you said?"

"Yes, the article in the paper reported that as his occupation. And his friend told the hair stylist they were heading out for a week. So I guess Harper may have a reprieve before he shows up again."

"The problem with these situations is that restraining orders often don't work. And the police's hands are tied unless he commits a serious crime. There's usually not much punishment for violating those orders."

Priscilla's heart sank at this news. "I don't like dealing with him, but maybe if he knows we're on to him, he'll stay away."

"Maybe. And if he tries to bother that young woman, he'll have me to deal with," Gerald promised, his voice gruff.

Headlights in the driveway announced Aggie's return. A few minutes later, they heard her enter the kitchen, and then she came into the living room.

"How'd it go?" Gerald asked.

Aggie was smiling. "Nick is doing great."

"It's snowing," Priscilla realized when they stepped outside a short while later. A couple inches already covered Gerald's SUV.

"Yep, sure is." He foraged for a brush in the back seat. "I guess that storm they've been promising is finally here."

The return trip to the cottage was a little slower, both because Gerald wasn't in a hurry this time, and because the roads were getting slick. Once in a while they passed snowplows, but otherwise the roads were deserted. Priscilla enjoyed riding in the warm cocoon of Gerald's SUV, sharing their favorite observations about the grandchildren.

"Here we are," he said, slowing to turn into her driveway. "Home at last."

Lights glowed in the cottage, including the outdoor light next to the door. Priscilla was glad she'd thought to leave them on, since more than once she'd had to fumble her way inside in the dark after forgetting.

"Priscilla," Gerald said in a strange tone, "you've got a visitor."

She glanced up from her purse, where she'd been digging for her keys, and saw a huddled figure lying on the front steps. To her horror, she recognized the woman, once again not appropriately dressed for the bitter weather. "It's Rebekah Alden."

CHAPTER TWENTY-TWO

R ebekah Alden? What is she doing here at this hour? Without a coat or hat, no less." Gerald flung his SUV door open, with Priscilla echoing the movement on her side of the vehicle.

"She did this once before," Priscilla called, running to the steps. "Somehow she gets away from her caretakers and wanders over here."

She crouched down to check Rebekah, praying that she was all right. How long had she been lying here? It could have been hours. Priscilla touched her neighbor's bare hand. Ice cold. She reached to check the pulse in her neck.

Behind the door, she heard whining and snuffling and a bark or two. "Just a minute, Jake," she called. "We'll be right in."

"Does she suffer from dementia?" Gerald asked, his voice low.

"I don't know for sure." Priscilla discerned a pulse and released the breath she hadn't realized she was holding. "She's usually very sharp, but once in a while she gets really confused."

"Let's get her inside and call an ambulance," Gerald said. "She might have been out here for hours." He made a hissing sound. "But I sure hope not."

He gently scooped Rebekah up while Priscilla unlocked the door and corralled an excited dog eager for company. "Jake, no," she said. "No jumping." He seemed to sense from her voice that something was wrong and settled down, contenting himself with a sniff at Rebekah's shoe, followed by a whine.

"Put her in my room," she told Gerald, leading the way. While he placed Rebekah on the bed and took off her shoes, Priscilla opened the blanket chest and found the thickest down comforter she had. Together, she and Gerald tucked Rebekah in, making sure she was fully covered, especially her feet and hands. Jake curled up at the foot of the bed on the floor, guarding Rebekah while keeping an eye on the proceedings.

Gerald called 911 while Priscilla tried the Alden home. No one answered. "This is really strange," she told Gerald when he hung up. "The Moodys are supposed to stay with her twenty-four hours a day."

"What about Bradley? Do you have his number?"

"I don't." Then she remembered that Bradley had given Candy his card the day of the fire. Maybe she still had it. "But I know someone who might."

"Try to get it. I'm going to watch for the ambulance." Gerald left her room, and she heard his footsteps crossing to the window near the entrance.

She dialed Candy's number, hoping she wasn't in bed already. To her relief, Candy answered after three rings. "Candy, I'm sorry to bother you this late, but I've got Bradley Alden's aunt here at the cottage, and I need to get ahold of him. It's urgent. Do you still have his card, by chance?"

Candy pondered this request. "You know what, I think I do." She chuckled. "I was going to throw it away, but I forgot. Good thing, huh? Hang on." Priscilla heard the clunk of the phone being set down, then footsteps and rustling sounds. Candy was back within a minute or so. "Here you go." She read off the number. "Is his aunt okay? She's a nice old gal."

"We don't know yet." Priscilla glanced at the unconscious woman, her slender body almost invisible under the heap of down comforter. "I sure hope so." She gave Candy a brief explanation.

Candy groaned. "That's awful. I'll say a prayer for her. Want me to put her on my church's prayer chain?"

"Would you? That would be wonderful." Priscilla felt tears come to her eyes as she verbalized this request. The initial shock of finding Rebekah had worn off, leaving fear and worry in its wake. "Please, Lord," she whispered after hanging up. "Let Rebekah be all right."

Gerald put his head around the jamb. "Were you able to get Bradley's number? I'll make the call, if you want."

"That would be great. I'm not in the mood to talk to him right now." She read off the digits, and he punched them into his phone, then returned to his post by the front door.

Her gaze never leaving Rebekah, Priscilla sank down into the overstuffed armchair in the corner. What if Bradley blamed *her* for his aunt's collapse? Priscilla shoved that thought away. Rebekah needed treatment for whatever was causing her to become disoriented and wander off. In addition, the Moodys should be fired for allowing it to happen. Who knew how many other times Rebekah had escaped their watch?

Fortunately Priscilla had intercepted her the night she went down to the beach wearing only a nightgown. Anything could have happened in that weather. Rebekah could have drowned in the icy ocean water or died of exposure. As for tonight, Priscilla prayed her neighbor hadn't been out on the porch long enough to become hypothermic or come down with pneumonia.

Whirling red and white lights announced the arrival of the ambulance. Priscilla left the comfort of the chair and stood by the bed, keeping vigil until the EMTs came to join her. She heard Gerald's familiar rumble at the door, along with two other voices, male and female. Shortly after, the EMTs appeared in her bedroom doorway, carrying a stretcher.

"Is this our patient?" the male EMT asked. He was short and stocky, with an air of brisk competence. His partner was tall, with a ponytail that swung when she moved.

"Yes." Priscilla moved away from the bedside to give them room to work, holding Jake back by the collar. Gerald observed from the doorway.

"Temp's low but okay," the woman said. "So is BP." Blood pressure.

"No to hypothermia then."

Relief swept over Priscilla. In that case, Rebekah couldn't have been outside all evening as she had feared. But another concern followed. *Why is she unconscious?*

The attendants seemed equally puzzled as they checked for other signs of injury or illness. They placed an oxygen mask over Rebekah's face, then prepared to load her onto the stretcher. "We're going to take her in now," the male EMT said. "Is she related to you?"

"No, she's my neighbor," Priscilla said. "Rebekah Alden is her name."

Someone banged on the front door. Priscilla gave Jake an order to stay and scooted out of the bedroom to answer, Gerald behind her. When she opened the door, Bradley Alden forced his way inside, practically shoving Priscilla out of the way.

"What's going on? I got a call that my aunt is here." His accusing gaze darted back and forth between Gerald and Priscilla.

"I left a message with your answering service," Gerald said, his calm demeanor in stark contrast to the other man's frantic movements. "When I brought Priscilla home a short while ago, we found your aunt unconscious on the steps outside. So we called an ambulance."

"Unconscious? Ambulance?" Bradley's head swung around. "Where is she?"

"In my bedroom," Priscilla said. "They're getting ready to take her to the hospital." She put her hands on her hips. "Where are the Moodys? No one answered the house phone." She heard the aggravation and frustration in her voice. *Calm down, Priscilla.*

Bradley held up both hands with a helpless shrug. "They had the night off. She's been doing better lately, and I thought she'd be okay alone. Guess I was wrong."

Wheels rumbled on the wood floor, and the male EMT began backing out of the bedroom. Bradley watched, his face twitching. Once the EMTs had pulled the stretcher fully into the hallway, he ran over and grabbed Rebekah's limp hand.

"Auntie. I'm here now," he crooned. He hobbled along beside his aunt all the way to the front entrance, still clasping her hand. There he was forced to relinquish his grip and stand aside so the EMTs could maneuver the stretcher out to the waiting ambulance. "What's wrong with her?" Bradley asked them. "Why isn't she waking up?"

"Don't know. We need to do some tests," the female EMT said. "I suggest you follow us to the hospital, if you're the next of kin."

Bradley sucked in a breath. "Yes. Yes, I am the next of kin. I'm the only loved one she has in the world." He wrung his hands, his lips trembling.

The trio watched through the open front door while the EMTs loaded Rebekah into the rear of the ambulance, its strobing lights made hazy by the falling snow. Moving in unison, the paramedics shut the doors and went around to the cab. Seconds later, the ambulance raced up the drive, the shriek of the siren cutting through the quiet night.

"You'd better go," Gerald said to Bradley. "They're in a hurry, and that's not a good sign."

Priscilla found herself gripping Gerald's arm, cold dismay trickling through her veins. Was Rebekah going to make it? "Please keep us posted, Bradley. We'll be praying for her."

Instead of accepting the sentiment graciously, Bradley's face twisted in anger. He clenched his fist and shook it in her face. "It's all your fault, Priscilla Latham Grant." His tone was sneering as he mocked the name his aunt used for her. "You put ideas into her head, and now she's sick. I told you before, stay away. You'd better listen this time."

Priscilla sagged under this onslaught of hatred, and only Gerald's arms kept her from falling to the floor. Arguments rose in her mind, seeking expression. It wasn't her fault, it was the Moodys and Bradley himself who weren't taking good care of Rebekah. Priscilla was the one who had rescued her, twice.

But before she could manage to formulate a single word, Bradley stormed out of the house, slamming the door behind him. His car roared to life, and he was gone, rocketing up the driveway.

Gerald was still holding her. "Hush, Priscilla," he said, somehow sensing her chaotic thoughts. "It's okay. People say bad things when they're upset." He ushered her to the fireplace, into one of the wing chairs. He lit the fire, already laid earlier and ready for a match. "I'll go make us a hot drink." Jake went with him to the kitchen, no doubt hoping for a treat.

Arms wrapped around her middle, Priscilla stared into the crackling fire, barely registering the sight she usually enjoyed. *It's all your fault.* Shivers ran through her middle, and she hunched over, sick to her stomach. Bradley had flipped the situation around in order to blame her, using words like fists and kicks to assault her.

Logic tried to assert itself. Maybe Gerald was right and an upset, frightened Bradley was merely striking out at the closest target. Certainly that was how some people reacted under stress. She'd seen it before. But then a treacherous thought trickled in, undermining this rationale the way the tide stole sand.

Something about Bradley's professed concern for his aunt did not ring true. More than once she'd witnessed him treating Rebekah like an errant, barely tolerated child. Maureen Moody did the same, perhaps reflecting her employer's attitude.

Thinking back to the scene in the hallway, Priscilla felt certain that she'd been watching Bradley play the role of a devoted nephew devastated by his dear aunt's illness. That act had dropped like a stage drape when he'd flown into a rage only minutes later.

And there was another odd thing. He had arrived at the house suspiciously quickly after Gerald's call. Where had he been that it took less than ten minutes to retrieve a message and drive to the cottage? Almost anywhere on the island was farther away than that, especially in a snowstorm. What if he had been at Rebekah's house and had known full well that she was out in the storm alone and underdressed? What kind of person did that? *Not a good one*, a little voice whispered.

By the time Gerald carried mugs of hot cocoa into the living room, Jake shadowing his heels, Priscilla had made up her mind. "Bradley Alden is not to be trusted. He's up to something, and I'm going to figure out what." She braced herself for his response.

He handed her a mug and sat in the opposite chair with his own. "You know, I agree with you. I take back the benefit of the doubt I gave him earlier. It may sound harsh, but I don't believe he has Rebekah's best interests at heart." He shook his head. "Let's keep an eye on her—and on him. He'll slip up sooner or later." He snapped his fingers. "And bam. We'll get him."

Heartened by his support, Priscilla took a deep breath, feeling stress and anxiety seep out of her muscles. "Thanks, Gerald. It's wonderful to have you on my side."

His eyes reflected the flickering firelight. "Where else would I be?"

The wind howled around the cottage like a banshee on the loose. After Gerald left close to midnight, the storm had intensified. Huddled under the covers, Priscilla tossed and turned, heartsick with concern for her friend. After a few hours of this, Jake jumped up on the bed and snuggled close, seeming to pick up on her state of mind.

She reached out a hand and touched his silky fur. "Oh, Jake, I hope Rebekah will be all right." A nudge of his cold, wet nose was his answer. She laughed and tucked her hand back under the covers. All she could do was pray and entrust Rebekah to God's keeping.

Gray morning light revealed the snow continuing to fall, although Priscilla thought maybe, just maybe, it was slacking off. Hopefully she'd be able to get to church. She'd need to give herself extra time to drive there. She had to pick up Harper too. Then she remembered the dinner party she was holding that night. She hated to cancel, but she'd have to check with the others to see if they wanted to make the trek.

After feeding Jake and letting him out for his morning constitutional, she made coffee, poured a fortifying cup, and called the hospital. Her fingers shook as she dialed the number. "Good morning," she said to the operator, trying to sound like she was entitled to call. "Rebekah Alden's room, please."

"Please hold." Canned music played, giving Priscilla time to fret about why she was on hold. Had Rebekah survived the night? If so, were they screening calls to avoid the troublemaker Priscilla Latham Grant?

Finally the music clicked off, and the operator returned. "I'm sorry, but Mrs. Alden isn't taking calls in her room right now. Can I take a message?"

Priscilla was swamped with sheer joy. Rebekah had survived her ordeal. "No, that's all right. When are visiting hours?"

"Noon to six on Sundays. Ten to eight all other days."

She could head over to the hospital after church. Rebekah would have at least one visitor that afternoon.

Due to the weather, church was sparsely attended, but Hugh and Gail made it, entering the vestibule right after Priscilla and Harper got there. Priscilla gave her uncle a hug. "I'm so glad to see you. Are you feeling better?"

"Much better, thanks." Hugh sent his daughter a sidewise glance. "I wanted to be out and about sooner, but my jailer wouldn't let me."

Gail gave a puff of exasperation, sending her bangs flying. "Now, Pop, you know we couldn't risk your cold going to your lungs. Last year you had bronchitis."

"Yeah, yeah. I'm not going to get bronchitis again." Hugh smiled at Harper. "I remember you from the bakery. Nice to see you again."

"Thank you," Harper said. "It's great to be here."

After the service, they went down to the fellowship hall to mingle. Priscilla was happy to see Harper talking to other people her age. One service, and she was already part of the congregation.

Priscilla poured a cup of coffee and joined Gail and Hugh, who stood near the refreshment table. "Are you two still going to come to dinner tonight? I thought maybe with the weather..."

"I won't miss lasagna for nothing." Hugh peered at the trays of homemade treats and picked a fat chocolate chip cookie. "I don't care if you-know-what freezes over."

Gail rolled her eyes. To Priscilla, she said, "We'll be there. If we Vineyarders allowed a little snow to keep us down, we wouldn't go anywhere from October to April."

"If we were stuck inside that long, one of us might not make it to spring," Hugh muttered.

Priscilla leaned over and whispered in her cousin's ear. "He's in rare form today."

Gail smiled. "Making up for lost time, I guess."

The hospital was in Oak Bluffs, a couple of miles from the church, so Priscilla headed over after dropping Harper at her apartment. Once she reached the hospital, Priscilla parked in the visitor area and hurried inside. Thinking she shouldn't arrive empty-handed, she detoured to the gift shop, located next to the cafeteria.

What to buy? The small shop was loaded with island-made crafts as well as the standard bouquets of flowers and toys. The flowers reminded her to call April Brown. She wondered if the dead bouquet had ever made it to the officer and what she thought of it as a clue to Harper's stalker.

She made a mental note to call April tomorrow. Finally she decided on a colorful bunch of flowers in a vase and a small stuffed dog that looked just like Jake. Rebekah would get a kick out of that. The friendly volunteer rang up the sale and gave her directions to the unit where she would find Rebekah's room.

At the nurses' station on the right floor, she asked which room Rebekah was in and if she was accepting visitors. "Room 215," the male nurse said. "Down the hall and around the corner. And yes, you can go on in."

Priscilla trudged down the hall, noticing how her boots squeaked on the shiny tile. Most of the rooms on both sides had occupants, with many of the doors halfway open. In one room, a family group laughed and chatted, no doubt bringing cheer to their patient.

Her steps slowed as she reached the numbers close to Rebekah's room so she wouldn't miss it. There it was, the next one on the right. Voices drifted out through the open door. She halted, not wanting to interrupt if Rebekah was being examined or was otherwise indisposed.

"I brought your favorite tea with me." The sound of gurgling liquid. "Here you go, drink up."

Unless she was mistaken, that was Bradley's voice. Priscilla tip-toed forward so her soles wouldn't squeak and give her away. She peeked into the room.

Rebekah lay in the hospital bed, an IV attached to her arm. Although she looked tiny and fragile, she was awake and her hair was brushed.

Bradley stood and leaned over her, holding out a mug. "Come on, Rebekah, take it. Your arms work, right?"

Rebekah pressed her lips together and shook her head. "I don't want it."

In response, he grabbed the back of her head with one big hand and pulled it forward, bringing the mug to her mouth with the other.

CHAPTER TWENTY-THREE

Excuse me," someone said right behind Priscilla.
She whirled around, relieved to see a nurse standing behind her. "Sorry." She moved aside to let the woman pass into the room.

"You can come in," the nurse said. "She's allowed visitors." She bustled ahead, calling to Rebekah and Bradley. "I'm here to see if Mrs. Alden wants lunch." Her gaze fell on the mug in Bradley's hand.

Bradley had dropped his hand from Rebekah's head. He set the mug on the bedside tray. "I brought her a thermos of her favorite tea."

"I don't want it," Rebekah said. Her gaze went beyond the nurse to Priscilla, her eyes widening. "Priscilla Latham Grant. You came to see me."

Bradley's scowl could burn through metal, but Priscilla ignored it. "Of course I did." She set the flowers on the windowsill and held up the toy. "Jake says hi."

Rebekah crowed in delight, reaching for the stuffed dog. "It's adorable. And it looks just like him."

The nurse had been standing patiently by. "Mrs. Alden, here are the lunch choices." She presented Rebekah with a menu.

"You're not on any restrictions, so you can have whatever you want."

Rebekah tucked Toy Jake in the crook of her arm and studied the list of food. "Chicken soup and crackers, please. Oh, and coffee." She slapped the menu down. "No tea."

The nurse took notes. "It's decaf, of course. But coffee it is." She turned to go. "Have a nice visit."

"Pull up a chair, Priscilla," Rebekah said. "Bradley, move aside so she can sit."

Whether it was the proximity of the nursing staff or the fact that he had almost been caught forcing his aunt to drink something, Bradley didn't argue. He edged away from the bed, leaving room for Priscilla to get to the chair.

"I should probably go," he said, screwing the cap back on his thermos. "I'll be back this evening to visit you, Auntie."

When he reached for the mug, which held a pale yellow brew, Priscilla grabbed it first. "Why don't you leave this? Maybe Rebekah will want to drink it later."

Rebekah opened her mouth to protest but stopped when Priscilla gave her a covert wink.

"That's right, I probably will," Rebekah said. "I never drink tea on an empty stomach. I'll drink it later, with a cookie maybe."

"I can get you a cookie," Priscilla said. "They have delicious-looking ones down in the cafeteria." She didn't really know that, but she assumed so.

With Priscilla holding onto the mug for dear life, Bradley couldn't really object to her plan, especially when another nurse popped in to check Rebekah's vitals. He picked up his thermos and slunk out of the room with a growled goodbye.

"Visitors with bad attitudes should be banned," Rebekah said, submitting to the nurse's examination. "He might have given me a setback."

The nurse gave a bark of surprised laughter at her remark. "I can bring it up with the attending doctor," she said, playing along.

If only Bradley *could* be banned from visiting. But since he was Rebekah's only living relative, that might be difficult to enforce. Priscilla contented herself with the knowledge that they had thwarted him, but in what, she wasn't exactly sure.

While the nurse examined Rebekah, Priscilla stared at the mug of tea in her hand. Unless Bradley was a devotee of herbal medicine, she saw no reason on earth why he would insist his aunt drink it. A terrible thought drifted into her mind.

The nurse had barely left the room when Priscilla said, "Bradley brought you your favorite tea. That was thoughtful." She placed the cup on the bedside table, out of the way.

Rebekah curled her lip. "He says it's my favorite, but I don't like it. It's some herbal concoction he swears is good for my memory."

Her supposedly failing memory was the reason Bradley had hired caretakers. Unease coiled in Priscilla's belly. "Do you drink it often?"

"Whenever he visits me. He drinks it too, says it helps him stay sharp for his business deals." She snorted. "Takes more than tea."

"I would think so." Priscilla made a decision. If Bradley was doctoring the herbal tea, that would explain why Rebekah's "dementia" seemed to come and go. She'd take the tea and see about having it tested, without mentioning her suspicions to Rebekah yet.

There was no sense in alarming her if she was wrong. *Or warning Bradley they were on to him.* Now, how to transport it?

She rummaged through her purse and found a small bottle of water. She could empty that and pour the tea in there. How to do it discreetly?

The nurse arriving with Rebekah's lunch provided the perfect distraction. Priscilla slipped into the bathroom and dumped the bottled water down the drain. Then she did her best to pour the contents of the mug into the bottle, not an easy task. She got a few ounces inside and screwed the cap on tightly.

"This soup isn't bad," Rebekah said when Priscilla came out of the bathroom. "Not as good as yours, of course." She picked up her coffee mug, sipped, and set it down with a grimace. "I can't stand decaf."

"Me neither, frankly." Priscilla sat quietly, letting her friend eat. She wanted to ask about the previous night but didn't want to ruin Rebekah's appetite. When she had spooned up the last bite, Priscilla asked, "What do you remember about last night?"

Rebekah tapped her pursed lips. "Let me take a step back. After Bradley and I left your house, we had quite the argument. He said he'd pulled the museum check out of the mail because I couldn't afford to make the gift. He told me I needed to conserve my money. I told him I was quite capable of managing my own finances."

"What did he say to that?" Priscilla was of two minds. Maybe Bradley was right and someone *should* manage Rebekah's funds.

She had heard of elderly folks who made bad decisions and were taken advantage of by outside parties. However, Bradley's actions were underhanded.

"He wants to take over my money with a power of attorney. I said no. Finally he dropped the subject, and we had a nice quiet evening. The next thing I know, I'm waking up in the hospital." Rebekah clutched at the sheet, her lips trembling. "What if he's right? What if I can't take care of myself?" Stark fear etched her features.

"I haven't seen any evidence of that," Priscilla said stoutly. But she did see a man up to no good. But again, rather than accuse him outright, she said, "Maybe you should speak to your attorney." Someone needed to be an advocate for Rebekah's best interests.

"Will you go with me to see him?" Rebekah's eyes were hopeful.

"Of course." Wouldn't Bradley love that? Priscilla got up and gave her friend a hug. "I'm on your side. So is Gerald."

"Thank you, dear." Rebekah blinked away tears. "How I wish Sally were here. She wouldn't let this happen to me."

Disturbed by Rebekah's predicament, Priscilla resolved to search for Sally. She'd made the promise but hadn't done a thing about it. Once she returned to the cottage, she stowed the tea sample in the refrigerator, then prepared everything for the dinner party at six. The leftover lasagna was ready to pop into the oven, and the table was set. Harper had made two loaves of bread, so she turned the untouched one into garlic bread and wrapped it in foil.

Priscilla found the albums Rebekah had given her and sat down with them in front of the fire to study the pictures of Sally and her friends. Bradley was in many of them.

Someone must have known where Sally went when she left the island. Kids that age were often closer to their friends than to their parents. Perhaps they'd even stayed in touch. Did the boy with the cross know, or the redhead with the ponytail, maybe? What about Bradley? He and Sally were cousins. Surely they'd confided in each other.

If only she could ask Bradley about Sally. She thought about it for a few seconds, then trembled at the thought. He was too angry with her to attempt such a thing. And besides, she doubted he'd welcome a return of the prodigal daughter at this point.

One photo of the teens showed them on the upper deck of the lighthouse, and she set it aside, planning to make a copy. Bradley posed with a spyglass, pretending to look out to sea while the others laughed. Sally's head was thrown back, her eyes squeezed shut in glee.

How sad to think she left the island soon after this happy day. *And so had David Castonguay, according to the newspaper,* she thought. Had he and Sally been together? Perhaps they'd run away and gotten married.

Priscilla set the albums aside and grabbed her laptop to search for Sally Alden online. She found a few women with that name, but none of the right age. With her new theory in mind, she then looked for Sally Castonguay. No luck there either.

The mantel clock chimed five, which meant her guests would be showing up soon. She reluctantly gave up for the time being and went to put the lasagna in the oven.

As she puttered around the kitchen, she thought about her quest. Unfortunately for her investigation, Sally had left the island before the internet became common. Nowadays she didn't know how anyone disappeared. With social media, legal records online, and newspaper archives readily available, it would be difficult to vanish. Someone would have to work at it.

Joan arrived first, bearing a lemon mousse for dessert. "I figured we'd want something light with pasta," she said, handing Priscilla the glass dish covered with plastic wrap so she could take off her coat and boots.

"It looks delicious," Priscilla said, admiring the pale yellow confection topped with mounds of whipped cream.

"I hope it tastes as good as it looks." Joan turned at the sound of a vehicle. "Here comes the rest of the crew."

Trudy, her husband, Dan, Hugh, and Gail had ridden over together. The next few minutes were an excited commotion as they all got settled. Jake was beside himself, dashing from one person to another to get his quota of petting and compliments.

"Dinner will be ready in fifteen minutes," Priscilla said once everyone was seated in the living room. She gestured to the sideboard, where the tray of vegetables Trudy had brought and apple cider and soft drinks sat. "Help yourselves."

Everyone served themselves drinks and nibbles. Trudy and Joan sat in the wingback chairs by the fire while Gail and Hugh took the sofa. Dan went over to the poster mock-ups of the museum exhibit Priscilla had made and studied them, stroking his beard.

"What do you think, Dan?" Priscilla asked. "I thought it was better to lay out the exhibits this way before going to the trouble of setting them up."

"I like it so far." He pointed to a picture of the lighthouse surrounded by pictures of the various keepers and short life histories. "This gives a good feel for the history of the place."

An idea sparked in Priscilla's mind. "I saw an interesting show about whales and sharks in the Atlantic the other night. Would you help me put together information about the creatures living in the waters off the lighthouse?" Dan was a marine biologist who worked at the Woods Hole Oceanographic Institution, so there was no better person to ask.

"I'd be happy to help," he said. "Lighthouses are excellent locations to observe fish and sea mammal migrations and populations. I'm sure past keepers were well aware of sea life."

"Seabirds too," Joan put in.

One by one, the others drifted over to the museum display. Priscilla was gratified by their interest and approval. After all, she was the newcomer interpreting family and island history.

Uncle Hugh picked up the photograph of Bradley and his friends on the lighthouse deck. He studied it closely, then waved it. "Here's a face I haven't seen in forever. David Castonguay."

CHAPTER TWENTY-FOUR

Priscilla's ears perked up. "Which one is he, Uncle Hugh?" Maybe putting a name to a face would help her find David, although so far she'd discovered only dead ends.

"This is him." Hugh stabbed his finger at the boy wearing the cross. "That summer he helped us paint the lighthouse. Good little worker. Came down from Canada. Always wondered what happened to him." He shook his head. "People come and go on this island. Here today, gone tomorrow."

Canada. Priscilla filed that away. She hadn't considered Canadians in her search for David. "Did you know Sally Alden?" she asked. She pointed Sally out to her uncle.

"'Course I did. She was always around. I knew her parents too, although I haven't seen Rebekah very often over the years. Henry's gone."

The timer went off in the kitchen. "Time to eat," Priscilla said. "Let's continue this conversation over dinner."

She bustled out to the kitchen, where she pulled the bubbling pasta dish and the garlic bread out of the oven. The cousins came in and helped her get the meal ready to serve. Gail tossed the big salad she'd brought and put it on the table along with two types of dressing. Trudy put the bread in a basket, and Joan ferried servings of lasagna to the table.

Once everyone was seated, Dan led them in grace, and they dug in. The salad bowl and breadbasket went around. For a few minutes, the only sounds were murmurs of appreciation and enjoyment and the clink of silverware.

"This is so good," Trudy said with a moan. "It's the best lasagna I've ever had."

"Not too shabby," Uncle Hugh said. "Nice thick layers of cheese and plenty of sausage."

"I'm glad you like it," Priscilla said. "It's one of my favorite dishes." She bit into a buttery slice of garlic bread. "Candy's new baker made this bread. Isn't it good?" The garlic bread got rave reviews, and so did the salad. Satisfied her dinner party was a success, Priscilla asked Hugh, "Speaking of Rebekah, she said to say hello to you. I've gotten to know her recently. She lives right next door."

"She's a good woman," Hugh said. "I felt bad for her when her daughter took off like that." He cut off another bite of lasagna. "I always thought it was her father's fault."

The cousins exchanged concerned glances. "Why's that, Uncle Hugh?" Trudy asked.

"Oh, he loved her in his own way, but he was a proud man, a little too good for the rest of us, if you get my drift. He had high expectations for his daughter, and when she didn't meet 'em..." He shook his head. "More than once I saw her sitting on the beach right out here, crying." He stared out the dark window as though seeing the scene in his mind. "She and David were as thick as thieves. And Henry didn't like that. He didn't approve of him, thought he was only a shiftless drifter. But in my view, he wasn't any worse than any of the other young people who come to Martha's Vineyard to work a summer and then move on."

The pieces clicked together for Priscilla. David had been important to Sally. They'd both left Martha's Vineyard. What had happened to them after that?

Hilda was seated in a corner by the window when Priscilla got to the bakery the next morning. Before ordering, Priscilla took a detour to drop her coat at the table and let Hilda know she was there.

"Thanks for meeting me," Priscilla said. "Can I get you anything?"

Hilda put aside the newspaper she'd been browsing and picked up her fork. "No, thanks. I'm all set with this awesome Tisbury Tizzy." She scanned the room. "I haven't seen Harper yet."

"She's probably baking." Priscilla went to the counter to order. What should she get today? The cranberry streusel muffins looked good, a slight change of pace from her usual plain cranberry.

"Good morning, Priscilla," Candy said. "What can I get you?"

Priscilla placed her order. "How's everything going?" she asked when Candy handed her the coffee and muffin.

Candy beamed. "Fantastic. I got my first online order yesterday. A dozen cranberry muffins delivered to Boston by express service. For a meeting, no less. The executive loves my muffins and thinks they'll help her seal the deal."

"Congratulations! That's wonderful news. I hope it's the first order of many," Priscilla said with sincerity.

"Me too." Candy put her hands together and looked heavenward. "I pray no other disasters happen for a while."

"I'll be praying too," Priscilla promised. "Can Harper come talk to me and Hilda for a minute? We're right over there." She pointed with her chin.

"Sure thing. Enjoy." Candy picked up a rag and began to wipe up a spill.

Harper popped out of the kitchen a few minutes later, wiping her hands on her apron and glancing around the room. Spotting Priscilla and Hilda, she headed their way.

"Good morning, ladies," she said, pulling out one of the empty chairs. "Thanks for coming, Hilda." Her smile was both eager and a little scared.

"No problem." Hilda reached into her bag and pulled out a couple of photograph envelopes. "It gave me a good excuse to get my photos organized. I only had about a thousand." She laughed.

"Me too," Priscilla said. "Don't you love the ones without names or dates? You always think you're going to remember..."

Hilda was sorting through the photos. "Thankfully we did include names on these, but I didn't find a Megan, I'm sorry to say." Her eyes were full of empathy. "I thought you might like to see them anyway."

Harper's shoulders slumped, and she bit her lip in disappointment. Then she blinked and took a deep breath. "Okay, it was a long shot. I knew that. Let's see what you have."

The waitress slid three pictures across the table. "These are for the year you mentioned as well as the one before and the one after."

Harper examined the first photo, then flipped it over to read the names. She handed it to Priscilla. She did the same with the second. On the third, she paused. "How many girls do you know who are named Zinnia?"

"Not many," Priscilla said with a laugh. Her fingers began to tingle. "What'd you find?"

"A girl named Zinnia Jones."

Hilda gave a squeak. "I remember her. How could I ever forget that name?"

Harper slid the photograph to the middle of the table so both Priscilla and Harper could see it. "Remember Mom's friend, Zinnia? Do you think this is her?"

"It must be." Priscilla studied the line of attractive young faces standing in front of the Inn, Tilly Snyder and Hilda on one end. "Which one is Zinnia?"

Harper pointed to a petite redhead in the front row, and Priscilla recognized her pretty face. It was the redheaded girl from Rebekah's photographs.

Another point of connection. David and Zinnia. It was starting to look like Megan and Sally shared the same group of friends. "Do you have a picture of your mom when she was this age?" she asked Harper.

Harper shook her head. "No. This diary is all I have. When I used to bug her about pictures of her or her family, she would tell me that she had lost them or they'd been burned up in a fire. I don't even have many baby pictures." She pushed the photos across the table to Hilda. "I'd better get back to the kitchen."

"Why don't you keep that one?" Hilda said, pushing the picture with Zinnia back toward her.

"Thank you." Harper studied it, then slid it into her pocket. "I really appreciate you trying to help me find information about my mom."

"I'm sorry these weren't of more use," Hilda said. As Harper strode across the bakery, greeting customers as she went, she added, "It looks to me like her mother didn't want to be found."

"It sure seems that way. We've run into one dead end after another." Priscilla thought about Zinnia. "Jones. Do you suppose she was any relation to Ida Lee Jones?" That was a long shot, since the name Jones wasn't exactly uncommon.

"I think Zinnia was her husband's cousin." Hilda laughed. "How could I ever forget that name? Sure is different." She crumpled up her napkin. "This has been nice, but I have to run."

"Let's do it again sometime." Priscilla had enjoyed Hilda's company and felt like perhaps she had a new friend.

218 | MYSTERIES of MARTHA'S VINEYARD

After the waitress gathered her things and left, Priscilla decided to stay for a while. She was in a quiet corner, a perfect place to gather her thoughts and make her plans. First she got a coffee refill and a glass of water, and then she settled in to think.

What next? The sight of Jason noisily stacking coffee mugs on trays reminded her of Harper's grocery store bouquet. She'd call April Brown and ask about it. She had called the police station so often, she didn't need to look up the number.

April was in, and Priscilla only had to wait a few minutes on hold for the officer to answer. "Officer Brown here. How may I help you?"

Priscilla explained who she was. "I left a bouquet for you at the front desk the other night. Did you get it? I thought it might be evidence in the Harper Jenson stalking case."

"I did receive that bag of dead flowers, thanks. Want to run your reasoning by me again? The note that came with it wasn't very explanatory."

"Harper found them in her mailbox the day before she reported the stalker. They weren't dead then, of course. We fished them out of her trash. She doesn't know who gave them to her, so I thought the stalker might have left them. You can trace where they came from by the label on the plastic wrap, right?"

"I suppose we could." April sounded doubtful.

"Then the store could let you see the tapes, and you'd see who bought them."

A long silence, then April cleared her throat. "Mrs. Grant, your reasoning is correct. We could in theory track that purchase.

But without a crime being committed, well, we don't have the resources to give or, quite frankly, the interest in doing so."

"I guess I understand that." Priscilla could see her logic. But it upset her that there was so little the police could do regarding Harper's dilemma. "But please hang on to them. For when a crime *is* committed."

She set the phone down a little harder than she planned, and it made quite a *crack* on the tabletop. She picked it up, grateful to see that it was still intact.

"Something get under your skin this morning, Priscilla?"

She looked up to see Gerald's laughing eyes looking down at her. "Don't mind me. I was just having a little hissy fit. I'm over it now." She gestured to the empty chairs at her table. "Have a seat."

He shrugged out of his coat and draped it over the back of a chair. "I think I'll take you up on that. Let me go get coffee and a muffin."

"I recommend the cranberry streusel," she called.

Gerald took her advice and returned with the recommended muffin. "Good pick," he said, taking a huge bite.

Priscilla thought about all that had happened since she'd last seen him. "Have I got news for you. But first tell me, how is Nick?"

"Nick is grand. He's home. A little sore, but he'll be back at work soon."

"I'm so glad." She glanced around the room, noticing that the tables around them had cleared out. They were in a lull that would last until late morning, if other experiences here were anything to go by. She lowered her voice to a whisper anyway. "Gerald, I think our friend has been giving his aunt doctored tea."

He understood right away. "And what makes you think our friend is doing that?"

"Because I caught him." Priscilla took him through the incident in the hospital room. "I think that tea is causing her cognitive problems."

"That's quite a leap, Priscilla. Maybe he really thinks the tea will be beneficial for her. I get all kinds of advertisements for herbal products to help my aging brain." He grinned. "Don't you?"

She waved that off. "He was forcing her to drink it. But when I showed up, she became brave enough to say no." She leaned across the table. "I saved a sample. I want to have it tested."

Gerald rubbed his chin. "You could do that. But I'm warning you, it will cost hundreds of dollars."

CHAPTER TWENTY-FIVE

Hundreds? She didn't have that kind of money to spend. "Then what can we do? I know he's trying to get control of her money. He'll probably use these wandering episodes as an excuse to have her put in an old folks' home."

"Where was he the other night?" Gerald asked. "He got to your place awfully fast after I left that message."

Priscilla nodded. "I thought the same thing. When I talked to Rebekah in the hospital, she said she and Bradley were alone that evening. According to her, he gave the caretakers the night off."

Gerald's eyes narrowed. "Boy, this is a tough one. If she speaks out against him now, he could spin it as her dementia talking. Unfortunately we have no proof that he allowed her to leave her house and wander off. He could say she slipped out while he was busy."

Priscilla thought back to her visit with Rebekah at the hospital. "She doesn't remember what happened. She said they were arguing at her house about the donation to the museum, and the next thing she knew, she woke up in the hospital."

Gerald perked up. "What's this about a donation?"

"She thought she made it, but he told Mildred she wasn't going to." She gave him a few more details of the incident.

"Is she still in the hospital?" He asked. He held his mug up for the waitress circling with a pot of coffee.

"I'm not sure. I'll call and check." Priscilla accepted a splash more coffee and thanked the young woman.

"When you find out, let me know. We're going to figure out a way to help your friend."

After leaving the bakery, Priscilla ran a few errands, then headed for home. She called the hospital and learned that Rebekah had been discharged that morning. That was good news.

Priscilla ate lunch and gave Jake a short walk, then sat down to continue researching David Castonguay online. This time she focused on Canada, based on Hugh's information that he had come from there. She did find a number for a David in Montreal. The age listed online was older, but maybe he was a relative.

She had to start somewhere. After checking to be sure international calls were covered on her plan, she dialed the number.

"Bonjour," a woman's voice said.

She'd forgotten many people in Canada spoke French. Priscilla didn't. "Hello?" she said, hoping the woman could speak English.

The woman switched languages. "Hello. How can I be of help?"

"My name is Priscilla Grant, and I'm calling from Martha's Vineyard—"

Before she could continue, the woman sucked in a breath. "The island?"

"Yes, the island. I'm looking for David Castonguay."

"David is my father. He's not well enough to talk, I am afraid. What is it you need?"

"Actually the David I'm looking for would be in his forties. I must have the wrong number."

"Well...I had a brother named David of that age. But he is gone. We don't know where he is." Her voice sounded forlorn.

"I'm so sorry." Priscilla took a deep breath, feeling terrible for intruding into this woman's grief. "Did he visit Martha's Vineyard, by chance?"

"*Oui.* Yes. He did. That is where we last heard from him. But he had a habit of dropping out of sight for long periods of time. He used to talk about going out to Alaska. Maybe he is there." She paused. "I hope."

Again Priscilla apologized for intruding. "I'm looking for someone too. A woman named Sally. She disappeared about the same time David did. I was hoping..."

"You hope they were together?" The woman's laugh was sad. "If you find out anything, please call me. My name is Angelique Girard."

"I will, Angelique, I promise."

Now Priscilla had made promises to three people to find loved ones. Perhaps she should open a service. That bit of humor helped lift the depression that had settled on her shoulders during the call to Angelique.

On to the next person on the list. Keep busy, that was the key.

Ida Lee Jones was at home as Priscilla hoped, since she usually worked the breakfast or lunch shift at the diner. "Hi, Priscilla. How are you?" In the background, Priscilla heard a refrigerator door shut, then a clatter of dishes. "Sorry, I'm in the middle of making dinner."

"I won't keep you long. Your husband's cousin Zinnia Jones came up in conversation recently. She may know a woman I'm looking for."

"Zinnia? Zinnia knows everyone." Ida stretched the last word out and punctuated it with a laugh. "She lives off-island now, in Falmouth."

"Can I have her number?" Priscilla picked up a pen and jotted down the number Ida recited from memory.

"Who are you looking for?" Ida asked. "Maybe I know her."

"Her name is Megan Elliot, and it's actually her daughter, Harper, who is searching for her. She thinks her mother lived on the island about twenty years ago."

"Hmm. Doesn't ring a bell. Maybe she was a summer kid. We've got plenty of those coming and going." Something clanged in the background, and water ran.

"That's what I think. We looked in the high school yearbooks, but she wasn't there."

"So why do you think Zinnia might know her? Hold on." The sound of muffled talking. "Sorry, Randy wanted to know what we're having for dinner."

"I won't keep you much longer. Megan mentioned a friend named Zinnia in her diary. We think it might be your Zinnia. She's about the same age as Megan."

Ida laughed. "Not many Zinnias running around, are there? You could be right. Zinnia was friends with everyone when she lived here—locals, summer people, you name it. Give her a call. Hopefully she can help."

After saying goodbye to Ida, Priscilla called Zinnia, but she only got voice mail. At least she could honestly say in her message that Zinnia's cousin had given her the number. That might encourage a call back from the former waitress.

At loose ends now, Priscilla decided to work on dinner. She'd bought a container of fresh shucked clams at the supermarket, so she decided to make Aunt Marjorie's clam chowder. She sautéed a little salt pork and bacon, then some minced garlic, celery, and chopped onion. Diced potatoes and clam juice followed to simmer. The clams and cream were last, added while homemade biscuits browned in the oven.

All the while, Rebekah's well-being nagged at the back of Priscilla's mind. Was she all right? Were Bradley and the Moodys treating her well?

When the telephone rang, it startled her.

"Hi, Priscilla. I hope I'm not interrupting your dinner," her neighbor said.

She was, but Priscilla didn't care. "Rebekah, how are you? I've been wanting to call but didn't know if you were up to it."

"I'm fine. The doctor said my episode was all due to my medication. Too much of one thing and not enough of another. I'm all straightened out now." Her laugh was dry.

"I can't tell you how glad I am. I was worried."

Rebekah lowered her voice. "I have something confidential to discuss with you and that nice gentleman friend of yours. What happened the other night was the last straw, I'm afraid. Do you think you could come see me tomorrow?"

"I definitely will, and I know Gerald will want to also. I don't know his schedule, but I'll find out. What time were you thinking?"

The next evening, Rebekah answered her front door, looking every inch the lady in her green velvet housecoat. "Come on in, Bradley, and have a seat."

Her nephew stepped over the threshold, removing his hat and kicking the snow off his feet. From her vantage point in Rebekah's living room, Priscilla saw his eyes widen in surprise. "You're looking well, Auntie."

"What did you expect, a deathbed visit?" Her laugh pealed out, and she seemed to overlook his flinch. "Do come in. We have a couple of friends here with us."

His footsteps faltered. "Friends? Where are the Moodys?"

"I gave them the night off and a gift certificate to the Colonial Inn. They're probably sitting down to dinner about now." Rebekah swept into the living room, her robe swirling around her. "You know Priscilla and Gerald, don't you, Bradley?"

He frowned, giving them only a brusque nod of greeting and ignoring Gerald's outstretched hand. "Not to be rude, but I was under the impression that you and I were having a discussion of a private nature tonight."

"And so we are. Have a seat, Bradley, and do stop dithering." Rebekah sat in her wingback chair and picked up the teapot to pour him a cup.

He hastened to obey, the stern note in her voice no doubt evoking an ingrained response to authority. He pulled an armchair up to the circle and accepted the cup of tea Rebekah pressed on him.

The group sat in silence for a minute, Gerald passing a plate of molasses cookies to Bradley, who took one and rested it on his saucer. Finally Bradley spoke. "So, Aunt Rebekah, can you please enlighten me as to why you called me over here at this hour?" His aggrieved tone made it plain he'd rather be elsewhere.

"As I said in my message, I've been doing some thinking." Rebekah gazed into the fire, her face somber. "You're decades from this yet, all of you, but there comes a time when you have to admit that…that…things are changing."

Bradley edged forward in his seat. "Yes, Auntie. That's what I've been saying all along. There isn't any shame in realizing that you might not, er, have the same grasp of matters as before."

Rebekah's answer was a laugh. She held up the teapot. "A little more tea, Bradley?"

He obediently held out his cup for a refill. "I'm glad you're seeing sense now, Auntie, and if your friends are helping with that, then I take back what I've said about them." He chuckled. "No hard feelings."

In response, Gerald and Priscilla smiled. "Glad we could be of assistance," Gerald said.

"You have no idea." Bradley laughed again and drained the cup. He set it down and dabbed his lips with a napkin. Pushing back in his chair, he propped his arms behind his head and stretched out his stocking feet, the very picture of a gentleman at leisure. "Why don't we get into the details tomorrow, Auntie? I'll call the attorney, and we'll have the papers drawn up."

Rebekah smiled. "There is one little thing I wanted to share tonight." She waited until he moved to a more upright position. "Remember the tea you brought me in the hospital?" At his confused nod, she added, "That's what was in your cup."

Priscilla held her breath. Here came the moment of truth. Either Bradley would laugh in disbelief and think his aunt really was nutty, or he—

"What?" His voice was a roar. He erupted out of his seat to a standing position, hands poised at his sides like a gunslinger ready to draw. "What have you done to me?"

"That's a question only you can answer, Bradley," Gerald said, his tone mild. "You know what was in that tea."

By the horrified expression on Bradley's face, Priscilla guessed it wasn't something he would choose to imbibe. He began to feel himself all over, patting his limbs and face as though checking for numbness. He wiggled his legs back and forth as though shaking ants off his skin and took great gusting breaths of air.

"Call the ambulance." His voice was hoarse. "I'm allergic to those medications." He put a hand to his chest, panting. "Call the police."

"They're on their way. You'll have plenty of chance to explain why you were overdosing your aunt." Gerald had talked to a doctor friend and figured out that Rebekah's prescriptions for high blood pressure could cause the symptoms she had been experiencing if given in the wrong quantities.

As Gerald's words sank in, the fear and terror on Bradley's face gave way to anger. "How dare you?" he bellowed, launching himself at Gerald.

Gerald was braced and ready, and with one neat punch, he knocked the other man flat. As Bradley hit the floor, his keys and loose coins flew out of his pockets, landing near Priscilla. Gerald followed up by flipping Bradley over onto his stomach and securing his wrists with cuffs.

"I know I'm on dry land, so let's consider this a citizen's arrest," Gerald said.

Bradley rolled around on the carpet, straining against the cuffs. "You'll regret this, O'Bannon. It will be my purpose in life to make sure you do."

Priscilla glanced at Rebekah, concerned how she would take this devastating turn of events. It was one thing to suspect and quite another to have proof that a loved one was trying to harm you.

But the older woman showed amazing fortitude. She pushed herself out of her chair and strode over to Bradley. "How could you do this? Henry and I treated you like a son. Everything I have is going to be yours." She thought about that. "Or it was. Now I'll leave it to charity."

Bradley curled up in a ball, his aunt's words striking him like arrows. "I'm sorry, Auntie. I don't know what got into me... I was always so jealous of Sally. She was your real child."

"We loved you too, you fool." Rebekah shook her head. "What was so urgent that you had to harm me? Why not ask? I would have helped you."

"I was sinking...my investments went south. I was desperate. I even went to the wrong people for loans."

"Nothing justifies you trying to hurt your aunt," Gerald said. "You'll be going away for a good long time if I have anything to say about it."

"It's nothing less than I deserve. I was wrong." Bradley rolled around in his anguish, and one of his feet almost struck Priscilla. She moved back a step and kicked Bradley's key ring. She bent to pick it up, noticing an ornate cross hanging from the bundle of keys. It looked familiar. She turned it over in her fingers, trying to remember where she'd seen something similar. Realization flashed into her mind.

"Bradley, why do you have David Castonguay's cross?" she blurted.

In response, he closed his eyes with a groan. "I guess the jig's up, as they say. Help me up and I'll tell you all about it."

Gerald hoisted Bradley to his feet and, after fervent assurances the prisoner was going to cooperate, took off the cuffs. Bradley sat in one of the wingback chairs, rubbing his wrists. To Priscilla's amazement, he appeared almost peaceful as he began to talk.

He pointed to the cross. "I carry that with me as penance," he said. "Every day, every time I use my keys, I see it and am reminded of my crime." He bowed his head.

Priscilla looked at the others, whose expressions reflected her own rapt attention. "David was with you on the boat, wasn't he?" she said gently.

He nodded. "Yes. I invited him to go sailing with me. I loved David. He was one of my best friends. But like all friends, he spoke the truth. And that was something I wasn't ready to hear." He gave a great, gusting sigh. "We got into an argument as soon as we left the dock. He was in love with Sally, and I was jealous of their happiness. I knew her father didn't approve of David, and I rubbed that in his face, that he'd never be accepted into the Alden clan."

"You were right," Rebekah said sadly. "Henry would have objected to Sally's involvement with David. In his eyes, David wasn't worthy. Oh, he was a nice young man, but he had no connections or money. Henry wanted more, much more, for our daughter. Whether he would have come to accept their union—if it went that far—we'll never know."

Bradley barked a laugh. "My real fear was that David would be accepted and that I'd be displaced. He told me I was spoiled and needed to grow up. He was right. By then we were out in the bay, and a storm had sprung up. But the two of us were more concerned about our argument. It escalated until finally I hit him. The boat came heeling around, and he fell overboard. I reached for him, but all I could grab was his necklace." His finger shook as he pointed at the cross. "It broke in my hand, and he slid under the waves.

"I had to fight for my own life, the storm was so bad. I ended up running the boat aground, and I was rescued. By then, I'd decided to say that David hadn't been with me on the boat, that he'd left before I set sail. It seemed simpler than explaining." He fell silent, his head bowed.

"What happened with Sally?" Priscilla asked. She had a strong suspicion that Bradley was involved in her flight from home.

"I told Sally her parents paid David to leave."

Rebekah gasped. "How could you do such a thing?" She clenched her fists. "Where did she go? Where is she?"

Bradley shook his head. "I'm so sorry. I was stunned when she ran away. I wish I could find her for you." He began to weep. "Oh, why didn't I fall off that boat instead of David? Everyone would have been better off."

Priscilla couldn't disagree with that assessment. His greed and insecurity about his position in the Alden family had conspired to create a selfish man with little regard for others. Only time would tell if he would truly repent.

CHAPTER TWENTY-SIX

S omeone here place a 911 call?" Chief Hank Westin was at the
door, accompanied by Officer April Brown. Chief Westin was
a tall, authoritative, but kind man with a thick local accent.

"Yes, we did," Priscilla said, opening the door to let them in.
Gerald was standing guard over Bradley, who still seemed cooper-
ative. Gerald had taken the precaution of slipping the handcuffs
back on, in case Bradley panicked when he saw the police.

"Good evening, Chief," Gerald said. "Officer Brown."

"Captain O'Bannon." Chief Westin nodded, taking in the
scene. Gerald stood next to Bradley, while Rebekah sat in her
chair by the fireside. Except for the handcuffs, one might think
the foursome was having a civil social evening. "What seems to
be the problem?"

"I made a citizen's arrest of Robert Bradley Alden tonight,"
Gerald said. "He confessed to doctoring his aunt's tea with the
intent of doing her injury."

Robert Bradley Alden? Priscilla didn't have time to think
about that. She picked up the jar of tea, still cold from the refrigerator. "I have a sample here. I got it when Bradley visited Rebekah
in the hospital. He was trying to force her to drink it. I heard
him."

"It's all true, officers," Rebekah said. "He's been making me drink that horrible brew for weeks. With the result that my medicine has been all messed up and I've had spells of confusion and amnesia."

"What do you have to say for yourself, Alden?" the chief asked.

Bradley refused to meet the chief's eyes. "It's true. I didn't want to hurt her, just make her realize I should be in charge of her affairs."

"Causing her to wander outside in her nightgown during a snowstorm might be considered harmful," Priscilla snapped. "She came to my house not once but twice, both times inadequately dressed for the weather. She might have frozen to death. Or ended up in the ocean."

The chief pushed back his hat and scratched his head. "So, Robert Bradley Alden, you're confessing to tampering with your aunt's beverages? And this confession is uncoerced and of your free will? Anything you say can and will be held against you in a court of law."

"Yes, sir. I'm guilty of tampering with her beverages."

"Well, we're going to take you in, Alden. We'll need statements from you other three, but that can wait until tomorrow."

"Hold on." Priscilla held up her hand. "There's more." She dangled the cross so both officers could see. "This cross belonged to David Castonguay, a young man who disappeared twenty-five years ago. Bradley was there when he fell overboard off Henry Alden's sailboat during the storm that wrecked it."

"Is this true?" Chief Westin asked Bradley. At Bradley's affirmative nod, the chief shook his head. "You folks have had quite a busy evening. We'll be in touch." To April, he said, "Take the tea and the cross into evidence."

The house seemed quiet after they left. Gerald added another log to the fire and stirred it into life. The mantel clock chimed nine o'clock. It felt much later.

"Thank you," Rebekah said with a shiver. "I feel so cold." She pulled her shawl more tightly around her shoulders.

"Can I get you something else to eat or drink?" Priscilla asked. Her own mood was an odd mix of elation and sorrow. They'd figured out why Rebekah had those dangerous wandering episodes, but her own flesh and blood had been revealed as the cause. Not easy for anyone to digest.

"No, thank you, dear." Rebekah stared into the leaping flames. "I have one more chore to do tonight. I must fire the Moodys. I want them gone immediately." Her voice held a note of steel, but Priscilla saw the fatigue on her face.

"I can do it for you," Gerald said. "And I'll supervise their removal. If they can't get all their things tonight, we'll have the police come over tomorrow while they clear out."

"And I'll stay here for the night," Priscilla offered. "Let me go fetch Jake. I hate to leave him alone."

Rebekah smiled. "No, you mustn't leave him alone. He'll be upset."

Priscilla dashed back to the cottage to pack a small bag and get Jake. She gathered his food and his leash. "We're going for a sleepover at our friend's house. What do you think, Jake?" His answer was a laughing doggy grin, his tongue lolling out. At the

236 | MYSTERIES *of* MARTHA'S VINEYARD

last minute, she grabbed the photo albums she'd borrowed. She didn't need them anymore.

By the time she returned to the Alden house, the Moodys had returned. She and Jake stayed with Rebekah in the living room while Gerald had sharp words with them in the kitchen. There was some banging around upstairs, and then their truck started with a rumble, and they were gone.

"Ed and Maureen have some more things to collect," Gerald said, "and they'll call to make an appointment. Let me know, and I'll be there if you need me." He went to the fireplace and poked the embers, then added another log.

"I can't thank you enough for all you've done," Rebekah said. "It's good to learn that I have friends on this island. I've shut myself away for far too long."

"There's a nice ladies' group at my church, Faith Fellowship," Priscilla said. "They meet every week for tea and Bible study. I'm sure you'd be welcome."

The older woman leaned her head back against the chair with a sigh. "I'd like to do that. And start going back to weekly services." A glint of humor appeared in her eyes. "I'll make that a requirement of my next live-in caretaker. 'Must go to church.'"

"Maybe one of my cousins knows someone," Priscilla said. "I'll give them a call tomorrow." If only she could find Rebekah's daughter. That was who she needed, not a paid servant.

"Sounds like a plan." Gerald was still standing by the fire, leaning on the mantel. "Is there anything else you'd like me to do, Rebekah? If not, I'd better head for home. I've got an early shift tomorrow."

Rebekah shook her head, and Priscilla said, "We'll be fine." She gave him a mischievous grin. "If not, I've put your number on speed dial."

He laughed, then bent to give Jake a pat. "I'll leave you be, then. Good night."

The next morning, Priscilla made the calls to the cousins as promised, with the result that Mrs. Ellie Doyle was located and hired. She was cheerful, strong, a good cook, and best of all, a devout member of Faith Fellowship Church. She was a retired nurse who did private duty work to supplement her income.

After Ellie was settled, Priscilla left Rebekah's house and went home. She was pooped. She'd barely slept in the comfortable but strange bed in Rebekah's guest room, startled all night by unfamiliar sounds and troubled by dreams of the evening's dramatic events. Once or twice she'd even heard engine sounds, but when she'd tried to listen harder, they'd faded away.

The phone rang when she walked into the cottage, and she almost didn't answer it. But it was Harper.

"Hello, Priscilla." The young woman's voice was bright and chipper. How Priscilla wished she could share Harper's boundless energy. "I've done a mock-up of a website for your lighthouse museum, and I'd love to show it to you."

Priscilla moved to the cupboard and pulled out coffee. She needed more caffeine. "Already? That was fast."

"Well, a lot of it has placeholders where pictures and text will go, but I have a basic design." She hesitated, then said, "If you're not busy tonight, I'd like to make dinner for you as a thank-you.

My special Portuguese fish stew. Then we can look at the website together."

Priscilla laughed. "You had me at fish stew. Sure, come on over. And thank you, Harper. I really appreciate your help with the museum."

"Ah, it's fun. I like doing it. See you at five or so?"

The wall clock said two. "Sounds good." After she hung up, Priscilla decided to take a cup of coffee and the book she was reading to the bedroom. A nap sounded lovely.

The throaty sound of a loud car muffler awoke Priscilla later. Jake leaped to his feet and barked at the annoying sound. Priscilla peered at the bedside clock with one eye. Five p.m. "That's Harper, Jake. Simmer down." She must have found a vehicle to use.

Groggy from her nap, Priscilla swung her feet to the floor and yawned. The bedside lamp was on, and the book still lay open to where she'd started. She must have fallen asleep almost immediately.

Jake was long gone, sniffing at the door and waiting for Harper. The young woman entered, lugging two sacks of groceries and her messenger bag.

Priscilla grabbed one of the bags, which held a sack of mussels and a packet of fish. "Ooh, this looks intriguing."

Harper set the rest of her things on the kitchen table. "It's so delicious. I got the recipe from a neighbor in New Bedford. She made it often, and one day I went over and demanded to know what smelled so good. She was kind enough to teach me how to make it."

Together they worked to prepare the stew, which featured tomatoes, garlic, potatoes, green pepper, onion, and chili flakes in addition to the mussels and fish. Harper then whipped up a batch of fluffy quick-rise rolls to go with the savory dish.

"Want to move in?" Priscilla joked. "Everything you make is fabulous."

Harper glowed with pleasure. "I adore cooking as well as baking. It's my dream to someday own a restaurant."

Over dinner, they discussed Harper's search for her mother's family. "I'm really sorry we haven't been able to get further with it," Priscilla said.

"I'm okay with it," Harper said with a philosophical shrug. "If it's not meant to be, well, I guess I'll move on. I'm making friends here on the island, and I have a great job. If only—" A shadow crossed her face.

Priscilla guessed what was troubling her. "Has the stalker come back?" Inwardly she groaned. She'd been hoping that he'd been scared away after they'd called the police.

"No, I haven't seen any more men lurking outside my window. But it's like waiting for a shoe to drop. You know what I mean?" Harper shivered. "I'm on edge all the time."

How terrible. A stalker could affect someone's life without even doing anything. "If you see him again, I'm going to pressure Officer Brown to do something. So let me know, okay?"

Jake interrupted the somber moment by bringing a tennis ball over and dropping it on Harper's foot. It bounced and rolled away, and he dashed to grab it.

They laughed. "He misses playing ball," Priscilla said. "If I threw it outside now, it'd vanish forever in the snow."

Harper reached down and stroked his fur. "I'll take him for a walk after we clean up. And then let's look at the museum website."

They spent a quiet evening doing exactly what Harper suggested, but when she went outside to leave, her borrowed car wouldn't start.

Priscilla offered to drive her home. "Leave the keys here. If it doesn't start tomorrow morning, we'll get a tow." She'd been through this drill with Rachel's friends, who often drove older cars with multiple issues.

Harper sighed in exasperation. "What a pain. Are you sure? I can call someone else to come get me."

"I'm sure." Priscilla reached for her coat. "Want to go for a ride, Jake?"

The route to Harper's apartment led past the bakery, and Priscilla glanced over, as she did at every familiar place she passed. The usual spotlight in the front window was on, but then she saw something strange and slowed the car for a better look.

What appeared to be a flashlight's beam was bobbing around in the kitchen.

CHAPTER TWENTY-SEVEN

Priscilla slowed the SUV to a crawl. "Harper, it looks like someone is in the bakery."

Harper craned her neck to see out the driver's side window. "You're right. Pull into the alley, and let's check it out."

Jake braced himself in the backseat, panting with excitement as they slowed down and pulled into the narrow passage between the bakery and the adjacent building. In the parking lot, a pickup truck was parked near the bakery's rear entrance. Priscilla braked, not able to pass the truck, which was blocking the route.

"That's Jason's truck," Harper said, already halfway out the passenger door. "What's he doing here?"

"Let's go find out." Priscilla turned the car off. "You're staying here, Jake." The last thing she needed was an agitated dog in the mix.

Harper put her finger to her lips. She shut her car door softly, and Priscilla did the same. Moving as quickly as possible across the rutted ice and snow, they crept to the bakery's back door. Harper reached out and turned the knob. It was unlocked.

The back door led directly into the kitchen. Harper pushed the door open and tiptoed inside, Priscilla at her heels.

Jason was kneeling beside one of the ovens, which had been pulled away from the wall. He was reaching behind it, and something clanked.

"What are you doing?" Harper asked. Her voice was soft, but there was no doubt she meant business.

Jason's head whipped around, and his face blanched even whiter in the pale beam from the flashlight he'd set on the floor. "Harper. What are you doing here?"

She crossed her arms. "I came to check on you. Now 'fess up, or I'm calling the police."

Priscilla sniffed, noticing a very distinctive and unpleasant odor. "I smell a gas leak."

"Yeah, that's it. I'm fixing a leak." Jason rose to his feet, rubbing both hands on his grimy canvas pants.

"How did you know there was one?" Harper asked. "The ovens were fine when I left today."

"Let's get out of here," Priscilla said. "Right now. We need to call the fire department." She tugged at Harper's arm.

Jason took a step toward Harper, his rubber-soled boots clumping on the tile floor. "I did it for you, Harper. And for Candy."

Harper's mouth hung open. "Did what? What are you talking about?" She whirled around. "Yeah, we'd better go. Quick." She let Priscilla run outside first, then followed.

Priscilla already had her phone out of her pocket. She dialed 911 on the way to her car. When the dispatcher asked, "What's your emergency?" she simply said, "Gas leak," and gave the address.

"Jump in, Harper," she said. "I'm moving the car." All she needed was her SUV and dog to go up in an explosion. After Harper got in, she backed out of the alley, driving with more skill than she thought she possessed.

She parked up the street on the other side. "Where's Jason? Do you know?"

Harper shook her head. "I think he's still in the bakery." She turned around in her seat. "What did he mean by doing it for me and Candy? Do you have any idea?"

The accidents and problems Candy had recently faced lined up in Priscilla's mind, creating a very interesting picture. "All Candy's problems started after she hired Jason, right?"

They could hear sirens in the distance. Good, the fire department was on their way.

"I'm not sure. We were hired around the same time, so I don't know about any problems before I got here." Harper absorbed this. "Do you think Jason caused them? The heating system problems, the fire, the flood?"

"It makes sense. He was on the spot to help after each one. But I can't figure out what he hopes to get out of it or why he says he did it for you and Candy."

A couple of fire engines and a police cruiser squealed to a halt in front of the bakery. "There's our cue," Priscilla said. "We should go fill them in."

The two women crossed the street, waving to get the attention of the firefighters. Officer April Brown got out of the cruiser, accompanied by Officer Teddy Holmes.

244 | MYSTERIES *of* MARTHA'S VINEYARD

April's eyes widened when she saw Priscilla. "You called this in? What's going on?"

Priscilla explained how they'd seen Jason inside and when they checked on him, they smelled gas.

"Good thing you called," one of the firemen said. "Gas leaks are nothing to mess with." He gave orders to the firefighters to turn off the main.

"Where is this Jason now?" April asked. "Do you have a last name?"

Priscilla realized she didn't know his surname. "Last we saw him, he was still in the kitchen."

The officer relayed that information to the fireman.

"We'll get him out of there." He got on the radio and called for an ambulance, just in case.

Within a couple of minutes, two of the firefighters returned with Jason in tow. They left him with Officer Brown and went back to work.

"Name and address?" April barked.

"Jason Dexter." Jason's grin was sheepish as he gave his address. "I'm glad you got here in time to save the building." He stared up at the bakery, that foolish smile still on his face.

April's brow furrowed. "Let's talk about that. What's your involvement with the bakery?"

"I work there. I'm the dishwasher. And I fix stuff." His gaze remained fixed on the building.

"Why were you here tonight?"

His eyes swiveled to her face, and he appeared confused. He stuttered, unable to form an explanation.

"I know why." Harper stood with her hands on her hips. "He just says he fixes things. He was tampering with the oven to make it leak. So he could fix it and be the big hero."

"Harper, why are you saying that?" Distress creased Jason's face. "Everything I've done is to help you."

"Help me?" The young woman scoffed. "By standing outside my window and leaving me tacky flowers? It was you, wasn't it?"

Jason's head went down, and he stubbed his boot toe into the crusty snowbank edging the sidewalk. His silence was all the answer they needed.

"Another exciting evening," Priscilla grumbled to Jake over coffee the next morning. "Too exciting, actually. When will it ever end?" Only a short while ago, she'd been housebound and bored, and now it had been one breathless adventure after another. Too much of a good thing could, well, be a bad thing, she decided.

The night before, Jason had been arrested for malicious mischief, having confessed to causing all the strange accidents and problems around the bakery. The charges against him included stalking and harassment for bothering Harper and Ida Lee Jones. Ida had come forward after Jason tried to use her as a character reference.

He truly didn't get it, Priscilla reflected. In his mind, he was saving damsels in distress.

"I hope tonight is relaxing," she told Jake, hoping that talking to your dog wasn't a sign of a problem. But he was the only one there, so she had a good excuse.

She had come home to a message from Aggie asking her over for dinner as a thank-you. Aggie had apologized for the short notice, blaming it on yet another storm approaching, this one threatening freezing rain. "We may be stuck inside until spring at this rate," she had said with a laugh on the message.

"Dinner with the kids," Priscilla said aloud, rising to refill her cup. "Is that the late-life version of meeting the parents?" Her mind skittered away from where that thought was leading. One step at a time. Right now she had to get back to work on her museum display, or it would never be ready by the end of May.

She enjoyed a productive day, which included making a pan of strawberry-rhubarb crumble for the dinner party using a jar of preserves she'd been gifted. Gerald picked her up, thankfully, because she didn't really remember where Aggie lived.

The crumble was a hit, the perfect topper to a dinner that included lots of laughter, Max's hilarious antics, and a star turn by the adorable baby. Nick, Aggie's good-looking and very nice husband, gave the crumble the ultimate compliment. "It reminds me of a dessert my grandmother used to make."

Aggie rolled her eyes. "You and your grandmother's cooking. I thought I was supposed to compete with your mom."

"But my mom can't cook" came the swift rejoinder from Nick. "It's a good thing my grandmother could, or I wouldn't be here today."

They were sipping decaf coffee when Priscilla's cell phone rang with a call from Harper. She'd meant to put it on silent, so she let it go to voice mail.

She checked the message in Gerald's SUV while they were pulling out of the driveway.

"Good thing we left when we did," he said, turning on the windshield wipers. The rain droplets running down the windshield were freezing on the glass. "It's getting nasty."

Priscilla hummed in agreement and pushed the play button. *"Priscilla...he's here. Ollie. Help."* A scream and a man's shout, then dead air.

Cold dread trickled down Priscilla's spine. "Gerald, we need to go to Harper's apartment. Ollie Perkins is there."

He didn't question her request. "Where does she live?"

Through teeth gritted with anxiety, Priscilla gave him the address. In response, Gerald sped up to as fast as was prudent on the increasingly slippery roads. She gripped the armrest and prayed, pushing away the distressing fears and thoughts that kept trying to intrude. Harper was all right, she had to be.

The street in front of Harper's apartment building was empty of cars due to the parking ban, and Gerald slid to a stop, the SUV fishtailing slightly. Lights burned in Harper's apartment. Priscilla jumped out without waiting to see if Gerald followed, but she heard his door slam and footsteps behind her. She clattered up the porch steps, hoping the outside door was unlocked. Otherwise they wouldn't be able to enter unless someone let them inside.

The outer door was ajar. Priscilla pounded up the staircase, taking the stairs two at a time, her heart racing. She gulped in air, and her lungs began to burn.

Harper's door stood open. Priscilla slowed, moving cautiously so as not to warn whoever was inside. Behind her, Gerald did the same. When she reached the open doorway, he nudged past. "Let me," he whispered.

After a long minute of listening, he gestured. "No one's here." He slipped into the apartment.

There had been a struggle, that much was evident—a chair lay on its side, sofa cushions were tossed about, and a lamp was broken. One of the curtain rods had been pulled loose, and the curtain dangled on the floor.

"He took her," Priscilla said. Her belly hollowed with shock and fear. "Where did they go?" Sleet ticked against the glass, melting and running down. The storm was intensifying. Had he taken her off the island?

Gerald's work phone buzzed. He pulled it out of his pocket and looked at the screen. "This may be a coincidence, but I find it hard to believe. There's a small boat in trouble out in the bay." He punched in a number.

While Gerald talked, Priscilla continued to look around, hoping to find a clue to indicate where they'd gone. Something silver glittered in the light of the overhead bulb. Priscilla picked it up. It was a cross, hanging from a broken chain. A cross identical to David Castonguay's.

At first Priscilla couldn't wrap her mind around what she was looking at. David's cross was safely in custody with the police. She'd given it to them herself. How did Harper get it?

Then a great gust of understanding swept over her, making her knees tremble.

Harper's mother was Sally Alden. She and David must have had matching crosses. Immediately, arguments against this theory reared up, but Priscilla disregarded them. She knew the truth now. Why Sally had chosen to call herself Megan Elliot was unknown. The Robert in the diary was Robert Bradley Alden. Sally had run away after Bradley told her David had left the island, paid off by her parents. She'd fled to the mainland, changed her name, and gotten married. She'd been so hurt and angry that she'd cut off any way for someone to trace her. Only the diary and this cross remained of that tragic summer on the Vineyard.

"Priscilla." Gerald's voice cut into her thoughts. "We need to go. The cutter is on a call, and we need to help the ship in trouble."

She stared at him, his face gradually coming into focus. "What? There's a ship in trouble?"

"Yes. Out near where Bradley ran aground. They're sending distress signals, and it's up to us to go. The cutter is too far away."

"All right." Still holding the cross, still half in a daze, she followed him from the apartment. They clattered back down the stairs and out into the storm. Moisture-laden wind gusted against them, sending needle-like frozen rain into their faces.

The SUV set off so fast that Priscilla was flung back against her seat. "Sorry," Gerald said. "We don't have much time. A rescue can easily turn into a recovery."

She knew what he meant. A recovery was when people died, when they drowned in heavy seas or their boat sank. "Who's out there? Do you know?"

His voice was grim. "It's a fishing craft registered to Ollie Perkins."

Priscilla's heart fluttered, waves of panic washing over her. She gasped for air, her chest constricting. She imagined the small ship foundering in the waves, sinking with Harper aboard. "No, this can't be happening."

"I'm afraid it is." He reached over and took her hand. "We're going to do our best to save her. So chin up. Focus on the job at hand." He squeezed her fingers and let go.

A few gasped breaths, and she rallied. "Well, at least we know where she is."

"That's the spirit." Gerald raced down a narrow lane to the harbor. "I dock my boat here. She's all gassed up and ready to go." He parked the SUV as close to the docks as he could, and they bolted down the gangway, which fortunately was kept shoveled.

At his ship's berth, a streetlight revealed the name painted on the side: *Aggie Jean*. Gerald helped Priscilla aboard and instructed her to put on oilskins and a life jacket. He turned on the radio and tuned in to the Coast Guard frequency. The engines started with a rumble that shook the deck under Priscilla's feet. This was one powerful craft.

She stood by Gerald's side as he took the wheel, grateful for the windscreen that shielded them from wind and precipitation. The hat and raincoat she wore were heavy and smelled of rubber and fish, but they kept her warm. With great skill, Gerald guided the boat out of the berth and maneuvered it through the harbor's obstacles to open water, where the seas foamed and seethed, and the wind hit them full force.

He throttled up, sending the boat skimming across the waves rolling in, creating swells and troughs. "Hang on," he yelled. "It's going to get rough."

After fifteen minutes of plowing through the churning water, Priscilla felt like she'd been on that boat forever. The lights of the harbor had receded, and there was nothing ahead or around them but inky black sky and water, sleet streaking down like gray pellets. As they came around a headland, she spotted the lighthouse beam and a surge of joy swept through her. There it was, her safe harbor.

The lights and instruments on the boat's dashboard kept them on target, although Gerald had to constantly fight the wind and waves trying to push them off course. Now and then the radio crackled into life, and he spoke to his fellow officers then gave her updates. "The cutter is on its way." He radioed back his location. "But we're still going to get there first."

As they approached the reefs, Gerald slowed. "It's treacherous through here," he shouted. "A lot of boats have gone aground." He

252 | MYSTERIES of MARTHA'S VINEYARD

didn't have to mention what happened next. If the sailors didn't have a lifeboat or weren't rescued in time, they would be stranded, helpless as their crafts gradually filled with water and sank.

Bradley had almost died that way. He'd gone sailing in a summer storm and had been unable to avoid the rocks. It was how David Castonguay had died.

The radio burst into life again. Gerald listened closely to the communication, which was coded so that Priscilla couldn't decipher what was going on. He gave a grunt of satisfaction and let them know he'd gotten the message.

"It turns out Ollie Perkins is one of the smugglers we've been tracking. And get this—he double-crossed his gang and took the shipment. Intelligence says he was headed for Canada with the load."

Ollie was involved with the smugglers? Most likely those men she'd seen him with in Falmouth. Priscilla thought about the rumbling engines she'd heard offshore, perhaps coinciding with Harper seeing her stalker. Yes, Jason had been pestering her, but apparently he wasn't the only one. The day Harper thought she saw Ollie driving around, she probably had. He'd tracked her to the Vineyard.

Why had he kidnapped Harper? Priscilla didn't understand that. Was he going to try to force her to stay with him? Or did he have something worse planned? She steered her mind away from that horrifying idea.

Gerald slowed the engines even more, to a low mutter. The boat inched forward, the spotlight sweeping the restless sea.

Nearby, a bell buoy clanged, a warning of shallow water. Gazing down, Priscilla saw how the water eddied and swirled and broke against the rocks thrusting upward.

"Is it much farther?" she yelled into Gerald's ear.

He shook his head. "We have to move slowly in case they're in the water already."

In the water. Priscilla knew how cold the ocean was, especially at this time of year. A person might freeze and drown after only a few minutes.

The light swung around again. This time Priscilla caught a flash of white. She yelled, "There they are!"

Gerald directed the beam at the spot. A fishing boat quite a bit longer than Gerald's was sitting half out of the water, bow pointing skyward. The stern had settled into the water, which was foaming over into the cockpit. Two figures came into view, clinging to the upper fishing deck.

"Ahoy the *Patriot*," Gerald called through his bullhorn. "Captain O'Bannon of the US Coast Guard here. We're going to get you folks off that craft."

A huge wave hit the grounded boat, and Harper lost her grip on the slick fiberglass. As Priscilla screamed, Harper plunged straight down into the surf.

Priscilla searched the water frantically until she spotted Harper's bobbing head. "There she is." She yelled to Harper, "Hang on, we'll save you."

"Take the wheel," Gerald ordered. He'd set the boat to stay in one place. He went to the rail and expertly threw a life ring down to the young woman. Harper grabbed it, and Gerald pulled her to safety using a winch. Once she was out of the water, he pulled her into the boat, and she fell to the deck with a thump like a sodden log.

Afraid to let go of the ship's wheel, Priscilla cried out, "Harper, are you all right?"

To her relief, Harper sat up. "I think so." Her teeth began to chatter. "I'm freezing, though."

"Go into the cabin in the bow," Gerald said, pointing to the small, glass-windowed enclosure. "There are warm clothes and blankets in there." He threw another ring out for Ollie to grab.

Harper stumbled toward the cabin, pausing to give Priscilla a soggy hug. "I'm so glad to see you. Ollie said he was going to make sure I couldn't ever turn him in. I was praying so hard we'd be rescued, and there you were. It's a miracle."

"I've got another one for you," Priscilla said. "I think I found your mother's family. There are a couple of details to check, but I'm 99 percent certain."

"I can't wait to hear about it." Harper's teeth chattering went up a notch. "But I'd better change first." She disappeared into the cabin, and a minute later the light came on.

Gerald got Ollie aboard without much trouble. Instead of letting him into the front cabin with Harper, he led him to the small cabin below and locked him in.

The Coast Guard radioed, and Gerald reported in. They tried to salvage the *Patriot* off the rock but abandoned the task when Gerald was cleared to take his passengers in and get them checked over by medical personnel. Then Ollie would be placed under arrest.

"I'll take the wheel now," he said to Priscilla. "Good job."

She relinquished it gladly, noticing how sore her fingers were from gripping it so tightly. As the boat began to move steadily toward shore, her heart lifted in joy. They had come through the storm, and Harper was safe.

CHAPTER TWENTY-EIGHT

The afternoon of the Share a Little Love event, Priscilla indulged in a long bubble bath. She sank down in the tub all the way up to her neck, allowing the deliciously hot water to soothe her aches and tensions away. She'd pinned up her hair, planning to use hot rollers after bathing.

What fun it was to focus only on getting ready for a night out. Perhaps the last time Priscilla had done this was the final anniversary she and Gary had celebrated. They'd always gone out for a special meal or taken a mini-vacation, from the first anniversary to their last. For a little while, she allowed herself to revel in bittersweet memories of what once was. They'd shared so many good times over the decades of their marriage.

At least she'd appreciated their relationship at the time. Her mother had told her once to enjoy the special moments in life so there would be no regrets later on. And indeed she had very few, really.

After getting out of the bath, she toweled off and slipped into a robe. Then she curled her hair, put on makeup, and slid on her prettiest undergarments. Feeling pretty started at the foundation, another truism from her mom. A spritz of her favorite perfume, and it was time to get dressed.

The new outfit fit as well as it had in the store, thankfully. Actually the waist was a tiny bit looser, she noticed with pleasure. Perhaps midnight rescues on ships in ice storms burned more calories than usual. Dangling rhinestone chandelier earrings and a bracelet provided a touch of bling.

After she was dressed and had admired herself from every angle, she did something unprecedented—she took a selfie with her phone and sent it to Rachel.

In response, the phone rang immediately. "Mom, you look gorgeous. Wow."

"You think so?" Priscilla still stood in front of the mirror, and she turned side to side to check her appearance again. "I feel pretty too."

"You'll be the belle of the ball, I have no doubt. Are you excited?"

At her daughter's question, anticipation and trepidation bubbled up in her belly. "I think so. Actually I'm a little scared."

Rachel laughed. "Don't be. Just be you. That's what you always told me when I had a big date in high school."

She was getting wisdom from her mom and now her daughter. Priscilla had to chuckle at the irony. She changed the subject. "What are you wearing tonight?"

As she hoped, that diverted Rachel, who squealed. "I found the cutest dress. It's red and knee-length and the skirt is kind of full. I'll send you a picture when I'm dressed, how's that?"

"Perfect. I'll look forward to it. Happy Valentine's Day, darling. Love you."

"Happy Valentine's Day to you, Mom. Love you too."

Rebekah rose to her feet when Priscilla and Harper entered the Alden home's living room. The older woman wore a long brocade skirt, a frilled white blouse, and an expression of hopeful excitement.

Priscilla said simply, "Rebekah, this is your granddaughter, Harper Sarah Jenson. Harper, your grandmother, Rebekah Elliot Alden." Emotion tightened her chest and she could barely get the last words out. She blinked back tears, then gave up and dug for a tissue, letting them spill. Sarah Alden had taken the name Megan as her alias, inspired by her middle name, Margaret. Sally was a common New England nickname for Sarah, Priscilla had learned.

Harper took a couple of tentative steps forward. "Grandmother? You're really my grandmother?"

"I really am." Tears glistened in Rebekah's eyes. "You look like her. Just like my Sally. Except for the dark hair, of course."

Harper had been the one who reminded Rebekah of Sally in the bakery, Priscilla realized.

"That's all my dad." Harper laughed and ran long fingers through her cropped locks, fingers as slender and expressive as Rebekah's own. She took another step toward the woman waiting beside the fireplace. "I've been waiting so long to find my family. I can't believe it's really happened."

"Oh, it has, my love, it has." Rebekah held her arms open wide.

In a blur of movement, they were in each other's arms, crying and hugging and talking. Priscilla melted out of the room and went out to the kitchen, where Gerald was waiting. He looked handsome in a gray suit, crisp white shirt, and red tie.

"How'd it go?" He cocked his head toward the living room.

Priscilla clasped her hands together, barely able to speak. So she didn't. She merely nodded her head and smiled through her tears.

"That good, huh?" He grinned and held out his arm. "Ready? It's time to go to Share a Little Love."

"I think we already did." Priscilla took his arm, warm satisfaction filling her heart.

Rebekah and Harper decided to stay home and get to know each other, so Gerald and Priscilla set off alone to the Valentine's Day benefit.

The high school gymnasium had been totally transformed into a winter wonderland. Garlands of little white lights and hearts crisscrossed the ceiling and adorned the walls. Columns stood here and there, guiding attendees into the space. Tables were dressed in snowy-white cloths and set with red electric candles and bouquets of red roses and white carnations. Near the stage was a small dance floor, and on stage, the first band played soft, romantic dinner music.

Priscilla glanced around at the crowd, spotting familiar faces. Ida Lee and Randy Jones. Mildred Pearson and her father, Fred. Tilly Snyder and Hilda, lovely in an emerald-green silk dress with a red floral design she must have purchased in Falmouth. Beau Ortmann and Candy Lane. Dr. Mike Morris from the veterinary clinic. Everyone looked fabulous in evening attire, the women in bright dresses or slacks and the men in suits.

"Priscilla. Gerald." Joan appeared out of the crowd, looking lovely in a silky red blouse, black velvet pants, and a jaunty red velvet beret trimmed with a flower and rhinestone beads. She greeted them with hugs. "You're sitting with us."

Her cousin led them to a table near the stage, where Gail, Uncle Hugh, Tommy Townsend and his mother, Marigold, and the Galvins were already seated. A handsome older man with white hair and a trim build rose to greet them.

"This is Giles Castonguay, David's brother," Joan said. She introduced Priscilla and Gerald. Giles had traveled from Montreal to speak to the police after Bradley's confession regarding David's death.

"How do you do?" Giles said. He had a slight, very charming accent. "You are the ones who solved the mystery of my brother's death, is it not so?"

Priscilla shook his hand. "Yes, we did. So sorry for your loss."

He shook her hand, then dropped it to grasp her shoulders and give her kisses on both cheeks. "My family will forever be in your debt." Tears stood in his blue-gray eyes.

Giles thanked Gerald with a hearty handshake. Then Priscilla and Gerald found seats at the table between Marigold and the Galvins.

Trudy leaned across Dan. "You look lovely tonight, Priscilla." She winked. "Glad you could join us." She was gorgeous in a cherry-red dress and matching hair bow and lipstick.

"So do you. It's great to be here." Priscilla unfolded her napkin and placed it across her lap. The servers brought salads around, and the meal began.

The Galvins had eyes only for each other, and Marigold was focused on Hugh, so Priscilla and Gerald spent dinner talking to each other. The food was fabulous, surf and turf with porterhouse steak and giant shrimp.

"This is a little different than what they usually serve at school," Gerald joked, cutting the melt-in-your-mouth beef with a steak knife.

"It certainly is. We had mystery meat and soggy green beans." Priscilla smiled at the memory as she took a mouthful of buttery baked potato.

Gerald named a few of his least favorite school cafeteria dishes, and then their discussion segued into exchanging memories of their younger days.

This was part of getting to know someone, Priscilla remembered from eons ago. Sharing life stories, the humorous, exciting, or just plain ordinary experiences that had made them who they were now.

After a dessert of strawberry crumble topped with vanilla ice cream, Pastor Katie Rona took the stage to make remarks. "Thank you for coming out tonight to Share a Little Love," she said, beaming. The crowd applauded with hoots and whistles. "I'm happy to announce that this year's fundraiser has been the most successful yet." She named the figure that had been raised, to more cheers. "Thanks to your generosity, we'll be able to offer additional beds in our shelter and more services for abandoned animals. As you know, it's been a rough winter, with some of the worst weather the island has seen in decades. Tonight I wished I had ice skates on my car instead of tires."

Everyone laughed.

Pastor Rona went on. "Those without a roof over their heads depend on us for shelter, for a meal, for a friendly face and a helping hand. We're truly their port in a storm." Another round of clapping echoed in the room. "Next up, we've got dance tunes, so get ready to burn off a few of those calories." Groans and laughter rippled through the audience.

Priscilla ruminated on Pastor Rona's words. A port in the storm. Everyone needed one at times. She had, after Gary's death. And now, thanks to God's help, both Harper and Rebekah had found each other after going through storms of their own. *God sets the lonely in families . . .* that verse drifted through her mind again.

The second band emerged onto the stage, an ensemble that included a saxophone, guitars, bass, drums, and keyboards. They swung into their first number, a jaunty rendition of "Homecoming Waltz."

"May I have this dance?" Gerald asked.

Priscilla smiled and nodded. He took her hand and led her to the dance floor. He put his arm around her waist and she rested her hand on his broad shoulder. One, two, three, and they began moving around the floor, their steps effortlessly flowing together. Around them, other couples waltzed—Beau and Candy, Gail and Tommy, Trudy and Dan, even Marigold and Hugh.

Priscilla's mother had loved this song, made popular by Guy Lombardo in the 1940s. As the vocalist began to sing, Priscilla echoed the sentiments in her own heart. When she'd lost the love of her life, she'd traveled a long, hard journey. But now, with God's grace, she'd found a new beginning. Like the singer said, she was home to stay.

AUTHOR LETTER

Dear Reader,

Welcome back to Priscilla Grant's world on lovely Martha's Vineyard! I wrote this story during a steamy New England summer, so I enjoyed the refreshing mental trip to frosty February. Best of all, a winter setting gives a writer the opportunity to explore the cozy comforts of home and hearth, often more appreciated in bad weather.

Judging by the number of visitors, many would say Martha's Vineyard is at its best during New England's all-too-short summer. Certainly hiking, swimming, boating, sightseeing, even lounging on the beach, are much more pleasurable in warm temperatures and sunshine.

But winter has its own beauty and allure. The leaves are gone, revealing the elegant bones of the land. Snow and ice transform pine forests and quaint villages into enchanted wonderlands. And for the hearty, the frosty outdoors offer a variety of sports and pursuits. Perhaps best of all, we can hunker down inside without guilt. One of my favorite winter activities is pulling an overstuffed armchair up to a roaring fire, hot tea or coffee in hand, and diving into a good book.

Winter offers not only a return to the interior physically but also mentally and spiritually. There is no summer without winter. And this fallow season is a time to rest, dream, and plan for spring.

Elizabeth Penney

ABOUT THE AUTHOR

Elizabeth Penney lives in the White Mountains of New Hampshire, where she pens novels, runs a small farm, and cans lots of vegetables and jam. Active in their local church and community, she and her husband enjoy a clan of three children and five grandchildren. They are also under the management of a bold hen named Pearl and a very spoiled cat named Noah.

AN ARMCHAIR TOUR OF
MARTHA'S VINEYARD

Visiting Martha's Vineyard in Winter

In the not-too-distant past, the idea of visiting Martha's Vineyard in the winter was met with disbelief and even derision. But many delights await those who dare to travel to the island during the off-season.

While the majority of island inns and restaurants close in the fall, many stay open until Christmas and others all year round. Off-season rates practically make a visit a bargain, and it's certainly easier to get reservations. A cozy weekend at a lovely inn or bed-and-breakfast could be the perfect cure for the winter doldrums. You'll enjoy meals out in the company of locals and other intrepid visitors, often while listening to live music. A handful of stores and art galleries remain open, so shopping for fine crafts and unique items can be added to your agenda.

If you want to breathe fresh salty air and get some exercise, try a winter hike or snowshoe at Cedar Tree Neck Sanctuary. Trails meander through woods, over streams, by a pond, and along a secluded beach. Access is free. Blackwater Pond Reservation is another free spot open all year. The park offers easy terrain and trails along the shores of an undeveloped pond. The lovely Lucy Vincent Beach is residents-only in summer but open to all the rest of the year.

Ferry reservations are recommended in winter too, but of course are much easier to obtain. The Steamship Authority is the only year-round operator of passenger and car ferries to the island.

Beautiful in every season, Martha's Vineyard is a hidden jewel in the winter months. Consider it for a perfect romantic, creative, or girls-only getaway.

SOMETHING DELICIOUS FROM OUR SEASIDE FRIENDS

Candy's Rosemary Shortbread Cookies "Love Cookies"

These cookies are a favorite at Candy Lane Confectionery, often purchased for that special someone. Candy, of course, makes huge batches, but she kindly revised her professional recipe for the home cook.

1 cup butter (two sticks), softened

¼ cup powdered sugar, (plus 2 tablespoons for decoration)

¼ cup granulated sugar

2 cups all-purpose flour

1½ teaspoons dried rosemary, finely chopped

1 teaspoon water

Instructions

1. Cream the butter and sugar until smooth and fluffy.
2. In a separate bowl, stir together the flour and rosemary. Add the dry ingredients gradually into the butter and sugar mixture, stirring until fully mixed. Add the water and stir again until combined.

3. Form the dough into a ball and wrap with plastic wrap. Refrigerate until firm but no longer than 1 hour.

4. Once the dough is chilled, preheat the oven to 325 degrees. Roll out the dough on a well-floured surface to ½-inch thick. Use 1–2-inch cookie cutters to shape the dough. Candy usually makes 1-½-inch diameter fluted circles but sometimes she makes hearts or flowers. Place on a baking sheet lined with parchment paper.

5. Bake for about 15 minutes or until the edges start to turn golden. Cool the cookies on the baking sheet for 5 minutes and transfer them to a wire rack.

6. Once cookies are cool, spoon the reserved powdered sugar into a flour sifter and sift over cookies.

Read on for a sneak peek of another exciting book
in the series Mysteries of Martha's Vineyard!

Thicker than Water
by DeAnna Julie Dodson

Priscilla Grant huddled under her driftwood-gray afghan before the living room's blazing hearth fire, warming her hands around a cup of scalding-hot coffee. Along with this cottage, she had inherited the Misty Harbor Lighthouse from her aunt Marjorie Latham, and she had been working hard the past few weeks on the small museum she was creating on the lighthouse's bottom floor, a tribute to the Latham branch of the family and to the old lighthouse itself. For today though, she was taking a break. It would be nice to just putter around the house for a while, reading, maybe working on her long-neglected appliqué quilt, who knew what? One thing for sure, she wasn't getting out in the cold April drizzle on foot again today. As much as she and her dog, Jake, enjoyed brisk walks all year long, she was sure he was as glad as she was to be back inside the cozy cottage now.

She smiled at the dog as he lay snoozing in front of the fire. Though he was well over a year old now, he was often like a puppy with only two gears: full speed ahead and full stop. He didn't even twitch when her cell phone rang.

"Have you heard?" Trudy said before Priscilla could even say hello. "Have you heard what's going on?"

Trudy was one of Priscilla's three cousins who also lived here on Martha's Vineyard. Unlike Priscilla, her cousins were natives of the island, and they were consequently rather protective of it and its history.

"Hi, Trudy," Priscilla said, hearing in her cousin's voice only her usual excitability and not anything to indicate a life-threatening emergency. "Have I heard what?"

"Caroline Waterman is selling!"

Priscilla had heard of the Watermans since she had moved to Martha's Vineyard. They owned acres of valuable land that had so far been left untouched, much to the satisfaction of the island's residents. Priscilla had heard much speculation, evidently a continuation of what had been going on for decades, about what it would take to convince Miss Waterman to sell, why she was so dead set against it, and what her mostly absent relations would do when she passed away.

Once she had surpassed the age of eighty, people finally began to believe she was serious when she said she wanted to leave the land in its natural state for as long as possible, at least during her lifetime. But now...

"Are you sure?" Priscilla asked. "I thought—"

"We all thought!" Trudy almost always talked in exclamation points. "She's closing the museum too, and selling off all the artifacts."

"Oh no, really? That's too bad."

Even after living in Martha's Vineyard for several months, Priscilla still hadn't had a chance to visit the Cavanaugh Museum. It was a little bit of an oddity. Not too different, she supposed, from the little Latham family museum she was planning, though the Cavanaughs were certainly better known and much more controversial than any of the Lathams had ever been.

"How did you find out?" she asked Trudy. "It's not already a done deal, is it?"

"I ran into Mildred at Ortmann's when I went to get vegetables and things to make stew for dinner. She's just sure that land's going to be crammed full of McMansions within a month or two!"

"I don't think they can do anything like that so fast."

"Well, that's what she thinks!"

"Wouldn't that kind of development have to be approved by—"

"Oh, you know how it is. People with enough money can do whatever they want. I just hate to see that part of the island spoiled that way."

"What else did Mildred say?" Priscilla asked. "Did she know who—"

"Nothing like that yet. It's only just come out!"

"Well, whatever actually happens, it's Miss Waterman's land. There's not a lot we can do about it if she wants to sell."

Trudy sighed. "I suppose you're right. But it seems like such a shame. I think Mildred was much more upset about losing the Cavanaugh Museum than anything else."

"It could be that whoever buys the contents will open it in a different location," Priscilla said. "Maybe in Boston with some of the other historical sites."

"You know I don't know anything about old stuff. But I do wish I had some of the clothes Rosie Cavanaugh had back in the forties. That woman knew how to dress."

"I suppose she had to if she was going to marry into that family and be on display all the time." Priscilla laughed softly. "Not for me, thank you very much."

"Well, I don't suppose either of us will ever have that problem," Trudy said, her voice wistful. "Anyhow, I'd better go. This stew is one of those Crock-Pot recipes that take all day to cook, and if I don't get it started Dan and I won't eat till midnight. I just thought you ought to know about Miss Waterman, especially since Joan and Gail are both at work and can't talk right now."

"We'll have a chat about it next time the four of us are together," Priscilla promised. "Maybe there's nothing to the story after all."

"Maybe." Trudy didn't sound at all convinced. "Hey, you haven't forgotten Joan's birthday, have you?"

"Of course not. I've been counting the days. I found the most perfect present for her. I can't wait till she sees it."

"Ooh! What? What?"

"Oh, no," Priscilla said. "I heard that Joan told you what she was giving Gail for Christmas a couple of years ago and everybody on Martha's Vineyard knew what it was by the middle of December, including Gail."

"Fine," Trudy huffed. "One little mistake..."

Priscilla laughed. "You'd better get back to your stew. I'll talk to you later."

Once she had ended the call, she picked up her coffee cup again and breathed in the dark, rich aroma, but she didn't feel cold anymore. She had too much to think about right now. Jake was still asleep on the braided rag rug on the hearth, but she decided maybe she would go out again after all.

A few minutes later, she put on her coat and headed out to the Cavanaugh Museum. She had been meaning to go anyway, if only to get a few ideas about how to organize her own displays, and it wouldn't do for it to close up before she ever got to see it. She didn't know all that much about the Cavanaughs, only that the family had made its money out West in the last part of the nineteenth century and then had come east to settle down respectably. Since then, their wealth and influence had grown until they were well known not only in Martha's Vineyard but globally. Priscilla didn't want to miss her chance to get an up-close look at whatever was on display, especially if it was going to be her last.

Cavanaugh Museum House wasn't all that large, but it was a lovely three-story Victorian with towers and turrets, gingerbread trim, stained-glass windows, and wraparound porches in enough profusion to ensure it was the grandest home of its day. Priscilla scolded herself for not finding out ahead of time when the museum was open, but there was a black Acura parked in the drive that led to what was no doubt originally a carriage house, so with luck someone was there to let her in. She had thought there would be other people wanting a tour of the museum, but there weren't any other cars. Still, it was midmorning on a cold, drizzly Tuesday in April. Probably not their peak time.

Not quite sure what to do, she tapped on the front door and waited. According to the sign on the door, the place had been open for over an hour already, so she let herself in.

"Hello?"

The foyer was well lit and lined with photographs, some tintypes, others very recent. Some of them were of people she recognized. Others she couldn't possibly identify. As she read the captions, she was more and more amazed by the sheer number of celebrities the various Cavanaughs had rubbed elbows with. Actors and actresses, presidents and kings, politicians, popes and philanthropists, mobsters, scientists, poets and soldiers, activists and revolutionaries. It was quite a gallery, and she had only just stepped inside the door.

"Hello?" she said again, and she heard a door close from somewhere in another part of the house. Then she heard rapid footsteps, and a door into the main parlor opened.

"Good morning."

The man who greeted her was in his fifties, maybe three or four years younger than Priscilla. His smile was polite but the eyes behind his thick glasses were rather impatient, as if she had interrupted something he was in a hurry to get done.

"Good morning," she said with a bright smile. "I hope it's all right for me to come in. The sign—"

"Oh, yes, we're open. For now at least."

She added a touch of sympathy to her smile. "I heard Miss Waterman might be closing this place. What a shame."

His slumped shoulders slumped even more. "Aunt Caroline is being very difficult, if you'll excuse my saying so."

Priscilla's eyebrows went up. "She's your aunt?"

"For all the good that does. We haven't really spoken for over twenty years, and now she won't see me at all." He made a sour face. "I'm Malcolm Waterman. My father was her brother, but I suppose I shouldn't bore you with my family, when it's the Cavanaughs you've come to see about. Well, it's a good thing you didn't wait too long to visit." He made a sweeping gesture with both thin arms, encompassing the parlor. "Help yourself. Or would you rather have the guided tour?"

"I'm sure there's a lot you could tell me about everything." She couldn't help wondering about this falling out between him and his aunt, even though she was quite aware it was none of her business. As she hoped, he followed her over to the first of the display cases. It was full of medals from conflicts throughout the world, from the Spanish-American War in 1898 to Afghanistan over a hundred years later. All of them had been awarded to Cavanaughs.

"Pretty amazing, huh?" he asked, looking over the display. "You know, I used to hate this place. I wanted Aunt Caroline to close it. But since then I've come to appreciate everything that's here. It's an incredible collection. A microcosm of twentieth-century America."

"It is that," she said, strolling from the medals to the display of an elegant white silk dress with handmade Irish lace and seed pearls and, if the placard was to be believed, a twelve-foot train. Displayed with it was a gorgeous lace veil and dainty silk slippers. The celebrated beauty Rosalie Millican West, daughter of Texas oil magnate Bronson West, had worn the dress when she was married to Rowan Neville Cavanaugh II on June 18, 1943.

"I'm curious," Priscilla said. "How did your Aunt Caroline get all these things? I would have thought the Cavanaugh family would want to keep them."

"Many of them are just on loan. Some of them have been donated or sold to the museum by the Cavanaughs or friends of theirs, by collectors, even by other museums. Mostly we have them because my father asked the family for them when he decided to open the museum in '52. This used to be their house, back when Samuel Cavanaugh came here in 1875. But they built that big place up-island in the late forties, so Dad bought this house and made it a museum. Old Sam and my great-great-grandfather Elias Waterman made a lot of money in San Francisco during those Wild West days. I won't admit exactly how, but the Watermans and the Cavanaughs have been great friends since then. Well, not that we run in the same circles anymore, of course, not after they went into politics and war heroics and all that. But yeah, everything here has a pretty interesting story."

She looked at him, not sure if she should be amused or irked by his casual admissions. "I don't suppose this is what you usually tell your visitors here."

He shrugged. "Does it matter anymore?"

"Are you sure your aunt won't discuss her decision with you? If I were to guess, I'd say there are a lot of people on the island who won't be happy if she sells this land and many others who wouldn't like to see this museum closed. Maybe someone in her family could—"

"Not me, thank you, if that's what you're getting at. She lets her lawyer contact me if there's something I need to know. Last time I tried to talk to her, her housekeeper threatened to set the dog on me."

Priscilla bit her lip, suppressing the urge to find out more. Instead, she had him show her the rest of the museum that documented the lives and accomplishments of six generations of Cavanaughs. As he had said, it really was a microcosm of twentieth-century America.

"I'll have to come back again sometime," she told him as they reached the entryway again. "There's so much to see and study."

"Better not wait too long," he said, and with a cynical smirk, he shut the door behind her.

Priscilla decided to stop by the bakery on her way home. She didn't know whether she would just pick up her usual cranberry muffin and chocolate chip cookies or actually stay and eat something a little fancier, but that would depend on what was written on the chalkboard menu for the day's specials.

"Hi, Candy," she said as she approached the counter, and she was met with a bright-eyed smile.

"Priscilla. Come in. How are you this morning?"

"Good. I was just over at the Cavanaugh museum, and I thought I'd stop by here for a treat."

The place was empty except for a woman in her fifties sitting near the windows that overlooked the harbor. She had looked up from the cream puff she was eating when Priscilla came in, and she was still looking now, frowning slightly.

"I suppose you've heard it might be closing," Priscilla said, turning away from the woman and back to Candy.

"Yes." Candy shook her head. "Such a shame."

"Excuse me." The woman at the table stood up, smiling apologetically as she approached Priscilla. "I'm so sorry to interrupt, and I didn't mean to be eavesdropping, but aren't you Priscilla Grant?"

Priscilla stared at her for a moment and then rushed to hug her. "Kitty! Oh my goodness, Kitty! What are you doing here?"

"What are *you* doing here? You can't have left the farm."

"I can," Priscilla assured her, "and I have."

Kitty shook her head, her brown eyes warm in her plump face. "I never thought you'd be able to pry Gary away from the place."

"I'm afraid I lost Gary over a year ago."

Kitty's smile faded. "Oh, Priscilla, I'm so sorry. I had no idea."

"It's all right." Priscilla swallowed down an unexpected lump in her throat and gave her a wry grin. "Most days." She looked at Candy. "This is an old school friend of mine from Kansas, Kitty Merrick. We haven't seen each other in at least fifteen years."

"Twenty," Kitty said.

"Well, it sounds like the two of you have some catching up to do over coffee and chocolate chip cookies," Candy told them. "My treat."

They thanked her and went back to Kitty's table, both of them in a hurry to catch up.

"But why are *you* here?" Priscilla asked once she had told Kitty about inheriting the cottage and the lighthouse. "You don't live in the area, do you?"

"Oh, no. After we left Wheatfield, Keith and I moved to Oregon. I'm here on a business trip. Well, I was on a business trip when I was in Boston, but since I was so close, I thought I'd come over to Martha's Vineyard and catch up with my aunt Katherine."

"I didn't know you had an aunt Katherine."

"I didn't know her very well," Kitty admitted. "She was married to my mother's brother, Uncle Bert, but he died in a plane crash on the day I was born. That's why I was named Katherine instead of Carole Ann the way my parents had planned. Anyway, she and Mom were great friends even after Aunt Katherine married again and moved out here. They wrote each other all the time, and after Mom died, I started writing to her too. Not as much, just a few times a year, but it's been nice getting real cards and letters once in a while."

"That is nice." Priscilla sipped her coffee, delighted to have a chance to chat with her old friend again. "Does she know you're coming?"

"Well, that's the problem. Or I should say, that's why I came. Like I said, we haven't written much. Mostly birthday and Christmas cards or a letter here and there when something exciting happens, but I haven't heard from her in five months. Not at Christmas. Not for my birthday in February or hers in March."

Priscilla frowned. "Couldn't you have called her?"

"I don't have a number for her," Kitty said with a sigh. "Just an address. When I tried to get a phone number for the address, all I found out was it was unlisted. So I thought, since I had to come out this way anyway, I'd make sure she's all right." There was concern now in her dark eyes. "She's pretty old now, and I'm afraid she might have just passed away, although I couldn't find an obit for her online."

"I guess that's possible," Priscilla said as gently as she was able. "But that ought to be easy enough to find out, right?"

"I think so. I just got in, so I haven't really gotten started yet. I thought I'd find the address where I'd been writing to her and see what they can tell me."

"Good idea. Want me to help you find the place?"

"That would be great." Kitty fished in her purse for a moment and brought out an index card. "Here's the address."

Priscilla looked at it and frowned. If she wasn't mistaken, she was looking at the address of Caroline Waterman's home.

Sign up for the
Guidepeosts Fiction Newsletter
and stay up-to-date on the books you love!

You'll get sneak peeks of new releases, recommendations from other Guideposts readers, and special offers just for you . . .
and it's FREE!

Just go to Guideposts.org/Newsletters today to sign up.

Guideposts®

Find more inspiring fiction in these best-loved Guideposts series!

Mysteries of Martha's Vineyard
Come to the shores of this quaint and historic island and dig into a cozy mystery. When a recent widow inherits a lighthouse just off the coast of Massachusetts, she finds exciting adventures, new friends, and renewed hope.

Tearoom Mysteries
Mix one stately Victorian home, a charming lakeside town in Maine, and two adventurous cousins with a passion for tea and hospitality. Add a large scoop of intriguing mystery and sprinkle generously with faith, family, and friends, and you have the recipe for Tearoom Mysteries.

Sugarcreek Amish Mysteries
Be intrigued by the suspense and joyful "aha!" moments in these delightful stories. Each book in the series brings together two women of vastly different backgrounds and traditions, who realize there's much more to the "simple life" than meets the eye.

Mysteries of Silver Peak
Escape to the historic mining town of Silver Peak, Colorado, and discover how one woman's love of antiques helps her solve mysteries buried deep in the town's checkered past.

Patchwork Mysteries
Discover that life's little mysteries often have a common thread in a series where every novel contains an intriguing whodunit centered around a quilt located in a beautiful New England town.

To learn more about these books, visit Guideposts.org/Shop